FANBOY
IN THE *Falls*

This book is for everyone else who didn't quite fit in at the middle school lunch table. I see you. You're welcome over at my table anytime.

Contents

About This Book		1
Author's Note		3
1.	43 Days to the Devon Falls Leaf Festival	5
2.	42 Days to the Devon Falls Leaf Festival	15
3.	40 Days to the Devon Falls Leaf Festival	23
4.	37 Days to the Devon Falls Leaf Festival	35
5.	37 Days to the Devon Falls Leaf Festival	45
6.	37 Days to the Devon Falls Leaf Festival	51
7.	32 Days to the Devon Falls Leaf Festival	61
8.	32 Days to the Devon Falls Leaf Festival	69
9.	32 Days to the Devon Falls Leaf Festival	77
10.	32 Days to the Devon Falls Leaf Festival	85
11.	31 Days to the Devon Falls Leaf Festival	95
12.	31 Days to the Devon Falls Leaf Festival	105
13.	31 Days to the Devon Falls Leaf Festival	109
14.	31 Days to the Devon Falls Leaf Festival	117
15.	31 Days to the Devon Falls Leaf Festival	125
16.	30 Days to the Devon Falls Leaf Festival	131
17.	28 Days to the Devon Falls Leaf Festival	141

18.	28 Days to the Devon Falls Leaf Festival	147
19.	27 Days to the Devon Falls Leaf Festival	157
20.	19 Days to the Devon Falls Leaf Festival	165
21.	12 Days to the Devon Falls Leaf Festival	177
22.	12 Days to the Devon Falls Leaf Festival	185
23.	11 Days to the Devon Falls Leaf Festival	193
24.	11 Days to the Devon Falls Leaf Festival	203
25.	11 Days to the Devon Falls Leaf Festival	211
26.	11 Days to the Devon Falls Leaf Festival	221
27.	10 Days to the Devon Falls Leaf Festival	229
28.	9 Days to the Devon Falls Leaf Festival	235
29.	8 Days to the Devon Falls Leaf Festival	247
30.	3 Days to the Devon Falls Leaf Festival	259
31.	1 Day to the Devon Falls Leaf Festival	267
32.	1 Day to the Devon Falls Leaf Festival	277
33.	0 Days to the Devon Falls Leaf Festival	285
34.	One Week After the Devon Falls Leaf Festival	293
Epilogue		306
More Books by J.E. Birk		319
About the Author		321

About This Book

My two celebrity crushes might both be into me. What could be wrong with that? As it turns out: everything.

The world has thrown me a lot of challenges over the years, but I've always tried to stay positive. Life's too short to dwell on the negative. Unfortunately, my situation just took a very complex turn: I'm raising my little brother alone right now, but I've got to keep that a secret. If anyone finds out, I risk losing Lou.

My secret gets tough to keep when two international celebrities show up in our small town and start paying me all kinds of attention. I've got zero dating experience and plenty of reasons to stay away from them both, but keeping my distance isn't going to be easy. First there's Colin, the quiet and brooding former race car driver who seems uninterested in everyone and everything... except me. And then there's Tom, the charming movie star, who flirts with me like it's his job. Oh, and did I mention the two of them are best friends? Or that I think Tom might have some *very* deeply hidden feelings for Colin?

I'm definitely in over my head here. If I want to keep Lou safe, I know it's best that I keep both men at arm's length. So what do I do? I start renovating a hotel with them.

Oops. But I'm sure if I just stay positive, everything will work out fine. Right?

Right?

Fanboy in the Falls *is an MMM famous people/commoner romance. It comes with a brooding race car driver, a hopelessly romantic movie star, and the sweet cinnamon roll who is not supposed to fall in love with either of them. It has a guaranteed HEA and no cheating. This is a Devon Falls book, so of course it also comes with a leaf festival and plenty of small town quirk. This is the third book in the Devon Falls series, but it can be read as a standalone.*

Author's Note

I know many of you, like me, visit Devon Falls as a means of escape. This town is my happy place: a place that celebrates inclusion and love. Devon Falls doesn't get everything right, as none of us do, but I have always wanted this town to be a part of the world where people can take ownership of their mistakes and fix them. I have always wanted Devon Falls to be a version of the world I would want all of my loved ones to live in.

This book celebrates the same tenets of inclusion and belonging that both of the first books in the series celebrate. But that feeling of belonging is hard-won in *Fanboy in the Falls.* This book has references to some queerphobia and genderphobia, as well as some references to fatphobia. Spoiler alert: hate does not win the day in Devon Falls. I share that spoiler with joy, because I believe that romance novels should be a place where we can breathe in the knowledge that happy endings are coming. The book does have the very happiest of endings. But the journey to that ending is not always easy.

Here are a few other things to know before you visit Devon Falls! As with all my Devon Falls books, I play with the edges of reality at times in this story. Expect to suspend some disbelief here and there, particularly where fire science, medical science, and social service systems are concerned. I always enjoy suspending some of my own reality while I'm writing for this series. Along with an occasionally tenuous relationship with real life, this book also has an age gap between characters, a nearly obsessive use of nicknames, and a very charming six-year-old who loves princesses with his whole being.

Early readers of this book: I am, once again, so very grateful for your time and wisdom! Big thanks go out to Dianne (aka Mom), Megan, Annabeth, Knox, Katy, Leslie, Rachel, Shantel, Riley, and everyone else who has helped me make Devon Falls the best town it can be. Great thanks go out to Kari Shafenberg, my editor, and her endless patience with my continued love of ellipses.

One last thing: typos are the nemesis of every writer! Should you find a typo in this book, please email jebirk@jebirk.com so I can fix it.

And now... enter Devon Falls at your own risk of falling in love with Gabe, Tom, Colin, and Lou. They've stolen my heart, and I hope they steal yours as well.

Love,

J.E.

Chapter 1

43 Days to the Devon Falls Leaf Festival

I'm a twenty-one-year-old who's never even been kissed. And I'll stay that way forever if it keeps my brother safe. —Gabe Gomez

I stand over a bowl of cereal filled with nothing but milk and purple marshmallows, wondering if this is the moment when my world finally collapses.

"Gabe? Gabe?" A small hand tugs at my sleeve, and I look up from Lou's breakfast to find him staring at me. He squints his eyes together tightly. "Were you daydreaming again?" he asks.

I smile weakly and try not to think about my cell phone on the countertop, the one that sparked my drift into la la land while I was supposed to be eating and enjoying the most important meal of the day with my little brother. Six-year-old Lou has no clue why my phone beeped with a message as I was pouring milk for him a moment ago, and there's no way I'm telling him. My greatest mission in life is to keep Lou safe and happy, and that means making sure he's completely shielded from text messages that turn my heart into the drum line of a college marching band and send my pulse rate through the stained roof of our tiny kitchen.

I reach across the table to ruffle his hair. "Sorry, buddy. I got distracted. Were you saying something?"

"Yes! I was telling you that I have twelve purple marshmallows left today." Lou digs his spoon into the bowl. "That's two more than yesterday."

"That's great. The more purple marshmallows, the better the day it's going to be, right?" Lou nods eagerly. He dressed himself this morning, and he's wearing his favorite green skirt over his jeans. It matches the green-and-blue flannel shirt he's got on and the Mary Jane shoes he fell in love with the last time we visited the secondhand store. His beloved morning ritual is painstakingly poking the purple marshmallows out of his way as he eats through the cereal and other colored marshmallows first. And every morning he tells me how many purple marshmallows he ended up with.

He slurps away at his cereal, and I give the top of his head another quick rub, relishing the bright grin he sends back to me. Our mornings together in this house are something I've really come to treasure. I'm going to miss them if... *nope, don't think about that. You can answer that message. You can figure this out. You can do hard things. You can do anything you put your mind to. You are all-powerful.*

It was my last foster mother who taught me all about self-affirmations. Saying them made me kind of uncomfortable at first, but I kept doing it to make her happy. That was always my most important rule of living with Dave and in every foster or group home I ever stayed in: *smile and do what people tell you to do.* As long as I never upset anyone, as long as I stayed positive and smiling, I knew I'd be safe. So I did the affirmations with Ja'nae every single day, and eventually, they started to become a habit.

"Gabe? I'm finished!" Lou holds up his bowl triumphantly, and I glance over at the clock. Shoot, we're going to be late if we don't get going soon. And letting my brother be late for school is never an option on any day, especially this early in the school year. Not if I don't want his teacher and principal to start asking questions.

"Let's go, kiddo!" I announce. I swipe my phone off the counter and drop it into my pocket without looking at the screen again. Then I throw my poor, ignored toast into a plastic container. Hopefully I'll find an appetite for it later. Bethany keeps making comments at work about how I'm losing too much weight, and that's not the kind of attention I need right now either.

I get Lou buckled into his safety harness in the small backseat area of my bright yellow '84 Ford truck, the one I inherited from my father. Then I put on the *Frozen* soundtrack, Lou's favorite, and we sing together about building snowmen as we coast down the main street of Devon Falls, Vermont, past the town square that sits off to one side of Main Street and the few small churches surrounding the large green lawn. My stomach clenches slightly at the sight of the Pride flag flying over the Devon Falls community church.

When I first realized this was where Lou's dad, Dave, took him after my mom died and Dave left me behind in foster care in Connecticut, I thought Devon Falls seemed like the perfect haven for Lou to be raised in. A small town filled with maple leaves and pride flags and people who waved at you when you drove down the street was almost too good to be true. Maybe Dave would be different here, I thought. Maybe he'd finally get off his favorite message boards and stop listening to all the nasty little voices talking to him there. But this morning's text message from him was just a reminder that things haven't worked out that way.

You can do hard things. You are a strong human. Breathe in courage. Breathe out doubt.

I vaguely recognize the teacher on drop-off duty when I pull up to Devon Falls Elementary. She sometimes comes to events at Northern Stars Winery, where I work, but I can't recall her name. The school is a one-story building, constructed in a T-shape that spreads out in four directions, with two long glass windows at the front entrance covered in children's artwork. A painting of Lou's, featuring a castle and two princesses holding hands while they stand next to a dragon, is front and center in that window. His art teacher gave it an award for best brushwork. I fed Lou so much congratulatory ice cream the night he won that, but I never texted Dave to tell him about Lou's prize. I knew he'd ask to see the picture, and that would only cause trouble.

I help Lou down out of the truck and sink hard into the deep, long hug he gives me. "I love you, Gabe," he tells my stomach, and I relish the words. Lou may be my only real family right now, but he's all the family I need. I brush his blond bangs out of his eyes. No one would ever guess that he and I are related by looking at us. Our mom had Italian heritage and my dad had Mexican heritage, and I've got a natural tan all year round. But Lou has Dave's skin, which is so alabaster pale he burns right away if I don't keep him slathered in sunscreen during the summer. My hair and eyes are both dark brown, a total contrast to Lou's. People in Devon Falls still seem surprised to learn we're brothers.

"Have a good day today, okay?" I tell him. "And remember—"

"I know," he interrupts cheerfully. "If people ask where Daddy is, he's still working! Bye, brother!" Gabe scampers off toward the school building, and I wave weakly before I hop back inside my truck. As soon as I'm back behind the wheel, I turn the *Frozen* soundtrack up as high as my truck's weak speakers will go. I sing as I drive to the winery, coasting down roads lined with grazing dairy cattle, brightly colored barns, and forest and grass that span every shade of green you can find in a box of sixty-four crayons.

It's some of the most beautiful scenery I'll probably ever see in my life, and I do my best to focus on it. I can't think about that text message right now. I have a long day of work ahead, and Dave's message is a problem for later on, when I don't have customers at the winery's inn who need welcoming smiles and their beds perfectly made.

Northern Stars Winery is about a mile outside of Devon Falls, placed smack in the middle of a long line of dairy farm pastures that roll into each other across the landscape. Evelyn Shoalski built the winery on some of her family's farmland, and the trip up the winery's long driveway has a view of her vineyards, tall and ready for the fall harvest that will begin soon, and trees just starting to think about transitioning into their fall colors. I arrive at the end of the driveway and pull into the side parking lot where all the winery and inn employees park, and then I take one more deep breath.

This winery and its inn are my happy place. They're both new businesses, and the winery is one of very few wineries in this part of Vermont. Evelyn and her friend Bethany Rutgers, who manages the inn, gave me my first full-time job in Devon Falls. After I aged out of the foster care system, I spent over a year saving up enough money to move to Vermont to be closer to Lou. For a long time after I got here, I was keeping up what felt like about a hundred part-time jobs just so I could eat, pay my rent, and help take care of Lou. Then Evelyn and Bethany saved me when they offered me a job at the winery's inn. My position even came with *benefits*. I was so surprised I knocked over two bottles of cab sav when they told me, but they didn't take back the job offer, even though one of the bottles broke. Now Northern Stars, with the old barn converted into a winery and tasting room, and the sturdy, massive farmhouse Evelyn and Bethany turned into a thriving inn, is my favorite place to be when I can't be with Lou. I don't want any part of that text message coming with me into one of my favorite places in the world.

I hop out of the truck, repeat a few more mantras, and I'm already on the inn's front porch when I see it: the dark green

Porsche that Colin Templegate drives around Lake Devon whenever he comes to Northern Stars Winery.

Oh no. I take a few deep breaths and start considering which
affirmations to say next.

I first met Colin Templegate, totally famous race car driver,
when he and his best friend, totally famous movie star Tom Evers,
visited Devon Falls last year. It still blows my mind that two people
as well known as they are have anything at all to do with Devon
Falls. But Tom is brothers with Dr. Sam Evers, one of the doctors
in town, and Colin's a friend of Sam's. His brother Christian used
to be married to Sam before he passed away. Tom, Colin, and I
had maybe the most awkward moment of all time at the winery's
soft opening last year. I'd like to forget that day ever happened,
but I kind of can't. Because Tom and Colin both started visiting
the winery a lot after that day, and now they're investors in the
business.

I frown as I stare at the Porsche. The car is sleek and perfect and
shiny, and I always imagine that my '84 truck is trying to think of
pick-up lines when Colin parks that beautiful piece of machinery
next to it.

"Yup, he's here," says a voice next to me. I look over to find
Bethany, black hair cascading down her back and hands on the
wheels of her chair, studying me with a crooked smile. She cocks
an eyebrow at me. "Think you'll be able to get anything done
today? Or will you spend the whole day flustered, just waiting to
lose speech the moment you see him?"

"Excuse me! I do not *lose speech* whenever I see Colin Templegate." Which is completely a lie, because I totally do. One day
he was standing next to the front desk when I turned around from
sorting some room keys, and when I saw him standing there I made
some kind of noise I don't want to remember and then threw every
single key across the floor. Colin helped me pick them up, but I
couldn't manage to say a word the entire time.

He hardly said a word either, though. Colin's not exactly a talker, at least around me. Or maybe that's just me projecting, since I can never quite manage to make myself forget that time last fall when I got drunk on a picnic blanket next to him at that soft open last year and blurted out to the entire world that I'm a virgin.

Like the world-famous Colin Templegate even cares whether I'm a virgin or not. I mean, based on everything I know of his public persona, Colin's straight. But then again, most of the world thinks I'm straight, thanks to the unofficial vow of romantic and sexual chastity I've taken in the name of Lou. I'm a twenty-one-year-old who's never even been kissed. And I'll stay that way forever if it keeps my brother safe.

And to be fair, I guess I could be straight? That just seems kind of unlikely given that I've been attracted to all kinds of people since before I even really understood what attraction was. Not to mention the whole "can't stop staring at videos of Colin Temple-gate and Tom Evers" issue.

Ugh, Tom Evers. If he's here today too, I may have to go into hiding. Because of course I couldn't have a giant crush on just *one* completely unavailable famous person. Nope, I have to have a crush on *two* of them. "Is Colin here... uh, alone?" I manage to ask Bethany. Part of me was thrilled when Colin bought an old farmhouse around the lake and started fixing it up. A chance to drool over Colin's sweet, rarely seen smiles, dark semi-curly hair, high cheekbones, and near-constant five-o-clock shadow? *Yes, please!* Another part of me was horrified. What if he ended up coming up for visits here all the time? He's still really close to Sam, after all. What if Tom started staying in Devon Falls with Colin all the time, too, and they both started spending more time at the winery?

I was sure I'd never be able to make another bed in a normal amount of time again. I'd get fired for sure.

Bethany laughs out loud. "Repeat after me, Gabey."

I try to glare at her, but I can't hold it. I pretend to hate her nickname for me, but I secretly love it. Not too many people have ever given me a nickname. My mom had a few she liked to use, but she died when I was sixteen. Since then, it's been just Bethany and...

Well, Tom and Colin.

"Tom Evers and Colin Templegate are normal people," Bethany goes on. "I mean it, Gabey, you have to repeat this after me: They are part-owners of this business now, and I will not gush every time I see them."

I completely lose the glare I'm still trying to keep hold of, and I end up laughing. Bethany shakes her head and grins. "Don't worry, babe. You shouldn't have to play it cool for too long. Colin will probably only stay in Devon Falls until the leaf festival, when we celebrate the opening of our new event space. After that, I'm sure he'll go back to New York. And Tom isn't even with him this time." She frowns. "Actually, I think he's already filming the second movie in that franchise of his."

"Yup. They're mostly filming in California, but also in Ireland. Not that I've got it on Google alerts," I add after Bethany laughs out loud.

"C'mon," she tells me. "We've got a busy day today." She starts wheeling toward the front door of the inn, and I follow her. "The green room and the blue room are clean and ready for check-in. Evelyn's got people working in the barn, getting ready for the harvest, so she asked that we keep the guests away from that area during the day for safety reasons. Oh, and she's going to do some work later with painting the new event area at the back of the inn, so that will be closed off. The rest of the property is still on-limits. But she did mention that the ducks at the lake are particularly loud right now. Maybe it's mating season or something?"

I make a mental note to look up mating seasons for ducks as I follow her. But before we can make it to the door, I find myself pulling my phone from my pocket. And then I'm hitting the unlock button.

I shouldn't read the text again. There's absolutely nothing I can do about it right at this moment, when I need to have my mind on my job. I need to stay focused on the inn right now, not this text message. But it's like my fingers have a mind of their own as I click open the message again.

Dave

> I'll be back for the leaf festival. Don't forget what I said, Gabe. I fucking meant it. Lou's my kid, and I'm the one in charge of him.

My skin thrums as I read the words one more time, and I think back to the questions I asked myself while I was staring at the purple marshmallows swimming in milk this morning.

How much longer can I keep Lou safe around Dave? What would happen if I tell someone what's been going on? Is it time for me and Lou to leave Devon Falls?

I glance over my shoulder at the Porsche. It sure must be nice to be a famous race car driver.

I bet nothing would panic Colin Templegate into thinking about kidnapping a minor and running away from a place he's come to love. Not even a text from a man with the power to destroy his entire world.

Chapter 2

42 Days to the Devon Falls Leaf Festival

Someday, Tom will find a romantic relationship with someone who can give him everything he wants and needs, and I know I can never be that person. —Colin Templegate

"There's something about the air in Devon Falls."

I murmur the words out loud to myself as I take a sip of the glass of marquette in my hand—a Northern Stars Winery specialty—and sink down onto the steps of the porch in front of the house where I stay when I come up to Vermont to visit the winery. That sentence is something my brother Christian used to say whenever he talked about Devon Falls. After he married Sam Evers, he and Sam would come up to Vermont with Jack Lancer, Sam's best friend during residency. Jack grew up here, and Jack loved showing this place off to his friends even before he moved back here to help his mom run her medical practice.

And of course, with Tom and Sam being brothers and with me and Christian being brothers, Tom and I ended up in Devon Falls fairly often. The jokes our parents used to make about the four of us being attached at the hip while we were growing up together stayed funny right through Sam and Christian's marriage and then steadily on through the media's obsession with our friendship while I was racing and he was finally getting big breaks in Hollywood.

But we buried those jokes in Colorado with Christian a few years ago. There's nothing funny, it turns out, about losing part of your hip.

"There's something about the air here."

I whisper the words again as I rub a thumb against brand new blue porch paint. I've spent the last few months renovating this house, and I was hoping at some point it would start to feel like a home. So far, no luck, and I still feel like a damn nomad checking into an Airbnb whenever I pull into the driveway.

My parent's house outside of Denver hasn't felt like home since they abandoned it after Christian's funeral to hide in a condo in the mountains. My apartment in Manhattan hasn't felt like home since Christian and Sam disappeared from Sunday morning breakfasts there and Tom started spending more and more time in LA.

I had hopes for Devon Falls. Sam's here permanently now, and I've gotten used to the idea that he's getting married again. Malachai's a good guy, and he makes Sam happy. I've spent this last year determined to find the next phase of my life after racing, and I was tired of fending off phone calls begging me to come back to the circuit. So fixing up a house in this area and trying to sell a bunch of wine in northern Vermont, of all places, seemed like as good a challenge and next step as any. But here I am, drinking alone and talking to myself on my front porch in front of a sunset full of purples and pinks, wishing I felt a hell of a lot more pride and excitement whenever I looked at the kitchen table I built entirely by myself.

My phone rings in my hand, and I don't bother to look at the name on the screen. I just came from dinner at Sam and Malachai's, so there are only two people this is likely to be: Claire, my former racing adversary/friend, demanding to know if

I'm finally coming out of the impromptu retirement I went into after Christian died, or Tom, who calls for updates and questions about everything from the deeply important ("we need to discuss the ROI percentage on the ads I suggested you and Evelyn run") to the deeply not-important ("my eighteen-year-old co-star says wearing your socks up past your ankles is cool now, but I don't know if I should trust this information").

"Hello?"

"Bestie!" Tom's voice rings over the line excitedly. "Did you miss me today?"

"You know it," I tell him dryly. "Placing stickers on wine bottles for four hours with Evelyn's crew would absolutely have been more efficient with you telling us every single time a sticker was a millimeter too high or low."

"I did that one time, and your sticker placement improved by four hundred trillion percent. I counted," he replies proudly. "So you did miss me!"

"Well, I only had to miss you for about ten minutes before I got an alert in my newsfeed about you." I pull up the headline that I couldn't stop staring at while I was eating lunch, pounding empanadas and meatloaf at Luis' Cafe and Bar in the center of town. "You're dating Beatrice again, huh?"

I gulp back the strange taste of something like unease that always creeps into my mouth whenever I imagine Tom finally settling down with someone. I know I've got no right to any of that unease. I've never been much into dating, and it was easy to swear it off completely when I first earned a spot driving a car for one of the top teams on the open-wheel racing circuit. The public loves to get all up in the personal business of every race car driver who makes it to the big tiers of the sport. Relationships are dissected across headlines, Reddit forums, and every hole of social media. I managed to avoid that scrutiny by avoiding romantic and sexual relationships entirely.

There were always some rumors flying around that I was asexual and aromantic, and for all I know, those rumors are right. I've always found it a lot easier to avoid relationships entirely than try to figure out anything about my romantic life or sexuality in the public eye.

But sometimes I wonder about a life where I could be in a deeper relationship with someone like Tom. Someone who makes me laugh and smile and keeps me grounded in the world in the way no one else does. Someone who would be *my person* whenever I needed them to be, like they say on that medical drama Tom loves to watch.

"Oh, Beatrice?" Tom sighs. "Love, the writer of that article is the same one who's still convinced you're going to marry Claire at any minute. So...."

"Questionable source," we both say together before we start laughing. Claire Bismark may be one of my best friends, but marrying a former rival driver would have implications I don't even want to consider. I'm pretty sure no one on the racing tabloid scene has ever speculated that I'm planning to wed one of my fellow male drivers, but they still love plastering me and Claire across the internet the moment someone sees us laughing or smiling at each other. Heteronormativity for the win, I guess.

"Highly questionable," Tom says. "Nope, I haven't seen Beatrice since the two of us had a *very* delightful afternoon with one of Bea's friends from the touring cast of *Wicked*. And yes, dancers are just as flexible as you might imagine."

I won't imagine that at all, thank you very much. Tom may fill the role of *my person* for me now, but I'm all too aware that he can't forever. I've just never been attracted to Tom that way. Hell, I've never been attracted to many people at all. Something about my wiring, I guess.

But Tom's not like me. Tom's wired for love and romance. Someday, he'll find a romantic relationship with someone who can give him everything he wants and needs, and I know I can never be that person.

I don't like to think about the day when Tom finally finds *the one.* Will he and I still take vacations together, just the two of us? I'm guessing not. He probably won't sleep in my bed when he stays with me anymore.

Change. Things will fucking change; I know that for sure. Just like they did after Christian died and I stepped away from racing, into this weird, long-ass abyss I'm in now, the one where I just keep trying to figure out what the hell my life is supposed to be from now on. I take a long sip of wine and decide it's time to change the subject. "I saw Gabe at the inn today when I was working there. All I did was tell him I was leaving some paperwork for him, and he almost dropped a whole case of wine on both of our feet."

Tom bursts out laughing. "Oh, little one!" he says fondly. *Little one.* That all started as a joke at the winery's soft opening last year, on that day when all three of us got kind of wasted and Tom and I ended up taking care of Gabe after he lost most of his cheese and cracker plate into some rhododendron. Tom and I learned two things that day: Gabe had never had wine before in his life, and I have a penchant for making up nicknames for people when I'm buzzed. "I suppose that means he's still not over his crush on you," Tom adds, his tone mild and teasing.

"I still think it's more hero worship than a crush," I answer. "And you know he worships you too, Tommy." Which is all fine. Gabe's thing for Tom doesn't give me the strange heebie-jeebies that thinking about him and Beatrice does. And over the years, I've gotten used to people acting strangely around me just because I had skills driving a car and won a lot of money and attention doing it. I was never in that car for the money or the attention. I was in it for the adrenaline rush. For the thrill of winning.

Still, I spend a lot of time hoping I'm right, and Gabe doesn't really have an *actual* crush on me or Tom. That would be complicated as hell for way too many reasons. Reason number one being that Gabe is one of the very few people I've felt any kind of real, immediate connection with in one hell of a long time. There's just something about the guy. Maybe it's his perpetual cheer, or his excitement for life, or the way he blurts out his life secrets on blankets and throws keys at me. Whatever it is, I know I have a hard time looking away from him when he's in the same room with me. And that's not something I can say about too many people I've ever met.

Until I figure all that out, it's easier to just hope Gabe will get over this hero worship he has for me and Tom so he can run the winery's inn without dropping hundreds of dollars of wine on both our toes.

"Ah." Tom sighs. "Our little fanboy. Well, slip him some Xanax, bestie, so he doesn't go apoplectic when I show up at Northern Stars tomorrow."

I nearly choke on my marquette. "Excuse me? What are you talking about? You're starring in a movie, Tom. You're filming. You can't come to Vermont right now."

There's a long silence on the other end of the line. "Schedule changed, darling," Tom finally says. "They finished up my part early, so I'm all wrapped. I figure I'll come out to Vermont and stay until the leaf festival, so I can help set up for the new event space opening."

Most of me wants to pump my fist and do what Claire calls my "white man's excuse for dancing," but the other part of me is stuck on questions. Tom was supposed to be filming for months. How the hell did they finish up his scenes so quickly? "Are you sure everything's okay?" I ask him. "You can just disappear like that? Don't you need to stay in LA for publicity or whatever?"

There's another long silence. Well, long for Tom, anyway. "I was just thinking," he finally says softly. "Do you remember what Christian used to say? He used to say there's something about the air in Devon Falls."

You know the worst part of having a best friend who's been in your back pocket since you were six years old? They understand every damn part of you. Every piece of every cell in your body. Every segment of your soul. And they always know how to make you shut up when they want to. They know the exact right words to say.

So I decide it's time to stop looking a gift horse in the mouth. The house behind me always feels much less like a rental when Tom is here. Having my best friend show up in Devon Falls is the equivalent of the first-place racer in front of me getting disqualified, and I'll happily take this victory, however unearned it may be. "Send me your flight info," I tell him. "What time are you—oh, crap." A beeping sound in my ear interrupts me. "Hey, Tom? Malachai's on the line. Let me call you back, okay?"

"Malachai's calling you? Of course," Tom says. He knows Malachai doesn't call me a whole hell of a lot. We get along fine, the two of us, but I think I still make him a little uneasy at times. That makes sense, given how weird I acted when I first found out about him and Sam getting together. These days, I'm determined to make up for my behavior back then and make sure he can feel comfortable around me. So if Malachai's calling, I'm picking up.

"Malachai, what's going on?"

"It's all over the town message boards," he practically shouts. "The inn's on fire!"

Chapter 3
40 Days to the Devon Falls Leaf Festival

Never fall secretly in love with your straight best friend, no matter how lovely his hair smells. The pining will have you in therapy by twenty-five. —Tom Evers

I could go my whole life without ever getting another call that a place I love is on fire, but firefighters? That's another story.

"Have I mentioned how much I love a town where the local heroes show back up after the tragedy?" I cross my arms over my chest and lick my lips. Next to me, Gabe Gomez bursts out laughing. His laugh is something like a high giggle: bright and clear, just like him.

"That's Doug and Zeke," he says, as we both watch the two large, tall, and rather broad men circling the room together. "They're the La Fierte firefighters who were here the other night putting out the fire. They do fire inspections around the county. Oh, and Doug's also the mayor of La Fierte."

I turn to face him. "You're joking. That's next-level small town life. Does one of them also run a small muffin shop or, say, an animal rescue?"

Gabe frowns and scrunches his nose the way he does whenever he's thinking hard. "I guess they did sort of rescue this cow once, but that was more of an accidental kidnapping. It wasn't their fault, though. The kidnapping, I mean. But it's a really long story," he adds, like he hasn't just dangled the strangest plot premise I've heard right in front of me.

I'm tempted to ask for more details, but there's already a lot going on today, and I frankly don't have the energy to add "accidentally kidnapped cows" to the list of things I need to focus on. Right now, I'm just grateful Gabriel Gomez is speaking coherently to both me and Colin without causing any physical disasters in the room we're standing in. Not that things could get much worse here.

I arrived in Devon Falls the morning after the fire at the inn to find all the guests relocated to another BnB while Bethany, Evelyn, and Gabe played damage control. Since then, we've all been waiting to get into the back half of the inn, where the fire broke out and was thankfully kept in check, to see the full extent of the damage. And I have to say: so far, this whole situation is all quite reminiscent of the time one of my co-stars took a chance on an ill-advised nose job. Not horrific, but certainly less than ideal.

I cast my eyes around the room we're standing in, which is scorched and scarred throughout, featuring half-burned furniture, walls grayed with smoke damage, and blackened chunks of carpet. It's a depressing space, to say the least.

Evelyn sighs as she appears next to me and Gabe. Her blonde curls are jumping from her head and her dark eyes are narrowed and serious.

I personally feel that it's best to keep a certain lightness in all situations, even those involving large flames and enormous property loss. "Well, doc," I say. "What's the damage? Are we looking at a full amputation?"

"Funny." But a corner of her lip does perk up in a slight near-smile, and I take that as a win. "It certainly isn't good, that's for sure." She crosses her arms. "But Zeke and Doug confirmed the outlet that caused everything was a lone problem, so there are no larger electrical issues we need to worry about. And luckily, none of the outbuildings were damaged. The La Fierte firefighters came to support the Devon Falls department, and they got everything under control quickly. Doug," she calls out. "I'm sending your department and the Devon Falls department cases of my best cab franc!"

Doug makes a motion like he's tipping a hat he isn't wearing. "That's very kind of you, ma'am." He frowns. "What's a cab franc, now?"

Zeke waves at Evelyn in a gesture not to worry about answering, and then he starts whispering to Doug.

"And," Evelyn goes on, "really, it could have been so much worse. Thank goodness they kept everything away from the wine production areas."

All those chemicals. All that alcohol. I shake off catastrophizing thoughts of all the horror that one errant outlet could have caused.

Evelyn sighs again. "Eric's just finishing up looking everything over. Then he'll be able to tell us more."

"Eric is Jack's former brother-in-law," Gabe mutters to me. "He's also a construction manager. Oh, and he's Evelyn's second cousin, I think."

When on earth did he find time to memorize the Devon Falls phone book directory? And is *everyone* in this area related?

I let my eyes drift around me to Colin, who's standing in the corner next to the remains of what used to be blue patterned wallpaper. He's got his arms crossed, and he's focused on a conversation with this famed Eric Maggio, who I've only just met. I had no idea he was a relative of Jack's. That's most unfortunate, given that

I will need to murder him if he stands even one half-inch closer to Colin. Even from this far away, I can visualize every sensory detail he's experiencing right now: the gentle comfort of Colin's low voice, the scent of his strawberries-and-cream shampoo.

Never fall secretly in love with your straight best friend, no matter how lovely his hair smells. The pining will have you in therapy by twenty-five, I swear.

I look away quickly as Eric and Colin make their way across the room to join us. "Well," says Eric. "The winery's all good to go, as you know. No problems there. And as far as the inn is concerned, the front check-in area, dining and sitting area, and front three bedrooms are fine. They weren't even touched." He frowns. "But all four bedrooms back here took a hit, and the attached shed area you were turning into that event space got singed too. You're pretty lucky, in some ways. The structure wasn't permanently damaged, so virtually all of the repairs you're looking at are cosmetic. But they'll still be expensive."

"And time-consuming," Evelyn mutters. She shakes her head. "Insurance money will take forever, and with how busy construction companies are right now, I'll never be able to find people to get us up and running again before the festival. You wouldn't be able to take this on, would you, Eric?"

Eric shakes his head apologetically. "No, I'm afraid not. The company I work for has all its crews on apartment builds in Burlington right now. It would be a hell of a thing finding anyone who could do the work with such a quick turnaround."

Evelyn frowns. "Then maybe it's best if we just call time on the inn and the event space projects for now. We can close the inn for the season and look at reopening next year."

Gabriel gasps, and my heart jumps in my chest as I watch all the blood drain from his face. "No, Evelyn!" he all but shouts. "No, please. I love this inn! And I need this job!"

Evelyn sends him a soft smile. "I know how much you love working here, Gabe. But you've had other jobs. We'll help you find a new one, I promise you that."

If I remember correctly, Gabe used to have approximately twenty-seven jobs. I couldn't keep track of them all. I wonder if this is the first full-time position he's been able to land in Devon Falls.

Gabe's Adam's apple bobs in his throat. I recognize the look in his eyes: terror. Desperation. Panic in the face of uncertainty. The rug of his world has just been pulled out from under him, and I have a feeling this isn't the first time he's experienced that.

It's a feeling I know all too well, unfortunately. And honestly? I'm quite tired of it.

So I clear my throat.

"We can do it. Renovate the rooms and the event space," I say.

The group turns to stare at me. Colin raises an eyebrow. "I'm sorry, what?" he asks.

"Pardon me, I misspoke." I smile at him. "Colin's the one who's been renovating a house for months now. He'll do most of the work that requires someone with actual skills in the area of saws and nails. I'll provide design input. And most likely sandwiches."

Colin snorts.

"And Gabe can help us," I add, because being out of a job is clearly one of that man's greatest fears right now. "He can stay on the books for the inn and assist us. If we work at a good pace, we can have everything up and ready for the leaf festival in October."

Gabe's mouth is open now, and he's staring at me, barely blinking. "You want to renovate an inn? You're, like, a famous movie star!"

Every muscle in my body tightens as I hear those words. But I don't correct him. Now is very much not the time for that conversation.

"And you." Gabe turns to Colin. "You're a race car driver!"

Colin's frowning now, as he looks around the room. He doesn't seem to hear Gabe. "I know how to do the drywall and the tile work. Eric, could you just oversee things? Make sure we're keeping things up to code and whatnot?"

And just like that, I know I've got him. Even this far away from racing, my best friend can never resist a good game. A challenge.

"Colin will make sure we do this right," I tell the group easily. "He can do anything he tries to do. He speaks three languages, you know. Besides English."

Gabe coughs. "Really?

"Si, oui, and... oh, I can't remember the last one. Colin?" Drat, I'm sure I'm making that face right now that I always worry will give away my true feelings for Colin. It's difficult not to smile as widely as possible when I think about all the things my brilliant friend is capable of.

"Ja," Colin says easily. "But I'm only conversational in German."

Evelyn shakes her head. "It's a nice idea, gentlemen. But who knows when the insurance money will come in and what it will cover. I don't have the cash funding for that kind of project. Not right now, at least."

"We can cover the gaps financially while you work with the insurance company," I tell her. "We're investors, after all. Aren't we?" I look over at Colin again, and he nods.

"Then it sounds like we've got a plan!" Eric claps his hands together excitedly. "This is great news. Colin, let me show you something on that wall you'll want to be thinking about."

He, Evelyn, and Colin head off to stare at a beam of wood, but Gabe keeps wide eyes on me. "I can't believe you just offered to do this," he says softly. "I mean, you're right in the middle of making a movie!"

Oh, dear. He's getting very close to asking some dangerous questions. I must distract him.

"I can tell this place matters to you," I say. "That this is more than just a job for you."

He tilts his head slightly to the side and frowns again. "Yeah," he says quietly. "It really is, I guess. Even if I may not get to stay here for too much longer. I want to work at the inn for every moment that I possibly can." He shrugs. "I love the winery and the inn, and I want both of them to succeed. I want to have been part of something that matters, you know?"

What on earth is he talking about? I don't remember Evelyn or Colin mentioning anything about Gabe leaving Devon Falls anytime soon. "Are you—"

"Okay," says a voice from behind us. Firefighter Number One. Doug. Never mind; I'll have to continue interrogating Gabriel Gomez later.

"Well," Doug says, "everything looks structurally sound. Zeke and I did a pretty thorough look around. I think we're about ready to head out."

Next to him, Zeke grunts. From what I can tell, Zeke is not a man of many words.

"Okay." Gabe nods. "Thanks, Doug. It sounds like we've got a plan to maybe get things fixed up here. Hopefully." He sends me a sideways glance, like he's not entirely convinced Colin and I meant what we just said about taking on this project. I have a sneaking and sad suspicion that Gabe is used to people letting him down.

"Hey, that's great news!" Doug claps his hands together. "I hope you all get this done before the festival. I was thinking of maybe booking us a romantic few days here that week. You know. Walk through leaves, enjoy some time away from mayoral duties and hockey tournaments and deadlines and whatnot." He winks at Zeke. Zeke rolls his eyes, but I see the corners of his mouth tilt up in a smile.

"So you two are a couple?" I ask. "Goodness gracious, does Hollywood know about you? Two firefighters in love and one of them is also the mayor? I see a film of the week right here."

Zeke shakes his head hard. "Over my fucking dead body is anyone ever making a movie about us," he says, but Doug just laughs.

"Babe, the movie star is just teasing us," he says. "And anyway, we're not a couple. We're a throuple. And there's our third now! Hi, Max!" A man approximately half the size of Zeke and Doug waves from the doorway across the remains of the room we're in.

"Hey!" He comes jogging over. He's wearing Chucks, tight jeans, and a salmon colored collared shirt, an outfit I immediately appreciate. I'll have to ask where he found the shirt; I like the fit of the collar. "I finished up my interview over at the Thai restaurant about the Devon Falls open mic night series, so I thought I'd come by and say hi."

"Well, hi." Doug leans down to kiss the apparent third member of their trio, softly and sweetly, and then Max jogs in front of him and over to Zeke, who borderline attacks him with his lips. Not that Max seems to mind.

Gabe makes a sound somewhere between a squeal and a sigh. "You three are couple goals, I swear. Or throuple goals, I guess."

Doug lets out a booming laugh. "Ask these two if that's the case when I leave my socks on the stairs. Anyhow, you two aren't exactly slouches in that department either, from what I can see."

The conversation falls silent as I process what he's just said. Goodness. Doug thinks Gabe and I are a couple?

Gabe catches on more quickly than I do. "Oh, it's nothing like that!" He squeaks out the words. "I'm, uh, not dating anyone. Definitely not Tom! And I've never dated a guy," he adds quickly.

Those words sting with sharp familiarity, a large needle directly to my chest. I swallow and force myself to take the medicine. Gabe's straight, then? I suppose I should have seen that news coming, given the marginal attraction I've felt for him since we first met last fall. I wonder if it's possible to hold a world record for being interested in unavailable people.

I force myself to smile and nod in agreement. "No, we're not a couple," I add.

Doug's eyebrows go up. "Well, my apologies. I hope I didn't just fudge anything up there. Zeke, let's go get this paperwork signed off with Evelyn. Max, want to head to the diner for some chow after that?"

"No one calls it chow," Max calls after him as Doug and Zeke walk away. Zeke makes a sound somewhere between a laugh and a grunt.

Gabe frowns as he pulls his phone from his pocket. "Bethany's texting," he says. "She needs help in the tasting room. I'll be right back." I nod, and he disappears through the blackened doorway of the room. A sense of loss rings through me, like a ghost passing through my body. Perhaps I've become lonelier lately than I've realized.

"Sorry about Doug," Max says. He shrugs his shoulders. "He's the kind of guy that sees love everywhere. Which is sort of ironic, since it took him forever to see it right in front of his face."

There's a story there, I'm certain, but I don't feel up to asking about it. Not when I can still feel the residual heat of Gabe's body next to mine. "It's not a problem," I murmur to Max. And I mean that. Because it's always better to know these things, isn't it? When something you want is completely off-limits, it's better to be aware of that. You can't be disappointed to lose something you knew you could never have. I swallow down all the obnoxious little feelings littering my stomach. "No problem at all," I add as I let my eyes drift around the room toward Colin.

"Listen," Max says, "I don't want to bug you about this, but I was wondering. I'm a journalist. Mostly freelance. And I've heard through some sources that there might be some odd things going on behind the scenes of *The Good Sword*. Is that anything you'd be interested in talking about?"

I barely manage to hide my flinch as I let out a strangled half-chuckle. "Oh, I'm afraid there's no story there. Nothing to tell."

"I see." Max frowns and narrows his eyes, and all too well I recognize the expression of a reporter who knows he's not being given the whole truth. "Okay. Well, listen. If that's the case, then I'm sorry I bothered you. But just so you know... if you ever do want to talk to me, I'd be happy to listen and make sure your story was shared fairly." My pulse immediately speeds up. "I'm sorry to tell you that there's no story," I repeat, keeping my voice as even and neat as possible. "I just finished filming for the second installment, actually. Now I'm here."

Max nods. "Okay, then." He shrugs. "Like I said, no pressure at all, ever. And I know you barely know me, but you can read some of my stuff if you want to see what I'm about. You're a great actor, and you seem like a really great person, the way you're supporting Northern Stars Winery and the people here. I'm just saying, if you ever need a megaphone to tell your story, I'm happy to help with that."

Doug calls his name, and Max and I shake hands briefly. Then he leaves. I stand stock-still in place, unable to process everything he's just said. The words of my final conversations in LA pulse through my brain.

Not sure this is working out.

Time to re-think this contract.

If you'd just keep your mouth shut, Tom.

Waves of failure push and ride through me. I glance at Colin, suddenly desperate to tell him everything. Desperate for his comfort. Colin is the first person I think of when I wake up in the morning and the last person I think of before I fall asleep. I've spent so many years imagining, wondering, what it could be like if he ever decided he felt the way for me that I do for him. But I know all too well that Colin doesn't feel attraction in quite the same way I do. And I'm very aware that he doesn't feel attraction to me.

Still, none of that knowledge stops me from craving his nearness, his touch, right now. I start to walk in his direction, only to hear a few phrases Colin is saying to Eric.

"Oh, Tom? Yeah, we've known each other since we were little kids. His family lived next door. Sometimes the tabloids like to get weird about us, but we've never been together or anything like that. Just friends. That's all we are."

All this pining might really kill me if I'm not careful. I quickly walk away.

Chapter 4

37 Days to the Devon Falls Leaf Festival

I'm being attacked by an onslaught of hormones my body has no chance against. —Gabe Gomez

So. It turns out I love demolishing things.

"Very impressive, little one," Tom says as he watches me haul the sledgehammer up over my shoulder, draw it down across my body, and crush it against the sheetrock. "You and that sledge-hammer are really having a moment together."

I'm definitely not imagining that the wall is Dave. Definitely, definitely not.

"Nice form!" Colin shouts above the music we've got playing in the background. Heavy metal, which is Tom's favorite. Colin, it turns out, is more into indie rock and rap.

I probably would have thought those preferences would be reversed. Three days into our renovation project, I'm learning all kinds of things about two of my heroes. Like how Colin doesn't like tomatoes on his sandwiches unless they're salted. Or how Tom once sprained his ankle when he tried to do his own falling stunt on the set of a comedy action movie and accidentally crashed into a wall.

Or how they look at each other every single time someone asks one of them a question. Like they're wired to always have a quick mental conversation with each other just to make sure they're both on the same page.

I bring the sledgehammer down a little bit harder against the wall as I wonder what it would be like to have someone like that. A guaranteed partner to look to whenever I needed them—even if they weren't *actually* my partner.

"Nice shot, Gabe!" Colin calls over the music. He drops his own sledgehammer easily over his shoulder and steps over to the pill-shaped speaker by the wall. He bends over to turn the music off, and I do everything I can not to stare at his ass.

If you want to stare at a guy's ass and you identify as a guy, that definitely means you're not straight, right? Or, if the ass in question belongs to Colin Templegate, does that mean you're just human? I really wish someone would explain the rules to me.

Tom wipes beads of sweat from his forehead. "When do we get to be finished with this part, bestie? I don't believe I enjoy destroying property nearly as much as the two of you."

Colin tilts an eyebrow. "There's a hotel room in Ibiza that suggests otherwise."

"I'm insulted." Tom huffs, but he's smiling. He drops his own sledgehammer and crosses his arms over his chest. "My dates were responsible for most of that damage, as you well know. Especially the sink that fell out of the wall."

I cough. "A sink fell out of a wall?" Now I grip my own sledge-hammer even tighter. What the heck were they doing to make a sink fall out of a wall? And *dates*? Multiple people caused the destruction of the sink together?

My brain's working overtime conjuring up fantasies, and I have to drop my arms to quickly cover my groin. Good thing I wore very loose jogging pants today.

Colin snorts. "If I remember right, the bed also withstood some serious damage." He smirks at Tom, who just smiles and winks. I tighten up my hands and pray that neither of them notice the slight rise in the cotton of my joggers.

"Well, good news," Colin says. "We're nearly done for the day. Eric said to take out this wall between the bedroom and bathroom; this is the only one that had serious drywall damage. So if we finish taking out this section, we should be good."

I feel like cheering. We're only a few days into this project, and we've already done most of the demo work on one of the rooms. Hopefully, this means we're on schedule for having everything finished by the leaf festival. I know Bethany decided to keep all the bookings for that week, which means we've got to be done by then if we want the inn to stay in business this year.

If only the Devon Falls Leaf Festival, one of my favorite weekends of the year, wasn't also hanging over me like some kind of ticking cartoon bomb clock. Dave texted me again yesterday, because I'm pretty sure he can sense my panic all the way from Rochester.

Dave

Everything good? You still able to work at that winery and take care of my kid? Make sure you keep Lou out of those skirts and tutus. And don't show him any of that weird shit you like. None of those shows with all the gay people.

I *might* have purposely let Lou wear his favorite purple tutu right after I saw that text. And I thought I'd hidden my favorite shows from Dave pretty well the last time he was in Devon Falls, but I guess not. Great. I texted Dave back that everything was fine and then repeated my affirmations for almost two hours straight.

And then I started looking up lawyers. And bus tickets.

"Excellent news." Tom raises the hammer back up over his head. "Honestly, if I'd had any idea how dreadfully boring renovation was, I may not have suggested we take on this project. I simply have no idea why on earth you two like this whole demolition thing so much."

"It's cathartic," Colin and I both say, exactly at the same time. He glances over at me in surprise, and I drop my gaze to the charred carpet below me.

Tom snorts. "Loves, I can think of *many* things that feel much more cathartic than this. Trust me." He starts to aim the sledge-hammer for the wall.

"Be careful," Colin says. "The pipes we're trying to avoid are—"

But he doesn't manage to get the words out before Tom's hammer hits, cracking a large hole into the half-collapsed, blackened drywall there.

And then the water comes.

It spits out from the wall, spraying all three of us, and it's so shockingly cold that I actually shriek like Lou does when I let him run through the sprinklers. "I told you to turn the water off!" Colin shouts at Tom.

"I'm certain I did!"

"Sure doesn't look like it!"

The two of them rush toward the broken pipe jutting out of the wall. "I'll get the water valve!" I shout. I rush past the stream, breathing through the shock of cold. I can't shut off the water to the whole inn, or the guests Bethany and Evelyn let back into the unaffected front rooms will be livid. Luckily, Eric showed us where to shut off different sections of the old house's water. I'm guessing Tom just hit the wrong switch.

I can hear Tom and Colin trading comments and barbs back and forth about wet t-shirt contests and useless YouTube videos all the way to the basement stairs. But the basement under this part of the house is small, more like a crawl space since this area of the building was actually added onto the original house sixty or seventy years ago. I move on my knees through dust, dirt, and cobwebs before I find and close the shutoff valve.

By the time I get back to the room we're working on, I'm panting and gross, and the dirt from the crawlspace has attached itself to my soaking-wet formerly yellow t-shirt, creating rivulets of mud and brown water. I don't even want to imagine what my face looks like right now. "It's off," I tell them, dropping my hands to my knees while I catch my breath. "And I—"

I can't finish my sentence, though. Because Colin and Tom are just standing there, and all of their clothes are completely soaked through. The outlines of Colin's pectoral muscles and nipples are clear and distinct through the blue t-shirt now clinging to his body, and the outline of Tom's belly and arm muscles is telegraphing the exact shape of his upper body.

I choke on my own breath. I'm being attacked by an onslaught of hormones my body has no chance against. My cock stands up so fast it almost hurts, and I know I have to get out of this room before either one of the men in front of me notice. Before they realize that I can't even be in the same *room* with the two of them like this without losing every ounce of control I have.

"I need to rinse off! Lake!" I call out in a choked voice, and then I take off out of the room again, rushing down the back hallway of the building, out the door, past the crawlspace I just came out of, and down to the edge of the small lake that butts up against the edge of the winery's property.

I throw myself into it.

The cold water hits me like a freight train, and for a moment, I have to fight not to panic as the frigid temperature sinks through my body. I manage to grab hold of my breath and hold it before water finds its way into my lungs. I let myself fall for a moment, drifting in the stillness of the water. The world goes still, just for a moment.

And for that moment, I wonder what it would be like if I let myself keep falling. Away from all the hardest parts of the real world.

My mom first got sick when I was fifteen, not long after Lou was born. And ever since then, it's like I've been treading water, just trying to stay afloat in a world that's determined to drown me. That was when Dave slunk out of the hospital room and into an online world, leaving me to take care of my mom and Lou while he just seemed to get angrier and meaner. Then Mom died and Dave took off with Lou, and I was alone and in foster care and so desperate to see Lou again that nothing else seemed to matter but that. And when I finally made it to Devon Falls and Dave started leaving Lou with me while he left to take road work jobs, I thought maybe I'd finally figured it out: how to tread water in my own life.

But then Lou developed a love for tutus, and Dave blamed me for that, and he started to say meaner and nastier things to me, and since then I've spent so many hours wondering if I should take the risk and tell someone what's really going on: how often Dave just disappears and leaves Lou with me, how bigoted and terrible Dave sounds when he talks to me now, how worried I am that he'll start saying the same kinds of things to Lou. But that risk just seems too dangerous, too huge. Dave is Lou's dad, and I'm just his older brother with an arrest record I'm not proud of. What if I said something to someone and Dave ended up taking Lou away from me permanently? Or worse, what if Lou ended up all alone in foster care, just like I did when Dave left me behind in Connecticut? And then there are all these *feelings* about butts that I can't even do anything about, because who knows what Dave would do if he ever found out I might like guys.

Treading water gets harder and harder when every move you make has the chance to sink you down into the water. Just for a moment, I wonder: would it be easier to stay here? In the stillness?

And then something tugs at my arm. *Someone* tugs at my arm.

I let the force pull me until my head bursts through the surface. Sounds come at me from all sides now: birds chirping at the feeder closest to the water, wind whistling gently in the trees. Tom's holding onto my arm as he treads water next to me. I gasp in quick breaths as my body readjusts to having access to air again. Tom tows me to the surface and keeps his hand on my arm, and we both step out of the water and up onto the grassy shore that Evelyn's lined with inviting Adirondack chairs. I feel like I could fall into one now and sleep for a week.

"Little one, did you honestly just dive face-first into that open water?" Tom asks incredulously. I can't tell if he's angry or laughing at me—maybe something in between? I run a quick survey of my body, and I'm happy to note that the cold shock of water did what I originally needed it to do: my erection is gone, and my poor dick has tucked itself between my legs. It's probably terrified I'm going to throw myself off a building if it decides to go rogue like that again.

"I'm fine," I tell Tom in between breaths. "Just needed to... um... cool off."

He arches an eyebrow. "From all that cold water a pipe just spit at us?"

"The crawlspace was hot!" I insist, but it's September in Vermont right now, and while the air isn't exactly chilly, it's not stifling either. Tom just cocks his head at me.

And then he leans. Just a little bit. Just ever so slightly into the space where I'm standing, unable to take my gaze off of his.

His shoulder-length dirty blond hair is curling in wet waves, his lips are bright, pink, and slightly chapped, and I can feel myself memorizing every crack in them the closer he comes. Is he going to kiss me? No. No way. Movie stars like Tom Evers don't kiss nobody inn workers who jump into lakes without warning. The cold water must have shocked my brain.

Tom brushes droplets of water off my forehead. "You scared the bejesus out of me, little one," he mutters. "You just dropped into the water and didn't come back up."

I wish I could lie and tell him that he imagined it; that I wasn't under for as long as he thinks I was. But I remember the intense calm of being underneath that water: the quiet, cold nothingness. It's a kind of peace that doesn't exist in many places in my life. "Sorry I scared you," I finally say instead.

"You should be, love." He brushes more wet hair back from the side of my forehead. My heartbeat speeds up slightly, and he takes a tiny step closer to me. My own feet slip against the ground beneath my soaked sneakers, but I manage to stay still this time.

I should stay still, right? Because this can't really be happening. "Gabe," Tom murmurs. He moves slightly again, and now our faces are only inches apart, his chest nearly bumping against mine. His hands are warm as he places them on my shoulders, and his breath is light against my cheek. It smells like the cherry strudel he had for breakfast. "I'm just so glad you're okay," he finally says. "For a minute I thought..."

He tilts his face slightly, and I study his lips again. What would it be like, I wonder, to have Tom Evers' lips be the first ones that ever touch mine? Would I even know what to do if he kissed me? Would I move my lips the right way? Where do you put your tongue when you kiss someone, anyway? My heart speeds up again, and then I do what I do best: I panic.

"I'm not into guys!" I yell loudly as I pull back away from him. The lie feels like the cold, hard water of the lake as I smashed into it, abrupt and shocking as it brings me back to reality. Because I know for sure now that those words are a lie; having Tom this close to me has definitely confirmed once and for all that I'm not straight.

But that doesn't matter. Not with Dave's presence looming from Rochester and Lou's future hanging in the balance of every rumor that might ever travel to his father from Devon Falls. And I'll lie every single day of my life to protect Lou.

"Oh." Tom jerks back, suddenly, and his eyes go glassy and a little dark. He shakes his head. "Of course. I overstepped. I seem to have quite the penchant for doing that. I'm so sorry, little one." He sighs and runs a hand through his hair. "I absolutely wouldn't blame you if you hated me right now."

"No! Never!" I shake my head hard, determined to wipe that regretful expression off his face. Tom Evers never deserves to look that sad. Especially when all he tried to do was give me everything I've ever wanted in the world. "It's not your fault," I whisper. "Not your fault at all."

Tom sighs. "I just don't know how I keep—"

"Tom? Gabe? Where are you?"

Colin's voice rolls through the air. Tom and I step apart like magnets turned to opposite forces. He wraps his arms around his chest. "We're by the lake, bestie," he says. And is it just me, or does his voice sound a little strangled?

Colin appears at the back lawn of the inn. "Oh, there you two are. Everything okay? I got that pipe fixed."

"That's good." I blink and do my best to nod.

"That mayor of Devon Falls, you know the one with the rainbow hair?" Colin asks.

"Her name is Amelia, love," Tom answers. But his eyes are locked on me. He never looks away, even as Colin keeps talking.

"She called. Said the town meeting this afternoon is all about the leaf festival, and Bethany and Evelyn are going to be updating everyone on the fire and what we're doing with the renovation. They want us to come."

It's like I'm frozen in place, the wet, dirty bottoms of my sneakers sucking at the soles of my feet.

Tom swallows. "Yes, of course. Colin, let's go back to your house so we can make ourselves more presentable. Gabe, will you be able to use the shower in the winery building?"

I nod jerkily.

"Wonderful. Let's meet at my car in thirty minutes."

He slogs across the lawn, and Colin announces that he'll clean up our workspace before he showers. They both disappear from my view, leaving me standing at the edge of the lake, slowly sinking in muddy grass.

Chapter 5

37 Days to the Devon Falls Leaf Festival

I still wonder if something happened when Gabe threw himself into the lake this afternoon. —Colin Templegate

There's something about the air here, bro. I swear.

I roll down the window a little farther in the Jeep that Tom brought up to Vermont with him this week. I'd rather be driving my Porsche 911, but Tom brought the two of us over to the winery today, so the Jeep is what we have right now. And that's probably for the best, since Gabe and his little brother would barely fit into my car's tiny backseat.

And yeah, it turns out Gabe has a little brother. Who we're picking up from school right now so we can bring him to the town hall meeting with us. I'm looking forward to meeting this little brother. I've never wanted children myself, to be honest, but I always liked the ones who showed up at racing events, shouting excitedly and asking ten thousand questions like how I pee when I race and what my favorite brand of chocolate bar is.

My answer was always Almond Joy, which never seemed to impress any of the kids. Poor Almond Joy.

I pull in a long breath and savor the scents that follow. Sweet-grass. Something floral. Maybe a little manure keeping Devon Falls honest. Next to me, Gabe's tapping his fingers against each other and looking everywhere in the car but directly at me or Tom. "Great weather we're having," he says to the windshield. "Don't you think? Not too humid or too much sunshine. And I hear it might rain this week. I hope that doesn't mess up haying season."

It's the fifth time he's brought up the weather since we got into this car. The last time he went on for almost three minutes about the potential snowfall for this winter. I choke back a small laugh. For all the time we've spent together in the last few days, it looks like Gabe still isn't quite over his nerves around me and Tom yet. I glance into the rearview mirror to look back at Tom, who's concentrating very hard on something outside of his window. I still wonder if something happened when Gabe threw himself into the lake this afternoon. I thought the two of them were acting weird when I found them outside together, but Tom said there was nothing to worry about.

Gabe taps his fingers against the console. "Could get more sun, though," he half mumbles. Then he shakes his head. "Shoot, I hope they're not livestreaming the town hall today. I forgot that Lou's wearing his blue tutu," he mutters.

I've got zero idea what he's talking about. I glance into the rearview mirror again and catch Tom frowning. "Is something wrong?" he asks Gabe.

"Wrong? Wrong? No, of course nothing's wrong," Gabe says, his voice so high and quick that he may as well be hiding something behind his back while he says the words. "Nothing's wrong at all!"

Both of Tom's eyebrows go up. I decide it's time for a gentler tactic.

"So tell us about Lou," I say. "He's six? And he's your brother?"

Gabe's eyes light up. "Yup, he's my brother. Well, my half-broth-er, actually. But I always thought that was kind of a strange phrase, you know? Because I don't love Lou halfway or anything like that. We just have different fathers. I mean, of course we do, because my dad died when I was just a kid. That's how I have my truck, actually," he goes on. "He left it for me in his will. He loved that truck."

"He had good taste," I say.

Gabe laughs. "Says the man who drives a Porsche!"

I shrug. "I have a '75 Ford F-150 too. I can drive more than just sports cars."

"Personally, bestie, I never understood the draw to collecting large hunks of metal," Tom says easily from the backseat. "I prefer that all of my cars are simply able to get me from point A to point B. So you and Lou share a mother, little one? Is she also in Devon Falls?"

Gabe looks away from us to stare out the window. "Uh, no. She died when I was a teenager and Lou was just a baby."

"I'm so sorry," I tell him, just as Tom says "Oh, little one! That's terrible."

"Yeah, it was really hard." Gabe turns again and gives us both weak smiles. "Especially since we were living in Connecticut at the time and my stepdad left and took Lou with him to Vermont. He inherited a house from his grandparents here. Anyway, I had to stay behind in Connecticut, in foster care. So yeah, that was... tough."

With every word he says, a fire of anger makes its way through my nervous system. "Excuse me?" I ask quietly. "Are you telling me your mother's husband left you in foster care and took your younger brother away from you while you were mourning the loss of your mother?"

In the backseat, I can hear Tom's breath hitch.

"Um. Well." Gabe makes an attempt to raise the corner of his smile higher, but it doesn't quite work. "I mean, Dave's not my dad, you know? It wasn't his job to keep me. And as soon as I aged out of the system and had enough money, I came up here to Devon Falls so I could be closer to Lou. Now I get to see him all the time. So it all worked out. Oh, we're here!"

I'm still trying to wrap my head about the newsbomb Gabe just dropped as I pull the Jeep up to Devon Falls Elementary School. Gabe basically leaps out of the front seat as we pull up to the curb. Tom and I, meanwhile, sit in silence.

"Is it just me, bestie," Tom finally says. "Or did Gabriel Gomez essentially just tell us a story of a horrific life trauma and smile the entire time?"

"Sure seems like it," I mutter. But I don't have time to say more before the front door of the school opens. Out comes Gabe, and now he's holding the hand of a cherubic little kid who's wearing a bright pink sweater and a blue tutu over jeans with Mary Janes.

Something else Gabe just said races through my mind: *I forgot that Lou's wearing his blue tutu.*

Tom hops out of the car to join me in the front, and Gabe helps Lou into the safety seat he moved from his truck to the Jeep earlier. "Lou," Gabe says gently, "this is Tom Evers and Colin Templegate."

The kid grins. "You're the famous people my brother always talks about!"

Gabe's face goes bright red. "Um, uh. I mean, when we met last year, I told you that I really liked your movies, Tom, and I used to watch your races sometimes, Colin, and—"

"It's always such an honor to meet a fan," Tom interrupts smoothly. He leans over the seat and holds out a hand. "I'm absolutely delighted to know you."

Lou nods. "Are you staying for the leaf festival? Gabe says I have to wait because it's not for a while still, but when it gets here we'll have maple cotton candy! And the dough that you fry and pour the maple syrup on!"

Tom glances over at me. "Yes, we're planning to stay for the festival."

"Oh, that's good! Because my brother likes you, and that means I'll like you too. And you like my brother, right?"

"Uh. Lou. That's not..." Gabe garbles his words as his face goes an even brighter shade of red.

"We certainly do," Tom says. His eyes are wide, the corners of his mouth lifted just enough to show off his dimples. "Yes. We like your brother very much."

Gabe's face stays bright red the entire time he's buckling Lou into his seat.

Chapter 6

37 Days to the Devon Falls Leaf Festival

I've never felt drawn to anyone the way I feel drawn to him—except for Tom, of course. But that's different. —Colin Templegate

"Order! Order, please!" Amelia, who I definitely think of as *the mayor with the rainbow hair*, taps against a podium with a wooden gavel. Then she points it at a guy with a pale complexion, long beard, and suspenders. "Burt, I already told you to stop talking once. You keep up the jibber jabber and I'm not bringing my famous lemon bars to the next church potluck."

"Amelia's also the minister at the local community church," Tom whispers to me. We're sitting all the way in the back row of the Devon Falls town hall, but he still glances up as he says the words. Probably nervous that the sixty-something-year-old with the gavel and pink, purple, and teal hair is going to come for him if he gets caught talking.

"Right. I forgot that part. And she's married to a nudist, right?"

"Yes, that's Ellie. She's Benson's partner at the law practice. Benson is Jack's husband," he adds.

"I fucking know who Benson Lewis is," I tell him as I roll my eyes. It's not like Tom doesn't also have trouble keeping track of everyone in this town. I keep meaning to ask Sam to draw me a murderboard of all the people in Devon Falls. I just never seem to remember exactly how everyone is interconnected.

Burt holds up his hands in surrender. "Sorry, Ames," he calls politely. "That's my fault. I was gossiping about the famous people in them back seats there." He turns to wave at us over his shoulder, and I swear, the entire town turns with him.

I've got no response to that, but Tom waves back and puts on his brightest smile. "Happy to be here, loves," he calls out. "We're only helping out at the inn. No plans to bring the paparazzi down on you all, I promise."

A woman with brown skin and a green-haired pixie cut crosses her arms. "I wouldn't be upset if you wanted to bring some paparazzi over to the Farm-A-Cy." The crowd starts mumbling and talking about whether Devon Falls could go viral. "Can you put us on one of those picture apps? Where the pictures disappear?" Burt calls out loudly.

Amelia pounds her gavel loudly again. "My good gracious! Town, we have business to take care of!"

Things settle down after that, and Amelia launches into the first item on the agenda: a proposal to purchase a giant leaf costume for someone to wear during the leaf festival. There are a few rounds of conversation about who should wear it, and finally they settle on asking Benson, who's missing from the meeting. He's still at work, Tom tells me. "And I do very much hope I get to be in the room when someone has to ask Benson Lewis to dress up like a giant leaf and dance around for crowds of tourists," he adds.

Bethany and Evelyn take the stage and lay out some of their plans for the events the winery will hold during the leaf festival, and then someone asks whether the inn will be fully open again by then. Bethany smiles tightly.

"We're hopeful," she says. "You know we've got people working on it. Tom, Colin, and Gabe, we're grateful to have you three on the job!"

She waves to us in the back row, and both Gabe and I sink down in our seats. Tom and Lou, on the other hand, sit up brightly and grin.

"Oh, Gabe! By the way," says Amelia. "Can I catch you after the meeting? I've been meaning to ask you when Dave's back in town. I need to talk to him about that large tree with all the dead branches that's crossing both our yards."

I watch as all the color seems to drain from Gabe's face. "Uh, sure. No problem, Amelia."

"Excellent!" She claps her hands. "I've been trying to chat with you for days now, but you're a busy little bee!"

Tom and I glance at each other again. I grimace. "Gabe looks like you did that time you entered that pepper eating contest back when you were in college," I whisper. He's biting his lip and clutching at the back of Lou's shirt as Bethany keeps talking about timelines and goals.

"I went all the way to the Scotch Bonnets before I threw up, at least." Tom frowns. "But yes. You're right, bestie. He does."

I'm not even a little bit surprised when Gabe jolts up from his seat at the end of the meeting. "Benson texted me," he says quickly. "He asked if we could come over to his and Jack's place and catch the two of them up on what happened." His eyes are darting across the crowds of people milling around. It's like he's a bank robber trying to escape a crime scene.

Tom purses his lips. "I think the mayor wanted to talk to you, little one. Is she your neighbor?"

Gabe gulps, "Um, yeah. Well, she's Dave's neighbor. It's no big deal, though. I'll just talk to her when Lou and I get back to the house tonight. Let's go, okay?" He basically runs out of the room ahead of us, holding onto Lou's hand tightly as he dodges small groups of people chatting. I watch as his eyes find Amelia at the edge of the crowd. He looks away, fast, and heads right for the door.

Tom raises his eyebrow. "Very interesting," he says softly.

Yeah. My thoughts exactly.

Benson and Jack live in an old Victorian house on Main Street. It's only a few blocks from the town hall, and I swear, the thing looks like it's right out of a Hollywood small town movie set. Front porch with a swing, flowers in boxes, bright blue and white paint, the works. It's about as many miles as you can get from the black, gray, and glass condo I call home in New York. I wouldn't mind if I could get my place on the lake to feel like this house, though. I always feel a weird sense of calm when I walk into the place. It's as if the space itself just invites you in or something.

"Hey, you made it." Jack pulls a pan out of the oven and sets it on the stove. "Thanks for coming over. Benson needs his fix of the town gossip. He gets antsy when they put meetings on nights when we both have to work late."

"Hi. Dr. Jack!" Lou waves and steps toward him. "Are those cookies?" he asks.

"Sure are." Jack comes over to lift Lou up so he can see the tray. "And Benson's going to grill hot dogs and zucchini in the backyard. How do hot dogs, zucchini, and cookies sound for dinner?"

"Yay!" Lou wraps his arms around Jack's neck, and Jack laughs as he hugs him and then sets him down.

"Your brother has a much better relationship with doctors than I did when I was his age," Tom says to Gabe quietly. "If I ever saw my doctor in public as a child, I'm quite sure I would have run in the other direction as fast as I could."

"He was terrified of needles," I fill in for Gabe. "Screamed bloody murder every time he had to have a shot."

Gabe smiles. "I think Lou's the one kid on the planet who probably likes going to the doctor's office. Jack and Benson kind of saved Lou's Christmas last year when... um, well, I was sort of struggling for money. They came to the rescue. Uh, never mind. Hey, there's Benson!" I catch Tom's eye and watch him raise an eyebrow again as Benson comes through the back patio doorway into the kitchen. He's wearing a green sweater and jeans, and his blond hair is sticking out in a few different directions.

"Benson!" Tom crows, and he runs to grab him up in a hug that Benson pretends to hate. I've seen the two of them do this dance before.

"Geez, movie stars," Benson mutters. "No concept of personal space, I swear. And who's this?" he scrunches his nose and pretends to carefully study Lou. "This can't be Lou Avid... can it? No, it can't be! This person is so much taller than the last time I saw him!"

Lou giggles. "Mr. Benson, it's me!" he throws up his hands. "My teacher says I had a growth spurt!"

Benson fake gasps. "Well. My my my!" Then the prickliest man in Devon Falls, as I've heard him call himself, reaches down and lifts Lou up in a hug.

Gabe's facial expression has gone back to that strange, almost wistful look. Tom's expression, on the other hand, isn't that hard to read. He's watching Gabe's every motion, staring at him like his gaze is tethered there. It's more focus than I've seen Tom give anyone in a long time.

Huh.

We end up in the backyard, sitting on Adirondack chairs under the falling sun, drinking beer and eating hot dogs while Lou does zoomies around the backyard like some kind of puppy.

"Your kid cracks me up," Benson tells Gabe.

"He's just my little brother, not my kid," Gabe says, but there's no heat in his words. He almost sounds wistful.

"Hey, now." Jack hands Gabe another hot dog and raises an eyebrow. "I'd say you're much more than a big brother, Gabe. You're the one who brought Lou in for his last three doctor's appointments. You're the one who was at Lou's field day with him during the opening week of school this year. When is Dave getting back from his latest job, anyway? Feels like it's been forever since I saw him at the diner during lunchtime." He frowns. "I'd eat with him whenever we ended up there at the same time. I noticed he was a little out of sorts the last few times I saw him. Is he doing okay?"

The color is draining from Gabe's face again. "Um, he's fine. He's been back and forth between here and New York for work a lot lately. Lots of chances to make money fixing up holes in roads, you know? But I don't mind helping out. I love spending time with Lou," he adds quickly.

"Your stepfather's gone that often?" I ask. I'm proud that I manage to call him "stepfather" instead of "demon hellspawn." After the story Gabe told me and Tom in the car today, I'm definitely imagining this guy as someone with horns, hooves, and a pitchfork.

"Like I said, he does road work," Gabe says quietly. "So I stay with Lou when he gets jobs he has to be away for overnight."

Tom leans over and squeezes Gabe's arm. "Well, I'm sure you deserve all kinds of credit for the way you take care of Lou," he says softly. Gabe looks back at him, his eyes wide and a little watery, and I'd have to be dead to miss the connection that passes between them just then.

I knew what I saw in the lake today was something more than the both of them cooling off. I swear, for a moment it looked like the two of them were going to kiss or something. And now my stomach's swirling as I think about the implications of that.

But there shouldn't be any implications, right? I've always known Tom would find someone who could return feelings for him the way he deserves. The way I've never been able to. And this weird pull I feel toward Gabe probably isn't anything real at all, anyway. Because I'm just not a guy who gets a whole lot of feelings like that. I never have been.

So why do I feel like I'm about to crawl out of my skin right now?

"Gabe," I blurt out. "Are you dating anyone?"

Tom looks sharply at me but doesn't say anything. Across the lawn, Lou giggles and collapses into a pile of clover. "I'll find us a four leaf one!" he calls out.

"Okay!" Gabe calls back. He looks over at me, and he stares for a long moment. "Nope," he finally says. He draws in a deep breath. "Lou takes up most of my time." I don't miss how his eyes meet Tom's quickly before he looks away. Tom's expression stays thin and unreadable.

What the fuck is going on between these two?

"You've got plenty of time," Benson tells him around a mouthful of hot dog. "I barely dated at all before I met Jack. College and law school kept me too busy. And Jack was practically ancient when he figured out he was bi, but things worked out great for him." He leers at Jack, who rolls his eyes and then leans down to peck him on the cheek.

"I'd throw back your snark, but we both know I hit the jackpot," he says to Benson. Then he goes in for another kiss.

"You didn't know you were bi until you were older?" I say the words before I can think too hard about them, and I don't miss the way everyone turns to look at me. Tom's eyebrows are raised again. If he's not careful, they're going to get stuck like that permanently.

"Nope," Jack says. "Well, maybe I *always* knew on some level. Or maybe not." He shrugs. "I don't spend too much time worrying about it, to be honest. I am who I am, and I'm happy." He leans over again to kiss Benson, and I fight the rush of heavy emotion moving up through my chest.

"Plus," Jack says as he straightens up, "I realized that there's nothing wrong with learning new things about yourself on your own timeline. If there's one thing I've figured out over the years, it's that sexuality and romantic love usually aren't straight lines."

"Pun intended?" Benson asks, deadpan.

Jack rolls his eyes and smiles. "Maybe. Maybe not."

My heart's going so fast now that I'm a little worried it might spring out of my chest. Words and phrases are running past my ears like the cars I used to lap on tracks.

Once you know how you feel about sex and love, that's it, right? That's what I always assumed, anyway. My brother was gay, and my former brother-in-law and my best friend both identify as bi or pan, and they all figured that stuff out back when we were teenagers. And up until recently, I've never been attracted to anyone who didn't identify as female. Not that I've been attracted to all that many people at all.

And then came Gabe Gomez, drunkenly falling across picnic blankets in front of me and lighting up rooms with his bright smiles. I've never felt drawn to anyone the way I feel drawn to him. But I figured whatever I feel for Gabe couldn't be attraction; not really. Because if a person is straight, they're straight forever. Right?

Except that logic apparently didn't hold true for Jack Lancer, who's now in one of the most stable, loving relationships I've ever seen. And that knowledge is a little bit of a mindfuck.

I let my eyes drift over to Gabe and Tom. Tom keeps looking over at Gabe, and Gabe's vision is locked on Lou, who's still playing in the same patch of clover, searching for endless luck. I swallow as I do my best to remember how to breathe.

"Colin, darling," Tom says. "Are you feeling okay, bestie?"

Four heads swivel toward me again. I panic. "Benson, the town wants to dress you up in a leaf costume!" I blurt out.

Benson studies me a minute, frowns, and then takes a sip of his beer.

"Yup," he finally says. "That tracks."

Chapter 7

32 Days to the Devon Falls Leaf Festival

Sometimes I can't believe how much we'll put off in our lives for someone we love. —Tom Evers

"Who knew hanging drywall would make me feel so jacked?" I throw up one of my not-quite-so-existent biceps and wiggle my eyebrows at Eric, who rolls his eyes and laughs. I've always had to watch my eating and my workout habits in order to maintain a body that Hollywood deemed "acceptable" for the sorts of parts I've been cast in, but I've never had a physique that naturally lent itself to GQ magazine covers. My stomach is just designed in a rounded form, it seems.

That topic came up during my final days of filming *The Good Sword*, as executives searched for more reasons to destroy my career. I can still remember the comments I had to sit in silence and listen to.

Just doesn't really have the shape to pull this off...

The look is wrong, you know? I hate to use the word fat, but...

Let's face it: you've put on some pounds.

Never mind that my trainer said I was in the best shape of my life during that segment of my career. I quickly drop my arm muscle.

Eric, who's got his hands on his hips as he studies the wall we've just finished hanging, doesn't seem to notice.

"It's looking good," he says. "And everything's on schedule. You, Colin, and Gabe are doing a great job, Tom. Sorry I can't be here to help out more." He runs his hand through his hair and shakes his head. "Between National Guard stuff, other construction jobs, and Elijah, my schedule just keeps getting busier."

I've decided I quite like Eric. It turns out he's always been a good friend to Jack, even after his sister and Jack got divorced, and Colin and I have both enjoyed meeting his son. Elijah's got spunk, heart, and based on what his band likes to play at local town events, he also seems to have excellent taste in music.

"Not to worry," I assure him. "You're keeping us on track, and that's what matters. Colin fills in the gaps with YouTube videos, and he makes sure to boss us around appropriately." I glance over into the attached bathroom of the room we're working in. Colin and Gabe are bent over the shower working on the tile. Gabe's got a look of concentration painted across his face, his eyes narrowed and his tongue sticking out slightly between his teeth and he follows Colin's lead.

I sigh. I feel as though I'm seeing Gabe Gomez's face everywhere these days. At night, as I work to fall asleep. His bright, energetic eyes are the first things that go through my head in the morning. And all day long I feel his energy in the spaces we share within these burnt-out rooms, zipping and shifting back and forth between us.

He feels it too. I'm sure of it. Ever since the day of the town hall, the day we nearly kissed, he's looked at me differently. There's a shy coyness to his looks. A curiosity that I know has been piqued.

But he told me himself that he isn't into men, and I must respect that. Even if I don't fully believe him.

He's still young. He's hardly had time to date anyone, as he told us at Jack and Benson's house that night. He's still figuring out how to fit into the world around him. And his behavior at the town hall and Jack's house that day confirmed for me, with certainty, that he's holding onto secrets that are weighing him down.

Colin's quietly explaining something to Gabe, pointing at a space in the wall where they're tiling some kind of pattern Colin drew up after watching a video about it. Colin's also been acting oddly lately. I didn't miss his reaction when Jack started talking about the discoveries he made later in life. I know my best friend better than anyone, and it's clear as day to me that Gabe is making him wonder about some later-in-life discoveries of his own.

I'm not sure which is worse, honestly: knowing that your straight male friend will never love you back because he's straight, or knowing that your male friend isn't so straight after all and simply will never love you back because he's more interested in someone else. I'd tell Colin that he may or may not be barking up the wrong tree with Gabe, but it's not my place to do so. As such, I'm stuck here in Devon Falls, hiding from the life I've been quietly blacklisted from while I fix up an inn with two men who I can never have despite the fact that they both hold all of my interest.

At least this drywall we just hung looks spectacular.

Eric steps back to look at the wall more fully. He smiles. "The three of you are a good team," he says easily. "I'm a little jealous of what you have here, if I'm being honest."

I snort. "Jealous of this? Yesterday Colin had to teach me and Gabe what a jigsaw was."

Eric grins. "Well, maybe not that part. But working with you three is a nice distraction from my work on sites where half the people don't get along or are just there to collect the day's pay. Which is fine. I get that life. I've been there. But putting up apartments in the suburbs of Burlington with people who couldn't care less about what they're working on isn't exactly a contractor's dream. You three get to work on a place you care about. This inn matters to all of you. You've got a goal, you're determined to meet it, and you're doing the best work you can for each other."

"Have you thought about starting your own construction company?" I ask him. "Getting away from the suburbs and doing more work that really interests you?"

Eric frowns. "Oh, all the time. But I'm retiring from the Guard this year, and Elijah's still got another year of high school after this. Doesn't feel like the right time." He shakes his head. "Maybe once he's in college. It's wild, isn't it? Sometimes I can't believe how much we'll put off in our lives for someone we love. But I'd do anything for Elijah. Hey, hand me that drill, would you?"

I pass over the drill, and he starts doing something with screws and the drywall while I parse his words. *Sometimes I can't believe how much we'll put off in our lives for someone we love.*

It's not the same, of course, his situation and mine. Eric has a son to look after. A living, breathing dependent who still needs him for financial and human security.

But—is that how I've been treating my relationship with Colin? Have I been putting off moving forward, letting myself fall in love, just to keep what the two of us have intact? I remember something Sheila, my last girlfriend said to me, not long before we broke up.

"I know, I know. You have plans with Colin, and he comes first. I get it, babe. He'll always come first."

I didn't bother to put up an argument, because we both knew she was right. I've always put Colin in front of everyone else, especially after Christian passed away. But Colin isn't a child. He's a full-grown adult, and even in his worst moments after Christian's death, he's always been a highly capable adult. That capability is on full display now, as he instructs Gabe on where to set tile after tile. The picture on the shower wall is coming to life now. It's a beautiful mix of hand-painted tiles Colin found at an artisan store, flooded with blues and greens and purples and reds that cross over each other in abstract patterns. Those are flanked with tiles of similar colors that Colin chose to frame them, and then he's boxed those in with a diamond pattern of white tile.

The sun moves through the open window of the bathroom, hitting the center of the tile just right, and now I see all of Colin's strength on full display.

It *is* wild, isn't it, how much you'll put off in your life for someone you love? Especially when you've trained yourself to believe that they need you just as much as you need them.

This epiphany is still swirling in my brain like the pattern on Colin's tiles when there's a knock at the empty frame of the room's door. I look up to see Bethany, who's holding Lou's hand. "Hi!" she says cheerfully. "Look who just got dropped off. Don't step over the doorway, Lou," she adds. "Looks like there might be nails on the floor."

"Best to stay where you are," Eric calls over his shoulder. "Hi, Lou!"

"Hi, Eric!" Lou waves back, always excited to see another friendly face. Today he's wearing a black t-shirt with leggings and the Mary Janes I've noticed he loves. And his purple tutu, which seems to be his favorite item of clothing.

I've gone my entire adult life without ever wanting to have children. But when I imagine the remote possibilities of anything ever happening between me and Gabe, it's strange how easily Lou slots into that picture. As if he was always meant to be there.

If only I understood better how this asshat stepfather factors into the larger snapshot of Gabe's life.

Gabe emerges from the bathroom, wiping his hands. "Hey, buddy. Can you hang out with Bethany for a minute? Then we'll head home."

"Yeah!" Lou claps his hands together. "And then we need to make the cake! For your birthday!"

Gabe goes scarlet as Eric and Colin both stop what they're doing. The three of us exchange looks with Bethany, and one thing is quickly clear: Lou just dropped a bomb on all of us. "It's your birthday?" Bethany asks, voice incredulous. "Why didn't you tell us? This must be your twenty-second!"

Colin snorts. "Were you underage at the winery opening last year?" There's a teasing note in his voice as he looks over at me. I know he's thinking about the many, many bottles of wine Gabe was carrying around that day.

Gabe's face goes so red I'm worried for a moment that he might pass out. "I'd just turned twenty-one," he finally says in a strangled voice. "And I was a mature twenty-one!"

"Tell that to the rhododendron you christened," I answer, but I send him a wink to let him know I'm joking. "How will you be celebrating your birthday?" I'm horrified he didn't tell us about this. Or even the people he works with, apparently. Bethany and Evelyn seem to be the two people he's closest to in Devon Falls. If he didn't tell them, there is only one assumption I can make: no one here except Lou knew when Gabe's birthday was.

"Nothing big." Gabe smiles slightly and wipes his palms on his work jeans. "But we've got cake mix at home, Lou, I promise. And I bought the good ice cream."

"Yay!" Lou dances around in a circle. "Let's go! Let's go!"

Oh, no. This will *not* be happening. I hold up one hand. "Time out, little one. You are not celebrating your birthday with a boxed cake mix. I will not allow that. Bethany, is the dining room available tonight? You don't serve dinner on Tuesdays, correct?"

"It's open and available," she says.

"Then we'll be borrowing it. I'm calling Luis and Thai for Two, and we're getting all your favorites. And a real cake, of course. Gabe, we're throwing you a birthday party."

Gabe blinks. "Uh, you don't need to—"

"We sure do." Colin interrupts him quickly as he sets one hand down on Gabe's shoulder. "Birthdays matter, little one. You matter."

Lou squeals. "Yay, a party! Can we have balloons?"

"Of course there will be balloons," I tell him. "Gabe, go home and get changed. We'll need you and Lou back here and ready at six. Casual clothes," I add when his eyebrows go up in alarm. "No need to break out a tux."

Gabe purses his lips and looks like he's going to argue, but Bethany cuts him off again. "Please say yes, Gabe. You've done so much for us. Let us do this for you."

When he drops his head in agreement, I notice my muscles going slack. *He's said yes.* I hadn't even realized how much I'd been hoping he would. I need to do this for him, I realize: I need to make Gabe the most important person in the world for once, because I'm not sure he's ever felt that way.

And then I need to let go of any feelings I have for him. I need to respect his wishes, his needs, and his timeline for whatever self-discovery he wants or needs to make.

But he's not the only one I need to let go of.

Chapter 8

32 Days to the Devon Falls Leaf Festival

Everything stops. —Gabe Gomez

The last birthday party I had is also the last great memory I have of my mother.

Mom had been trying her best since she'd been diagnosed with breast cancer. She hung up streamers and invited my friends over and bought cake and chips. She smiled and wrapped presents—all from the dollar store, I'm sure, because we had basically no money at the time—and sang and pasted on a bright smile.

But even then, I knew that might be the last real party I'd ever be able to have with her. I remember spending every single second of it as close as I could to her, determined not to let her out of my sight. I wanted her in all the memories I had of that day.

Dave had already started to fall down his internet rabbit hole by then. He'd been spending more and more time online after my mom was diagnosed; he was determined to find some kind of treatment that could save her, and then he fell into video game platforms, and then who knows exactly where he went after that. I don't remember even seeing him at my party that day.

Mom died before my next birthday.

So, yeah. Birthday parties? Not a thing for me. I bring out the cake and ice cream for Lou, but he's the only reason I bother to remember my birthday at all.

All of which means that when I walk into the winery wearing my best unwrinkled chinos and my orange polo, the one you can't see the stain on if you don't look too hard, I'm not sure what to expect. Lou, who's in front of me and wearing his favorite Prince Charming costume (clearance at the Burlington Walmart, I'm proud to say), pushes open the door to the winery's mid-sized dining room and gasps. "Gabe!" he shouts. "Look at all the balloons!"

Because there are balloons *everywhere.* In every color of the rainbow, and they dance and bounce along the edges of the ceiling. Round mylar balloons announcing *Happy Birthday* in every possible font line the walls, flanked by streamers, and giant balloon letters proclaim WE LOVE YOU, GABE on the back wall of the room.

And there's cake, because of course there's cake. Three of them, actually, and I can tell just by looking that these came from Marion's bakery, not from the grocery store. They're smaller, round, and all in different colors, and I'm betting they're whatever she had available in the shop today. And I already know I'm going to love them more than any other cake I've ever tasted. Behind the cakes are platters filled with almost every kind of food Elmer sells at Thai for Two. The platters are flanked with trays of empanadas, and I'd bet my life those are the ones Luis makes at the cafe. I wonder who figured out I'd sell my soul for one of Luis' famous empanadas.

"Not so surprise!" Tom comes charging through the side door of the room with a whole group of people behind him. Sam and Malachai are there, and Benson and Jack, and Evelyn and Bethany, of course. Some of the other seasonal winery workers are there too, and everyone's clapping and cheering. I let out a breath when I don't see Amelia and Ellie in the small crowd. Phew. I've been avoiding Amelia ever since that town meeting, and yesterday she left a note on our door reminding me to call her.

"Too much?" Tom appears in front of me, beaming. Colin's standing off just to the side of him, studying me intently. "Eric's bringing Elijah and the band over soon and then we'll have music! Colin and I were a touch worried we went overboard; Colin says I always go overboard, but I said—"

It's anything *but* too much. It's everything I never thought I'd have again after my mother died. It's everything I desperately wanted during those years I was just surviving alone, first in foster homes and group homes and then in dirty, cheap apartments with roommates who barely noticed I existed.

It's everything I could have wanted and never would have thought to ask anyone for.

I cut Tom off by grabbing him up against me in a hug. His body is warm and strong against mine, and I'm highly aware of the many inches and pounds he has on me. I like being wrapped up in his weight. His strength. When I finally pull away and hug Colin too, I feel both of their strengths merging together around me, like an addition problem that always adds up to the right number.

"Happy birthday, little one," he whispers in my ear.

The cheering goes louder, and I blush as I pull away from Colin. "You didn't have to do this," I tell them. "I didn't need a party."

Tom scoffs. "Nonsense. Of course you did. No one deserves to be celebrated more." He winks easily at me, and all I can think of now is that moment we had together in the lake. I fight back a shudder as I remember what I said to him. *I'm not into guys.*

Sometimes I feel like I tell lies for a living these days. But that particular lie still feels like one of the deepest and darkest I've ever said to anyone. Because the way Tom looked at me in that lake... I don't think anyone's ever, ever looked at me that way before. One of my very first crushes, a man I've admired for years, looked at me like he wanted to make me his entire world.

And I had to destroy the moment by telling him something I know in my soul isn't true.

I swallow as I look away from him. "Thank you," I whisper.

"Eat, everyone! Drink!" Evelyn calls out. "Bethany, grab us some wine?" Bethany nods and heads off to the cupboard on the other side of the dining room, and Lou squeals and runs over to Jack and Sam to show them his new costume. But me? Well.

I can't keep my eyes off of Tom. I can't stop wondering. Imagining.

I eat my weight in curry and rice and empanadas, and I let Lou eat so much cake that at some point he crashes out across Benson's lap on one of the couches in the sitting area next to the dining room. "It's cool," Benson tells me as he pulls out his phone. "I've got some reading to do anyway. Enjoy your party, Gabe." He waves me back toward the door of the dining room.

"If you keep this up, you're going to end up wearing the leaf festival costume *and* working the pie-in-the-face booth," I tell him.

"Over my dead body am I wearing that costume," he tells me, but it's hard to sound fierce when you're whispering so that you don't wake up a sleeping elementary schooler.

"Benson and Jack are good with him," I tell Malachai, who's standing next to me. "I wonder if they'll ever have kids of their own."

Malachai smiles. "I bet it won't be that long before they do. They still watch Elijah, Jack's nephew, a lot when Elijah's dad is out of town. Did you know they met when Elijah was living with Jack? They've basically been parents-in-training their entire relationship."

From what I've heard, it was more than that. Benson offered to fake date Jack to make sure Elijah could stay with him, or something like that. Parents-in-training is probably pretty accurate. I take another glance at Lou, who's snuggled up tightly against Benson's stomach. It's moments like these when I really question if I'm doing Lou a disservice by not telling someone in Devon Falls what's been going on with Dave. Dave's family is from here, after all. The town would do right by Lou, wouldn't they? If I told them the whole truth about Dave?

But it's not the town of Devon Falls I'm worried about. It's how Dave might react if I did that, or what could happen if the state got involved. And that's the thought that is still twisting and knotting its way through my stomach as I follow Malachai back into the dining room, closing the door tightly behind me and pausing for a moment to watch the scenery that's unfolded. Elijah and his friend Pat are playing on a makeshift stage Bethany puts up when the winery hosts open mic nights. They're keeping the volume low and playing through a list of songs from so many different decades that I don't even recognize half of them. People are dancing and talking and laughing, and it hits me all at once: I'm having a *birthday party.*

Whatever happens with Dave in the coming weeks, whatever else he might try to take from me and Lou, he can never take this. Just like he can never take away the last birthday party I had with my mother.

Wetness hits the corners of my eyes, and I'm suddenly having to take deep breaths to keep down the ball inside of my throat. Pat announces the band's next song, but the words are muffled in my ears. I feel almost dizzy on my foot, even though I've hardly had anything to drink. I stumble toward the back door of the dining room and manage to get to the section of the large wraparound porch there without anyone noticing.

I sink back against one of the white porch beams, and I breathe. I breathe in the cooling air of the Vermont fall, watch as the lights from the porch illuminate an orange leaf drifting down from a tree that rises above the roof of the building. I look up at the sky, perfectly clear tonight, and blink back more wetness.

What happens when you try to build a life you can't keep? A life that's built on a foundation of milk and soggy purple marshmallows?

Or something like that.

I gulp back something like a sob just as the door opens. Tom steps onto the porch and closes it behind him. "Are you okay?" he asks. "You just disappeared there." He sighs and wrinkles his nose. "I knew it. Colin was right. Don't tell him, okay? He's absolutely insufferable when he's right. The band is too much, isn't it? I was worried, but Elijah and Pat offered, and Eric told me they like getting practice playing in front of crowds, and I just…"

That's when it all crumbles around me, that lie I told at the lake. All I want in the world is to find out what it would really be like to kiss this man, Tom Evers. And it's my birthday, isn't it? So I decide to give myself the most impossible present I could ever imagine having.

I step up against Tom's body and press my lips to his.

He stops talking. Everything stops. I'd swear that the stars, the wind, the music from inside the dining room all stop at once. The entire world pauses while I kiss the man who just gifted me the best birthday present ever: two hours of believing this life that Lou and I have here, just the two of us, is real.

His lips are soft and lightly chapped, but I only feel them for a few short seconds before he pulls away and holds up his hand. "Gabe," he says hoarsely. "This shouldn't happen. I need… I need to respect what you told me at the lake."

I shake my head. "It was a lie," I whisper. "I had to say that. I can't tell you why, exactly, but I did. I didn't want to say that. I mean, I thought what I was saying was a lie, anyway. And now I know for sure," I add, and my voice sounds small in my ears.

Tom's eyes widen. He stares at me for a long moment. Then he turns to look back at the inn behind us and frowns. "I shouldn't," he whispers. "We shouldn't. I don't know... I don't know if he..."

He doesn't finish his sentence, but somehow I'm sure he's talking about Colin. I wrap my arms around myself, feeling like an idiot. Tom might have almost kissed me in that lake, and I know Colin's straight, but of *course* Tom would think of Colin now. Colin comes first for him in every way. Maybe Tom's supposed to be doing something inside with Colin right now, and I'm getting in the way. "Never mind!" I burst out. "Can we forget I ever did what I just did? Please?"

Tom turns back around, slowly, as he takes my face in his hands. He's studying me intently now, and I fight the urge to blink and turn away. No one's ever looked at me like this: like they're memorizing every part of me, inside and out.

"Sometimes," he murmurs. "Sometimes I can't believe how much we'll put off in our lives for someone we love."

And then he leans over to kiss me again.

This time neither of us pulls away. My lips relax against his, and pretty soon it feels like we're catching a rhythm, letting our lips and then tongues work together. Lightly at first, and then deeper and deeper, and it isn't long before he's pulling my body more tightly against his, pressing our chests and pelvises together, and I realize at some point that I'm so fucking hard it hurts. This is the most intense, perfect moment of my life, and I never want it to end.

But then there's a noise off to our side. A strangled sound, almost like an animal that's been caught in a trap. We both turn fast and look off to the east side of the porch.

Where I see Colin. And he's walking away from us.

Chapter 9

32 Days to the Devon Falls Leaf Festival

Hey Google: How do you know if you're bi? —Colin Templegate

I'm not exactly sure how I end up at Luis' Cafe and Bar. All I know is that after I see Tom and Gabe kissing on the porch outside of Gabe's party, I find myself in my Porsche. Driving. Maybe it's because I'm not sure where the hell else to go. The majority of the people I know in this area are at that party, and there's no way I'm going back inside there right now. It's way the fuck too confusing in there.

Watching Tom kiss Gabe made one thing way too damn clear: *I* want to kiss Gabe. And I've never wanted to kiss another human before in my entire fucking life the way I wanted to kiss him just now. Hell, I watched an entire orgy unfold the night I won the Monaco Grand Prix and didn't have a single urge to even take off an article of clothing all night.

But I watched Gabe Gomez make out with my best friend, and I had that same instinct I used to have right before I made an impossible pass on the track: the urge to go for what I wanted. And what I wanted was to see what Gabe Gomez's lips would feel like against mine.

So maybe I'm not straight after all, and I'm definitely one hell of a terrible best friend.

"What the fuck," I whisper to myself, as I do a few circles around Devon Falls and try to get my thoughts in some semblance of order. Driving used to be the one thing that could give me a guaranteed feeling of calm and relief, and even after I left racing I'd still use driving as my favorite "self-care tool," as my therapist likes to call it.

But tonight, driving isn't helping much. Visions of Gabe keep swirling in my mind, doing cartwheels on top of each other. Eventually I give up on driving and end up parking at the town square.

It's dark outside now, but the lights that dot each section of the Devon Falls square keep it illuminated well enough that I can see the fucking ridiculous statue at the center of it. I'm told it was supposed to be a statue of kids playing with leaves and that it was put up to celebrate the leaf festival. Somehow it ended up looking like a total joke instead.

I frown at the statue. Then I stare at it for a long moment. "So," I finally ask it. "How'd you come out looking exactly like a poop emoji?"

The thing doesn't answer. But I know I'm not the only one who sees the resemblance. Tom told me the last time he posted a picture of it that the post went viral in about five minutes.

I shake my head. "Man, do I feel for your artist," I tell the statue. "Imagine how much time they put into designing and creating you. Maybe they thought you were their life's work. And now all that energy, all that focus, is nothing more than an internet laugh."

Still no answer.

I have a sudden, strong urge to get as far away as I can from the thing, so I start walking. And that's when I find myself at Luis'.

What the hell, I figure. Alcohol isn't exactly my vice of choice, because vices have never really been my thing. But I wouldn't mind a beer or a glass of wine right now.

The bells above the door jangle as I enter, and I breathe a sigh of relief when I see that the place is mostly empty. Just some teenagers in the back goofing off on their phones and drinking milkshakes, and over in the corner I see the two firefighters who did the inn's fire inspection. They're sitting with a smaller guy I remember seeing that day too. The three of them are all in a relationship together, Tom said.

I shake my head and walk toward the bar, because there's another mindfuck I can't quite wrap my brain around. Three people in a relationship together? Is that really a thing that can happen? It's not something I've seen all that much of, actually, and I've literally been all around the world.

"Hey, Colin." Luis greets me cheerfully, but his expression quickly shifts to a frown. "Isn't there a party at the winery right now? I dropped off like ten tons of empanadas there earlier."

I gulp down the blob of who-the-hell-knows-what in my throat. "Still going on." I shrug. "I just needed... a quick escape, I guess."

He smiles. "I get that. Want something?"

I order a craft beer made with maple syrup because it's not like this evening can get any weirder. Luis pours while I close my eyes against those swirling thoughts. That picture I can't get out of my head.

Gabe's hand, soft and light, against Tom's arm. His hair messy, his eyes wide as he touched his lips to Tom's.

Part of me wishes I'd picked any other moment to take a walk around the winery and get some space from the party crowd. The other part? The other part knows that I didn't move when I saw them. I stayed in place. I stayed in place and I *watched.*

And then I couldn't stop watching. I couldn't stop watching Gabe make out with my best friend.

"Hey there, famous new buddy." I look up as a cheerful voice appears out of nowhere. The blond firefighter, Doug, has landed next to me on a stool. "Luis, can I grab the check whenever you get a chance?" he asks.

"No problem." Luis sets my beer on the counter. "Just let me get food out to those kids." He hustles off, and I'm left sitting alone with Doug. Great. Because small talk is exactly what I need right now.

"Good beer," Doug says. "You like that one?"

"I haven't tried it yet." I frown and study the beer.

Doug nods. "I was super skeptical, darn it. I mean, who the heck puts maple syrup in beer? But it turns out those brewers have a gosh darn good thing going. Made me glad I decided to try something new."

I'm getting the impression this guy doesn't swear much. I shrug. "Guess we'll see. New things aren't usually for me."

Doug nods and turns all the way on his stool to look at me. "Why's that?" he asks.

I could tell him that's none of his business. He's a stranger, and I don't talk to strangers. I barely talk to anyone since I retired, actually. But then I look over at his booth, at his two boyfriends, who are laughing and holding hands across the table, and I can't help but ask the one question that's on my mind.

"How's that work?" I blurt out. "All three of you? Together?" I immediately realize what a fucking asshole I just sounded like. "Shit, I'm sorry. I—"

But Doug just laughs jovially. "You're not the first person to wonder." He shrugs. "Heck, I couldn't figure it out when things first started. I thought I was only interested in women most of my life. Next thing I know, I'm falling for my best friend and some guy we both just met."

I nearly choke on my sip of beer. "I'm sorry?"

Doug shrugs. "I know. Sounds wild, doesn't it? Turns out Zeke over there," he says as he gestures to the other firefighter from the inspection, "had feelings for me for years. Never said anything."

He shakes his head. "I mean, I miss a lot of things, but I still can't believe I missed all *that*. I found out, and it opened up a whole mess of feelings."

Well. I guess that's one thing I've got going for me. I may be a hot damn mess where Gabe's concerned, but at least Tom's never given any indication that he's interested in me.

I swirl my beer in its glass. "How'd he get up the courage to tell you?" I realize something else. "And how'd that work with the other guy getting involved?"

"It's a whole story." Doug laughs again. "And as far as Zeke telling me goes..." He looks over at the booth where his two guys are sitting and smiles wistfully. "He says he'd been living a half-life for a long time, not telling anyone he was bi. And Max pushed him to see a bigger world, a world where he could finally be all the way himself. See what living all the way really felt like." Doug turns back to look at me. He shrugs. "Max changed us," he finally says. "Just made me see things I'd never seen before, I guess. Things that were buried down some place I didn't know about."

Luis comes back with Doug's check, and he and Luis start discussing some fire code Luis has a question about while Doug signs it. I just sit there, staring at my beer and swirling.

And then I pull out my phone, because it feels like it might be time to consult Google on some things.

> *Hey Google: How do you know if you're bi? Especially if you're not attracted to people all that often?*

And wow, does that search bring up a whole lot of terms.

Terms like *pansexual* and *demisexual* and *demiromantic* and *gray asexual* start appearing on my screen. They're all terms I've heard before, except maybe the gray one, but I never spent too much time thinking about them very hard. My life's always been pretty straightforward when it came to relationships. First I was a guy who dated girls once in a while, but not very often. Then I was an open wheel racing driver. Then I was... well, nothing.

Now, for the first time, I find myself searching through all these categories and trying to find the terms that fit best. Because *straight* doesn't feel like it fits anymore, but I'm not sure what does, exactly. I haven't been sure about much since the day almost a year ago when Gabe Gomez drunkenly fell across my lap.

I need to drive. I need to get back to the Porsche and drive and drive and drive until my brain stops going in circles. "Thanks, Doug," I tell him as I throw a fifty on the counter and head toward the door.

"Don't you want change?" Luis calls out.

"Keep it or donate it to the fire department!" I answer. Because car. I've got to get to the car.

I'm back at the edge of the town center when I spot Tom and Gabe both standing next to Tom's Jeep, which is parked next to my Porsche. Tom's staring down at his phone, and Gabe's looking around him wildly. "Colin!" he calls out when he sees me.

Tom looks up, and I watch his shoulders drop as he lets out a long sigh of relief. "Oh, thank goodness, bestie," he says as I reach the two of them. "You haven't disappeared like that since the night Sam told us everything about his new relationship with Malachai." He shakes his finger at me. "You promised me you'd never leave me like that again!"

I grimace. "Oh yeah. Shit." Sometimes I forget just how fucking much Tom has worried about me since Christian died, and I really put him through the ringer that day I took off. I know he and Sam panicked when they couldn't find me right away. I hope I didn't just re-traumatize my best friend or something. "That was a dick move," I blurt out. "Leaving like that tonight. I should have told you I was just going for a drive."

Tom raises his chin haughtily. "You certainly should have. Luckily, this town is all of three square miles, so it didn't take us long to find the Porsche."

Gabe lets out a laugh that sounds more like a snort. "Sorry!" he says. "That probably wasn't supposed to be funny, huh?"

"Anything to make you smile, little one." Tom beams at him, and Gabe's face goes pink. Then Tom frowns and takes a step closer to me. "Listen," he says. "I have to ask—you saw me and Gabe together on the porch tonight, didn't you? Is that why you left?"

Gabe stands quietly behind him, pushing at a rock with the toe of his sneaker. Damn it. I've probably just ruined his whole night with my stupid selfishness. It's his birthday, for crying out loud. And it's pretty clear he likes Tom as much as Tom likes him; I never should have interrupted them on the porch. I swallow.

I know what I should probably do here. I should walk away. Tell neither of them anything about what I've been thinking and feeling and fucking googling. I should let my best friend and sweet Gabe have whatever they're going to have together.

But I can't get Doug's words out of my head. *Half-life. Half-life.*

That's what I've been living since Christian died, when I walked away from my entire life's purpose. I know that. I've always known that. I just... I couldn't get back in that damn car again. It's like my whole life's been separated into *before Christian drowned* and *after Christian drowned.* One moment the world seemed simple and straightforward: drive car. Win races. Collect prizes. Repeat. The next minute, everything about that existence seemed stupid. Pointless, somehow. Did I even really like racing, or just winning? What was I even racing toward? An end like Christian, who died alone in a pool, all for a good time at a party filled with people he barely knew?

I couldn't fully explain to my team or friends why I left my sport. I mean, I couldn't even explain it to myself. All I know is that ever since then, I've been chasing *more.* More than what I had before

Christian left this world. But more hasn't seemed to be out there. Just wineries and reno projects and maybe, if I'm lucky, a decent glass of wine or an empanada.

Is more in front of me right now? More than the half-life I've been living? Or is this the moment where I'm supposed to walk away and look for that "more" somewhere else?

But Zeke didn't walk away. And look at him and his boyfriends now. All he had to do was say some words out loud.

I wonder what Christian would do right now—but only for a split second. That's how long it takes me to figure out the answer. My brother never stepped back from anything that mattered to him. He went for everything he wanted with full force. And he never struggled to say the hardest things out loud.

I swallow, and then I open up my fucking mouth.

"Here's the thing," I say. "And it's probably the wrong thing to say, but I'm going to say it anyway. I think I might not be straight." Gabe's eyes widen slightly, and Tom's eyebrows go up.

"Excuse me?" He whispers.

I shrug. "And I've never been attracted to people a whole lot. I'm not sure what that means exactly. Maybe I'm gray asexual or demisexual or something, too?" I shake my head. "Maybe. I mean, Google said maybe. But that's not the point." I'm rambling now, and I know it. Time to get to the point, or I'm never going to say what I need to say right now.

I take a deep breath. "Here's the thing. When I saw Tom kissing you, Gabe..." I shrug again. "What the hell; I'll just say it. I saw that, and I realized. I realized that I want to kiss you too."

For a long minute, the three of us stand there in total silence. And I've got to say: it feels like the same silence that hangs in the air right after you take a car right into the wall.

Chapter 10

32 Days to the Devon Falls Leaf Festival

Love requires sacrifice. —Tom Evers

Well. There's nothing quite like discovering that the straight best friend you've pined for your entire life is not only not straight but also interested in the one other man you have serious feelings for.

This year is beginning to make me wonder if I've angered the universe somehow. Perhaps this is all payback for the time last year when I accidentally kidnapped my neighbor's dog for a week? In my defense, I thought it was just a stray who needed a home. Still, the events of tonight, stacked on top of everything else that's happened in my life recently, are suggesting that I've definitely upset some sort of deity somewhere.

But I can't let on to either Gabe or Colin how shaky and out-of-balance I feel right now. Colin's just shared so much of himself with both of us, and I won't take away from his moment by demanding to know why he can't find some bicurious feelings for me as well as Gabe. So I'll just do what I do best as we sort all of this out: keep my impossible feelings for Colin buried far within me.

We all have our talents, I suppose. And I've certainly become a master of that one.

The three of us find ourselves back at Colin's house, sitting on the large wraparound porch that glints under a combination of moonlight and the solar lights Colin's installed across his property. Gabe's gotten a text from Benson saying that the party is winding down at the inn, but Lou's still asleep, and that there's no need for Gabe to rush back right now. Benson and Jack are still keeping an eye on him.

Benson doesn't even seem to be making any snarky remarks about my disappearance with Gabe. He's being such a dear tonight. Perhaps I'll decide to make an argument against him wearing the leaf outfit at the next town meeting.

Gabe's sitting on the wide porch railing, his knees crossed (he referred to the position as "criss cross applesauce" when he sat down), and I'm fighting the urge to put a hand behind him to make sure he doesn't topple off the railing and into Colin's rose bushes. Logically, I'm aware that Gabe's perfectly capable of making sure he's chosen a seat where he can sit without falling over. What can I say? I'm an overprotective, difficult man at heart.

Gabe clears his throat. "You two have probably noticed that I try to stay a pretty positive person."

I nod. "Yes, little one. Pollyanna's somewhere taking notes."

Gabe frowns and cocks his head. "Who's that?"

"Never mind; sometimes I forget just how young you are. Anyway, you were saying?" I do my best to ignore the rush of humming energy that I'm so certain is thrumming between Colin and me. Energy that's clearly all in my head, as tonight continues to confirm.

Because Colin, as it turns out, does feel romantic attraction to men after all. He simply does not feel attraction to *me*. No point thinking about that now. I clear my throat. "Go on, little one."

Colin nods shortly. How dare he look so confident when he makes mute gestures like that.

"Yeah. Okay." Gabe draws himself up straight on the railing. "Anyway, I'm pretty positive and all... about most things, anyway." I don't miss the quick grimace that passes over his face. *More secrets.* But now's not the time to suss those out. "So I'm just curious if maybe my own optimism has, like, gotten the better of me or something and now I'm dreaming and I don't realize it?" He blurts the last words out.

"Excuse me?" Colin asks at the same time I say "Come again?"

Gabe throws his arms up in the air, and both Colin and I jolt toward him as he rocks backward on the railing. He rights himself quickly, though, and we both sit back down. "You! You two!" He points at me. "You're a famous movie star! I used to watch you while I—um—never mind, but the point is that you're *famous* and you gave me my first kiss tonight!"

Colin's eyes widen as he turns to look at me. I, for my part, can only think about that kiss right now: the way Gabe explored my lips and his hands moved gently up my sides. Like he was trying to memorize every detail of me while I did the same for him. It was, to be honest, a level of emotion I'm not generally used to feeling while kissing someone.

"And you." Now Gabe points to Colin. "You've won a World Driving Championship! But first you decide to help me save an *inn*, and now you say you want to kiss me too?"

"To be fair, I'm also saving the inn," I point out.

"*Saving* is a bit of a strong word, don't you think?" Colin says as he turns to me, but he's smiling. "Yesterday you carried in three rolls of wallpaper and then spent an hour sitting on the floor while you showed me and Gabe pictures of carpeting options."

"You'd be lost without my supervisory capabilities, darling. You wanted to choose *marigold* as a paint color." I shudder. "The horror."

"Anyway." Gabe interrupts us and crosses his arms. "I'm just a little confused here, okay? Because I still don't get how even one of you could like me, let alone *both* of you."

It's on the tip of my tongue to say one word in response, but Colin gets there first. "Why?"

Gabe frowns. "What do you mean, why? I'm, like, *me*."

"Precisely," I say, and Gabe laughs.

"I mean that I'm a five-six nobody who works at an inn that may have to be closed, and I spend most of my life taking care of my little brother, and nobody else has ever wanted to kiss me until you, Tom, and my stepfather doesn't even like—"

He stops suddenly and clamps his mouth shut. Colin leans forward and steals my words again.

"Doesn't like what?"

Gabe takes in a long, deep breath, and then his face explodes in a sudden smile. "Never mind!" he says, aggressively cheerful. "I just meant that none of this makes sense, especially since you two are best friends!" His eyes stop on me briefly as he says that, and then he looks away again.

I look up toward the sky, where white dots float in a sea of black, and I think of the strange series of life events that all had to conspire in order for me to arrive in this one place, at this one time. Christian's death. Sam becoming friends with Jack and eventually moving to Devon Falls. Me taking on *The Good Sword* part. Colin leaving his career so abruptly.

My twenty-plus year secret love for Colin.

I'm so very tired of the secrets. The secrets surrounding my acting career right now are enough to hold onto, and my secret love for Colin is nothing but endless, meaningless, exhaustion. And these stars are so beautiful. So bright and clear and real.

That's what I would like to be tonight. Bright and clear and real.

I stand up. "I can't speak for Colin," I say. "But I can tell you, Gabe, that I can't fathom how you could have had a childhood where anyone wouldn't want you near them at all times. You are kind and sunny and caring. You look out for everyone around you, especially your little brother. You, Gabriel Gomez, are absolutely the furthest person from *nobody* that I could ever imagine."

Gabe sits, his eyes wide and his body frozen in what appears to be stunned silence. Colin sits back in the porch swing and crosses his arms. He glances over at me as he sends me a half-smile. "What Tom said," he says softly. "I mean, I never thought about kissing a man in my entire life before I met you, Gabe."

That comment stings slightly, but I brush it off.

Colin stands up. "Listen," he says. "I care about you both. Tom, I've cared about you since the two of us could barely walk. Gabe, I barely met you a year ago and I already know I'd walk through fire for you. Hell, I could have had the chance not that long ago."

Gabe's eyes get even wider.

"The point is," Colin goes on, "that I really don't want to get in the way of whatever you two have started here, and I can step back now. We can pretend I never said anything tonight." He shakes his head. "When I said that, I was just trying... to live all the way again for once, if that makes any sense. Because it's been a long damn time since I did."

"Oh, Colin." Gabe jumps up off the railing and rushes over to throw his arms up and around Colin's shoulders in a hug. He's so much shorter that his legs lift slightly up off the ground when Colin hugs him back. "That's terrible," he mutters into Colin's sweater.

My heart splits against its own seams. This man who is bleeding emotion across the porch for my best friend. Because of course he is. He's Gabe.

Gabriel Gomez deserves to be happy. No one deserves that more... except possibly for my very best friend in life.

That means I'm going to have to be noble here, aren't I? It's obviously the right thing to do. I clear my throat. "Actually," I tell the two of them, "I think I'm the one who should step back."

Gabe drops from Colin's arms as they both turn to look at me.

I paste on a smile. "Colin, I've known you a long time. You've barely felt attraction for anyone until you met Gabe. Whatever that means, it seems important." I stand up so that we're all at even height—well, not exactly even. Colin and I still tower above Gabe. "You two should see where this leads," I say, and my voice doesn't even sound like it's fighting against my body. But I mean what I'm saying. I know that I do. "See what you can become together."

Later on, I know I will probably remember saying these words as I sob in my bed upstairs in Colin's guest rooms. But sacrifices must be made sometimes, right? Love requires sacrifice. I turn to go inside the house.

"Wait!" Gabe calls out, and there's a sort of desperation in his voice that has me immediately turning back around. Colin and I both stare at him.

"I don't even know how to say this," he whispers. He crosses his arms, then gulps, then looks back and forth between us. "This still all feels like a dream." He shakes his head and drops it down. "I can't be with either of you anyway," he finally says, softly. "Not in public at least. I'm sorry. But I just can't."

Colin's eyes leap to mine. I shake my head.

No, I don't understand either.

"Why not?" I ask.

Gabe pulls his arms more tightly against his body. "My stepfather," he murmurs. "Lou's dad. He thinks I'm straight. He wouldn't like it."

I can't help the scoff that escapes me. "Lou's dad grew up here, in a town with more rainbow flags than cows. Are you telling us he's homophobic?"

Gabe sighs. "After my mom got sick, he changed. A lot. He started spending a lot of time in these online chat rooms, and he started saying things he never would have before. Stuff about gay people, and lesbians, and anyone who doesn't fit his idea of what a man is supposed to be." He shakes his head. "He wouldn't like it if he found out I was dating a guy, and I don't know what that would mean for me and Lou. Anyway, the point is that I can't date either of you. No matter how much I want to." He shrugs and sends me a soft, half-smile. "At least I finally got my first kiss tonight. I'll always remember that, Tom."

My mind boggles. "That was your first kiss?" Colin and I share another quick glance.

"I really wasn't kidding about the virgin thing." Gabe shifts back and forth gently from one foot to the other. "Do you think—" He shakes his head. "No, never mind. It's ridiculous. I don't think that—"

"Gabe," Colin interrupts, and I recognize that voice. It's the same voice he used to use with driving rookies who were psyching themselves out before a race. He'd put his hands on their shoulders, look them in the eye, and talk to them like a spooked horse. His technique always worked to get them out of their head and into the car.

"Gabe," he says again. "Just tell us what you're thinking."

Gabe coughs slightly, and he opens his mouth. And then he blurts out, "What if I got to kiss both of you? And it's okay with me if, like, Tom watches while I kiss Colin. And the other way around. And we just never told anyone?"

Colin lets out a choked laugh. "You want to kiss me while Tom watches? And you want Tom to kiss you while I watch?"

Gabe winces. "I know, it's a terrible idea! I was just thinking that I really like you both, a lot, and I never got to kiss Colin." He shakes his head. "But now I wouldn't want to kiss one of you while the other isn't there, because that might feel, like, weird or something? Like I was cheating on one of you with the other, I guess. And even though I really liked kissing you earlier, Tom, I know we both felt awful when Colin found out by accident. But we could never date or anything, and no one could ever find out since secrets in

Devon Falls are like milk that gets left out, so, yeah. Like I said. It's probably a terrible idea." He lets out a long breath, one he's definitely earned after that speech.

"Milk that gets left out?" Colin mumbles.

"It spoils," I mutter back. And then I find myself speechless. Because the idea of kissing Gabe, and possibly doing more with Gabe, with my best friend there watching doesn't turn me off... quite the opposite, in fact. That particular type of scene may have appeared in more than one fantasy I've had.

But I could never ask Colin to engage in this idea. His feelings for Gabe are something so new and strong for him. He deserves to keep them between himself and Gabe.

But Colin only shrugs. "Sure, why not?" he says. "If Tom's good with it, I mean." He laughs. "Those firefighters seem happy enough with their situation, even though what they have is a little different than what we're talking about. I want to kiss Gabe, and so do you, right, Tom?" He turns to look at me, and I can only nod, speechless. "So let's try this out. I'm cool with the idea if you both are." He takes a step toward Gabe. "But if your stepfather's putting you in some kind of danger, Gabe..."

I'm still gaping at Colin when Gabe's phone starts vibrating. He pulls it from his pocket. "You don't need to worry about me, I promise. I can take care of myself and Lou. Oh, and Lou's awake. I've got to get back to the inn." He shakes his head. "Listen, Tom, you don't have to say anything. It was a stupid idea, and I—"

"Tomorrow," I interrupt him before I can change my mind. "Tomorrow we finish tiling the shower in room four. Well, you two will be doing the tiling; I'll be choosing new drapes. Then all three of us will come back to Colin's house before you pick up Lou from school."

Gabe shakes his head back and forth wildly. "I can't believe any of this is even happening," he mumbles to himself. "But I really have to go. I'll see you both tomorrow." He jogs off the porch and down the driveway.

And then Colin and I are left alone on the porch. We both sit there in silence for many, many long minutes before Colin finally stands up and goes inside.

Chapter 11

31 Days to the Devon Falls Leaf Festival

I still remember the way he shouted at me that night. —Gabe Gomez

My phone rings while I'm staring at purple marshmallows again. And there were only eight of them this morning, so of course I'm getting this phone call.

I force myself to take a few breaths while Lou hums at his cereal. "I've got to answer this, buddy," I tell him. "Finish your breakfast, okay?"

Lou nods and stays focused on his marshmallows, while I take the phone into the living room.

"Hi. Um, hi Dave." And I really, really hate how much my heart rate goes up these days the minute I say his name.

"Hey, Gabe." There's noise in the background, and I wonder if he's already on a job site. "Just calling to check in. Did you get rid of those fucking tutus yet?"

Not even a *"how's Lou"* before he jumps right to the tutus. I squint my eyes tightly. So many days, lately, I've regretted buying Lou his first tutu. But I never stay regretful, because then I remember how Lou put the thing on and started twirling around, hands high in the air while his entire expression lit up. Every time I think of that memory, I love that first tutu almost as much as Lou does.

I force a wide smile onto my face, even though Dave can't see me. Smiles help me just as much as they help other people, I've realized over the years. They help me remember that there's always going to be happiness available in the world, no matter what anyone else tries to tell you. "He really likes them, Dave," I say.

Dave makes some kind of noise between a sigh and a growl, and I remind myself that I *really* can't blame a poor tutu for this mess. The truth is that Dave and I had all kinds of disagreements about what was best for Lou long before the tutu.

You can do hard things, I remind myself. And then I do what I always do when I have to talk to Dave: I try to conjure a memory from before my mom got sick, back when Dave was a different kind of person. Someone who laughed and threw baseballs with me and came to my plays. He cried when Mom told us she was pregnant with Lou.

Then the cancer came, and that all changed. Dave was on his phone in message boards more than in the room during the days Mom was leaving us. And while I was stuck in Connecticut and he was up here in Vermont with Lou, it's like the transformation became complete. By the time I got to Devon Falls, Dave was a completely different person from the man who used to ruffle my hair and make me homemade pizza.

He was someone who bought his kid football bedroom decor sets even though Lou really wanted the *Frozen* sheets. Someone who got upset when Lou asked for princess *and* prince costumes and muttered under his breath whenever Lou wanted to wear pink or asked for ballet lessons.

Then he started leaving Lou for weeks at a time. He'd tell us he had to go away for a job, assuming I'd take care of Lou, but then he wouldn't come back after the job was over. The first time he stopped answering his phone while he was gone, I panicked. At the time, I was barely making enough from odd jobs to feed myself, and Lou and I lived off a lot of ramen and hot dogs in those weeks. But the next time Dave disappeared, I was prepared. I'd socked money and canned goods away, and Lou and I did just fine.

I really did wonder, then, if I should tell someone what was going on. About Dave leaving all the time and about all the other concerns I had about him. I really did.

But.

I can't take the risk that Dave would manage to keep custody and take Lou away from me again, or that the state would decide to place Lou in some stranger's home instead of with me. Especially with my arrest record.

An arrest record for a stupid choice I'd take back over and over and over again if I could.

Since I've never been able to tell anyone that Dave disappears for long gaps of time or that I worry he might start saying damaging things to Lou about his clothes and interests, I've gotten along with Dave by doing what I do best: playing damage control. I've made sure Lou only wore his most favorite outfits when Dave was gone on jobs. I've fudged the dates of Dave's absences with teachers, with his doctors, with everyone. And that all seemed to be working... until I bought Lou a tutu he saw at a secondhand store the night before Dave left for a job in Rochester, and Dave saw it in our shopping bag.

I still remember the way he shouted at me that night, after the tutu was put away in the back of the closet and Lou was tucked into bed.

"I should've known you'd start trouble when you followed us up to Devon Falls," he raged. "You always were a weak little pansy-ass. It's bad enough that my neighbor here has to be that rainbow-haired pastor who's always walking around holding hands with her wife. It's not that I've got a problem with a lesbian being the mayor. I just don't get why they both have to flaunt it like that! And now you're buying fluffy skirts for my son!"

Flaunt what? I wondered. Amelia's just holding hands with the woman she's married to. But I decided not to risk more of Dave's wrath by pointing that out.

"Anyway," Dave went on. "It doesn't matter." He shook his head. "The tutu was a fucking wake-up call. When I get back from Rochester, things around here are going to change. Maybe it's time for Lou to spend a little less time around you, Gabe."

My vision went fuzzy around the edges, and for a second I swore I was reliving all the worst moments of my past. "But you can't take him away from me again," I whispered to the room.

Dave threw his hands up behind his head and started pacing again. "You think I wanted any of this, Gabe? This isn't what I signed on for," he muttered. "Things were never supposed to work out this way. Me taking care of a kid alone, living back here in this podunk town. This was never supposed to happen, you know? None of this ever would have happened if your mom was still alive."

And that was the crux of the whole problem, you know? My mom *was* supposed to be here. She was supposed to do so many things. Finish raising me. Raise my little brother.

Only things didn't work out that way. And now here I am, on the phone with my ragey former stepfather, trying to calm him down and keep my own heart rate in check. Not for the first time since the tutu incident, I seriously consider calling someone up and telling them what's going on. Benson's a lawyer, and he might help me, right?

Or... Tom would help me. Colin. If they knew what was going on. I think they would. I really do.

But then I remember that moment when Dave's car took off down the road, and I was left alone with a social worker, still shaking with the grief of my mother's loss. I will never, ever forget how horribly alone I felt in that moment. How lost.

Anything I do to upset the balance I have with Dave could cause Lou to end up alone without anyone who really cares about him; I know that all too well. So. I'm just going to have to figure out a different solution to keep Lou safe before Dave gets back. Thoughts of taking Lou and running float briefly through my brain one more time, right before Dave starts speaking again.

"So," Dave says. "Did you get my message? I'll be back in time for the festival, and then you and me are going to have a long, hard talk about Lou's future. Oh, and make sure you keep the lawn mowed while I'm gone. Since you're staying there anyway."

Sure, Dave. I'd be happy to do all your chores while I'm working a full-time job to feed your kid and also keeping the whole town from realizing you're a total fuck-up. No problem.

He's never even asked if I have a place of my own here. He probably doesn't realize I gave up my apartment when he last left town a few months ago. He never leaves extra cash when he goes away. I wanted to make sure we had enough money to eat.

I wanted to start saving up, too. Just in case I had to pull the nuclear option and get me and Lou away from Devon Falls.

"And what's this I hear about you spending time with that weirdo movie star who hangs around Devon Falls sometimes? That guy's a total poof."

Only he doesn't say "poof." He says a word that's so nasty it makes me want to scream through the phone at the top of my lungs. Tom Evers is twice the man—three times the man—Dave will ever be. But I force myself to stay calm. "He and Colin Templegate are working at the winery with me. They're investors, remember?"

"Oh, that's right. Well, at least it's kind of fucking awesome, I guess, that you're hanging out with a damn race car driver. Introduce Lou to Colin, will you? Maybe being around a guy like that will toughen him up. But keep Lou away from that Tom dude. I don't trust Hollywood types. No damn values out there."

Every single insult or cruel word makes me want to throw my phone across the room. The Dave I grew up with never, ever said mean things like this about people. This Dave? He'll say whatever he wants about anyone who doesn't embrace his new brand of toxic masculinity.

And my greatest fear is that someday soon he'll start saying these exact same things to Lou.

Dave sighs. "Just remember what I said before I left. No more tutus. No brainwashing my kid into thinking it's okay for him to dress like that."

Brainwashing? Lou's the one who squeals every time he sees a pair of ballet slippers. Lou's the one who watches *Frozen* on repeat but can't decide if he wants to be Snow White or Prince Charming for Halloween. Lou is who he is, and he's *perfect* the way he is.

I'll never understand why Dave doesn't see that. I can only imagine what would happen if he found out I was getting ready to try dating one guy he calls those horrible names *and* another one he thinks is a perfect model of "maleness" for his son. He'd probably have Lou out of Devon Falls so fast Lou's tutu would still be spinning in the closet.

Dave hangs up then, and somehow I manage to hang up too without destroying the phone or any of Dave's walls. "Gabe?" Lou peeks his head into the living room. "Are you done with your phone call? Can we go to school now?" Oh, shoot. We've got to get going. As we rush through backpack prep and I help Lou slide on his Mary Janes, the ones I trade out for sneakers whenever Dave's home, I can't stop myself from asking him a question I never ask. "Lou, do you miss your daddy when he's gone?"

Lou frowns. "Sometimes, I think. But he's sad and mad a lot when he's here, and you're never sad and mad. So I don't mind when it's just me and you, Gabe. C'mon! Today's pizza day in the cafeteria!" He grabs my hand and leads me out of the house.

"Gabe! Gabe Gomez!"

Oh, crud. Amelia's waving excitedly from her yard. Her pink bangs stick up in excitement as she jogs past a lawn gnome and over to me. "My goodness, you're a hard man to catch these days! I thought we were going to chat after that town hall meeting, but you just disappeared!"

"Sorry about that!" I say, and my voice sounds so high in my ears it could be a balloon about to pop. "I, uh, had to help some friends with something. Didn't mean to run away from you there." Which is a total lie, of course. I very, very definitely meant to run away from her.

"No problem at all," she says brightly. "I'm just glad I caught you today. I really need to talk to Dave about that tree our backyards share; it's an absolute menace to the tomato plants Ellie and I are growing. Attracts every squirrel in town. So when will Dave be home? Seems like he's already been gone quite a while."

I open up my mouth while my brain processes what to say. Maybe I should just tell her. Tell her that Dave's basically an absentee father, and when he is here he's more focused on what Lou's wearing than what Lou eats.

The words are nearly at the edge of my mouth when I remember: I remember how I felt watching Dave drive away. I remember the social worker, his hand on my shoulder as he walked me to his car to take me to a building filled with bunk beds and strangers. I curled up in a corner of one of those beds and cried all night that night, wishing my mother or Dave or Lou or *anyone* I knew and loved was there with me. Anyone at all.

That stupid arrest record hovers above me, and nasty voices chant in my head. *The state isn't going to take Lou away from Dave because Dave doesn't like when he wears dresses. And even if they did take him for neglect, they'll never give him to you. Not with that charge on your record.*

That stupid, stupid charge.

I can't do it. I can't say the words. So I swallow hard, determined to keep my smile firmly in place. "Um, I'll talk to Dave about the tree."

"Wonderful!" Amelia says cheerfully. "I'm sure we can get this all sorted out. Dave doesn't seem to spend much time in that yard, anyway. Thank you, Gabe." Amelia starts back across her lawn, and I breathe out a long, quiet sigh of relief.

Annnd then she turns back around. Drat.

But she stays standing where she is. "Gabe," she says. "I just wanted to let you know... I've noticed Lou's really coming into his own with his wardrobe choices, isn't he?"

I freeze. Where's she going with this? "Um... yes?" I finally say.

She nods. "Well, I just wanted to make sure you knew that you and Lou and Dave are always welcome at the Devon Falls LGBTQIA2S+ society meetings. Once a month, on Wednesday nights at my church. We have great cookies."

If I had time and energy to cry right now, I probably would. Because in so many ways, my little brother and I are the luckiest people on the planet. We live in a town with a thriving LGBTQIA2S+ society and a population that never even blinks when my little brother puts on a skirt or Mary Janes or wears prince costumes to birthday parties.

I manage to keep the smile on my face, though. Because I'll figure out how to keep Lou safe, and loved, and protected. I *have* to. "Thanks, Amelia," I finally say.

I drop Lou off at school, but I don't leave right away. Instead, I park the truck in a far corner of the parking lot and pull out my phone. Then I ask Google questions I hate asking, because it never gives me the answers I want.

Yes, Google reminds me. Arrest records are taken into account when determining foster placements.

No, Google reminds me. There's nothing illegal about parents telling their child they cannot wear a skirt or dress or certain shoes.

Yes, Google reminds me. Siblings have minimal custody rights while parents are still alive.

Yes, Google finally says. Buses leave the Burlington station regularly, with routes going through New York, Boston, and Maine.

I can't kidnap my little brother. That's not me. I'm not a kidnapper. Lou and I can't live on the run for the rest of our lives. How would I even keep us alive? Fed?

But I can't let Dave take Lou away, either. I can't let Dave spend the rest of Lou's childhood telling him there's something wrong with him. Not when I could have stopped that from happening.

I sink my head down on the steering wheel of the truck and run my hands across its damaged leather seats. My father sat here once. My mother, too. She drove this truck sometimes, back when it was just sitting in our garage in Connecticut, waiting for me to inherit it.

"Mom," I whisper. "Dad. I really, really wish you were here right now."

And then I do something I don't let myself do very often. I cry for a long time, and I cry hard.

Chapter 12
31 Days to the Devon Falls Leaf Festival

And then my thoughts took a hard left turn right into Anxiety Land.
—Gabe Gomez

When I finally get myself together and start my drive to the winery, I wonder if anyone here has told Tom and Colin about the LGBTQIA2S+ society. I've never had time to go before, but I know Sam and Malachai and Jack and Benson go a lot. I wish the three of us could bring Lou together.

Too bad that can never, ever happen. Too risky that news would make it back to Dave.

I'm trying to imagine what it would be like to walk into a Devon Falls LGBTQIA2S+ society meeting with Tom and Colin when I finally arrive at the inn. I step into the room we're currently renovating as I pull on the old, dirty sweatshirt I wear when I'm working.

And then I realize something: today's the day. *The* day. After work, Colin and Tom and I are going to go back to Colin's house and *kiss.*

I got so distracted by Dave and Amelia this morning that I wasn't even thinking about this afternoon. Now I can't stop thinking about it. Should I really be spending time with them both when I have to keep the three of us a secret and I don't even know whether I'm going to be able to stay in Devon Falls? And is it weird that I basically asked them both to kiss me while they're around each other? Because maybe asking people not to tell anyone that they're kissing you and then kiss them in front of other people is rude, and—

"Good morning, little one."

The voice behind me is low and deep, almost a whisper. I whirl around and let a rush of wonder flow through me as I stare up into the smiling face of Tom Evers.

Tom Evers the movie star.

Tom Evers the movie star I've crushed on since I was seventeen.

Tom Evers the movie star *who kissed me last night.*

I swallow hard and take a breath. I didn't sleep much last night. I spent most of it wide awake, imagining what it would be like to lie across a bed in Colin's house, kissing Tom over and over, maybe exploring even further than that, while Colin watched from the chair that sits just to the right of their bed.

And then I pictured the scene in reverse. Me and Colin, with Tom watching.

And then my thoughts took a hard left turn right into Anxiety Land. What if Colin changes his mind about wanting to kiss me? What if Tom changes his mind? What if they both decide this is the stupidest idea ever? Not to mention that I'm pretty sure Tom has some kind of feelings for Colin—what if Colin realizes he feels the same way, and they both get together and decide to leave me behind? Or even worse than that, what if they find out I'm lying to the whole town about Dave and they decide to hate me and—

"Is everything okay, little one?" Tom lifts up my chin and frowns. "You were smiling just a minute ago. Now you're frowning. I do not like it when you frown."

I burst out laughing and throw my arms around his chest, because I really need a hug right now. "Sometimes my brain just takes off on me," I say into the cloth of his shirt.

"That's something I can certainly understand." He hugs me back, letting his arms rest around my shoulders, and for a moment we just relax into each other. This is the most physical comfort I've really felt from anyone besides Lou in a long time. Probably since my mom died.

Someone clears their throat loudly next to us. I look up and see Colin standing there, a box of tiles in one hand and a large bucket in the other. His expression is completely neutral, and I can't read it.

"Let's get this shower done," he says gruffly as he turns and heads for the ensuite door.

"Very good, captain. Because we have plans afterward!" Tom calls after him.

Colin doesn't answer. I follow him without looking at Tom, because right now the only place making eye contact with Tom can possibly send me is straight back to Anxiety Land.

Colin turns on the Bluetooth stereo while the two of us work and Tom bustles around the area, talking about drapes and occasionally correcting the way Colin's laid out a tile and giving Colin orders that make him roll his eyes and half-smile. I like tiling, as it turns out. It's a lot of finicky, detail-oriented work that doesn't leave much room for me to get lost inside my head, and I feel so accomplished when it's finished. From this day forward, for as long as this shower stays in place, there will be a visual record of something I did in this world. Something I made.

"Done." Colin sets the last tile in place and stands up as he places his hands on his hips. "Now it all needs to set."

"Perfect. Then let's head back to your place, Colin. I'll go start putting the leftover materials away!" Tom whirls around and disappears, leaving Colin and me alone.

"Listen," I blurt out as I turn around to face Colin. "We don't have to do this, okay? I would never want to get in the way of your friendship with Tom, and I know you're figuring some things out, and I *really* get that because I am too, and last night when I said we should try this, I just meant that—"

"Hey, calm down." Colin lays his hands down on my shoulders. "Take a breath, little one."

I swear, all he and Tom have to do is call me *little one* and it's like a shot of Xanax—not that I would know, I've never tried Xanax—to my whole brain. I take the breath.

"Whatever is about to happen," Colin says to me slowly. Carefully. "Know one thing for sure. I'm not going to do anything I'm not sure I want to do. And as long as you don't either, and Tom doesn't either, everything will be fine." He smiles slightly. "Consent. Communication. Right?"

Right. Right. Right. He has to be right.

And we can keep this a secret. No one has to know. Dave never has to find out.

Right?

I charge out of the room, ahead of Colin, before I can change my mind. Because there are just too many sharp turns into Anxiety Land laid out in front of me.

Chapter 13

31 Days to the Devon Falls Leaf Festival

"Whoa."

Gabe stops so suddenly in front of me that I nearly run into him. He stands in the front doorway of my house, eyes wide as he takes in the large open concept floor plan I've spent the last two months working to create. A sitting area is on one side, flanked with soft, gray sofas that line walls in shades of blues or beiges. One of the three giant flatscreens I had installed in this house is the centerpiece of the space, and it hangs in its own frame above a reclaimed fireplace.

I still don't quite understand why I don't feel more pride when I look around this space. I definitely honed plenty of my DIY skills over the hours I spent working on fixing it up. Hopefully I'll feel differently when we finish our work on the inn.

"I took charge of the design!" Tom chirps from the kitchen, which sits on the other side of the large space. The stairway to the second floor cuts cleanly up the middle of it. Tom opens the restaurant-style fridge and pulls out a Diet Coke. "Goodness knows what sort of color scheme Colin would have settled on without me. Did you know he once paired teal and maroon?" He wrinkles his nose.

"The teal and maroon thing was a racing uniform. Nobody gave me a choice in the matter," I remind Tom. "Want anything, Gabe?"

Gabe takes a step toward Tom. "Those countertops," he whispers.

"Imported from Italy," I mutter as I walk past him and toward the island. I let Tom get a little audacious when he was helping me pick out kitchen fixtures, and they're all gold against dark gray cabinets. I was skeptical, but I have to admit, it's a pretty stunning look with the marble countertops. Especially when you add the high-end stainless steel appliances I put in.

I pull out a Coke for Gabe and hand it to him, because he's still gaping. I mean, I get it. I know all too well not everyone has the luxury to install a kitchen like this in a home they may not even live in all that long. So every time I buy something expensive for myself, like all the shit in this kitchen, I donate the same amount of money to a charity or organization that can pay it forward to people who need it. This kitchen financed a hefty donation to The Trevor Project, a charity I've supported for years.

Race car drivers can end up making a lot more money than they need. Money that can help so many other people who really do need it. Why the hell would I hoard it when I could put it out into the world so it can do some good?

Gabe takes another step and slides one hand over the marble countertops. He shakes his head and takes a step back. "I think I should go," he blurts out.

"What?" Tom and I say the word at the same time, and Tom immediately jogs around the countertop to put a hand on Gabe's shoulder. "Little one, what are you talking about?

"This!" Gabe gestures wildly at the room. "You're, like, celebrities! Both of you! What the hell am I even doing in your house? In one of my group homes I used to sleep on a blow-up mattress in a sleeping bag!"

"You slept where?" I stalk to the other side of Gabe, like I might be able to protect him from the horrible sleeping arrangements of his past. If only.

"I should definitely go," Gabe says. He puts his soda can down on the counter and starts to head toward the door.

"Wait." Tom steps in front of him. "Of course you should leave if that's what you really want to do. But Gabe... money and countertops and things like that have nothing to do with me wanting to kiss you right now. And." He swallows. "I have a sneaking suspicion Colin feels the same way."

I mean, I'm not too sure of very many of my feelings right now. But I am sure of *that* one. I nod slowly.

"So," Tom goes on. "Let's just take this slowly. What if I just kiss you now? Just once? Then we'll see how you feel."

Gabe swallows, and I watch his Adam's apple move in his throat. "Are you sure," he whispers, "that we can keep this a secret? Not tell anyone?"

I don't have to even look at Tom to have this silent conversation. I know exactly what he's thinking.

I don't like this stepfather character. We'll have to do whatever we can to keep Gabe and Lou safe.

Agreed. And if this stepfather is the asshole he appears to be, I can take him down the moment I need to. I won't hesitate to do it.

"We're sure," I say firmly.

Gabe takes a deep breath. I can hear him counting as he lets the breath back out again. "Okay, then," he finally whispers.

And then I watch my best friend hold Gabe's face in his hands as he bends down and kisses him like Gabe's his life energy. Gabe's hair is messy and askew, his eyes wide and bright one minute and closed the next, and the two of them seem to fit perfectly together.

Gabe's pressed against Tom's chest, and as he pulls away slightly, panting, I realize something: I'm hard.

I've never gotten hard watching two men kiss before. Hell, I'm not sure I've ever gotten hard watching a man and a woman kiss. Porn doesn't do much for me. But here I am, standing stock-still by the fridge, my jeans fully tented.

Tom's head whips around as he turns to face me. He tilts his lips into a half-smile. "You look as if you need to go somewhere more comfortable, Colin. Let's find a bedroom posthaste."

We're all messy from the morning's reno project, so we speed-shower in the three separate ensuites I installed, and I've never been so glad I decided to put a bathroom in every bedroom of this house. It's way too early to start talking about any of us showering together, and I'm too impatient to even imagine waiting for all three of us to shower one by one.

I step out of the shower in my master bedroom to find Tom and Gabe already making out next to the California King bed that takes up most of the space. Tom's wearing nothing but his jeans, and Gabe's got on a t-shirt and some exercise shorts that look three sizes too big for him. I nearly do a double-take when I realize they're mine.

Tom pulls gently away from Gabe. "First rule, little one," he says. "You will say stop to either one of us if you need to stop. And when you do, we stop."

Gabe gulps and nods shakily, and then he leans over to bring his lips back against Tom's. But Tom shakes his head.

"One more question first," he asks softly. "Do you want to do more than kiss today?"

Gabe sucks in a long breath that sounds more like a gasp. He looks back and forth between us. "Yes," he finally says. Or whispers, really. "I think I do."

Fuuucccckkkkk.

I can't look away from them as Tom lays Gabe across the bed. I'm so hard it hurts now, and I can't resist moving my hands to my crotch and rubbing myself over my jeans as Tom strips Gabe's sweatshirt and t-shirt over his head. "I'm feeling a little sad now that we didn't do any co-showering today," he says.

Gabe gasps lightly. "Maybe we could do that later?" he asks in a strangled voice.

Tom laughs. "You're dangerous, little one." He leans over and starts kissing down Gabe's neck and across his chest. "Perhaps little one is the wrong nickname for you, Gabe Gomez. You're more like a little minx."

Gabe's smile grows wider. But that name's not quite right.

My legs are going weak, and I take a few steps so I can ease myself into a sitting position on the edge of the bed. It creaks slightly as I lower myself. Tom glances over, and his eyes widen as he sees me stroking myself over my jeans.

"Not minx," I whisper. "Little fox. That's what you are, Gabe. Intelligent. Adaptable. Energetic. Resourceful. Resilient."

And you're taking me on the wildest chase of my life, I add in my head.

Tom traces a finger down Gabe's cheek. "Yes," he says. "Little fox. That's exactly what you are, Gabe." He draws the finger across Gabe's lips, and Gabe moans. The sound is like a shockwave through my body. I've got no fucking idea exactly what's happening to me here. I've never, ever been this turned on in my life; I'm sure of that. I never understood what other men meant about feeling some kind of desperate need for sex; I don't even have the urge to masturbate all that often. But right now I feel as though I might die if I can't touch Gabe soon. Kiss him myself.

It's like I'm driving down a straight road at top speed with no idea when a curve might be coming, and all I want to do is press down on the gas.

I push my hand harder against my dick as Tom goes back to kissing across Gabe's body. Gabe arches his back when Tom starts teasing his nipple, and then it's like my body has a mind of its own, like I'm outside of myself watching, as my other hand reaches over to stroke Gabe's other cheek. I play with his earlobe. I tease against his neck. Gabe lets out a strangled cry and Tom sits up, away from Gabe. I lean over.

I press my lips to Gabe's, and now we're flying down the straight so fast the world is blurred. And for the first time ever, I get what people have been saying about sex in books and movies for all these years. There's a thrumming energy pulsing through my entire body as Gabe's lips press back and forth against mine, as our tongues start exploring.

My hand's moving again. Touching Gabe's hand where it's lying next to his chest, running up his arm, his neck, and then up to his ear.

"Oh wow," Gabe whispers. I look down.

And I realize he's got his hand down his waistband.

Tom falls onto the bed on the other side of Gabe, the two of us bookending him while he and I kiss. Tom goes back to kissing across Gabe's upper body, then his neck, his cheek, down the side of his lips. Gabe's hand is moving faster now, and Tom slips his own hand on top of Gabe's shorts. No, *my* shorts, because Gabe Gomez is wearing my clothing. "Let it happen, little fox," he whispers. "Come for us."

Not come for *me*. But come for *us*.

Gabe whimpers sharply, and then his entire body seems to jerk upward as he spasms wildly against the bed. It's beautiful. Watching him is beautiful. Watching Tom's lips and hands move across his body is beautiful. The scene in front of me is so bright and striking that it seems to be lighting up the room around me with some kind of shocking glow. It's as if my world, which has been so dark for so long now, is suddenly illuminated and bathed in sunlight.

"I can't—I can't—I need—"

When Gabe uses the word *need* I swear it's like some kind of code word in my ears, scurrying me to action. I bring a hand to the top of Gabe's shorts as Tom falls across Gabe, kissing him hard. Gabe lets out a high, sharp cry as he spasms against our hands once again, and then he falls back against the bed.

Tom and I fall next to him, cradling his head between ours. This was Gabe's very first sexual experience. And I was part of it. There's a strange, heady power in knowing that, and I can't stop myself from pressing my hand harder against my jeans.

I glance across the bed and realize Tom's doing the same thing. And then he does just a little more and slips his hand down his own pants.

I'm thinking of nothing and everything when I follow his lead and shove my own hand into my boxers.

I'm so close that it only takes a few strokes and tugs before I'm right at the edge. I glance over at Gabe. He looks wrung out and strung out, the way I know I always looked after a race. His mouth is hanging open as his eyes track back and forth between me and Tom.

"You two," he whispers. "I can't believe... I can't believe any of this."

The sound of his voice pushes me another step closer to the edge of the cliff I'm standing on. I hear Tom panting hard and then crying out across the quiet room. I navigate the car in my brain straight down the road and into the hardest, strongest orgasm I've ever had in my life. Less than a few minutes later I'm asleep.

When Tom and I wake up hours later, Gabe is gone.

Chapter 14
31 Days to the Devon Falls Leaf Festival

It's the only way I know how to exist with him. —Tom Evers

"Gabe? Gabe, where are you? Little fox, call me back immediately. Please."

I hang up the phone and set it down with a sigh as I rub my hands through the sides of my hair. Colin sits up next to me on the bed, his eyes heavy with sleep. He looks over at me and clamps his lips together so hard I'm surprised he doesn't break a tooth.

Ah, wonderful. Here we are. The Morning After Awkwardness. One of the most shockingly beautiful and sensual nights of my life has resulted in this: my lifelong best friend is staring at me as though he's never seen me before, and the complete disappearance of the sweetest young man I've ever met, who may or may not be in a total panic after said best friend and I extricated a not-insignificant portion of his innocence from him.

Colin swallows again. He blinks and looks away from me. "Where's Gabe?" he finally asks. His voice comes out as a croak.

I shake my head. "I'm not sure. We were all lying here... together. He was in my arms. I must have fallen asleep, and I assume you did as well. When I woke up, Gabe was gone." I look for the blaring light of the clock on the nightstand, which reports that it's 10:45 p.m. "I assume he needed to leave to pick up Lou after school, but now he's not answering my calls or texts."

Colin lets out a long breath in the stillness of the room. His face is shadowed with the light from one floor lamp standing in the corner; it must have been on when we fell asleep. The rest of the room is bathed in blackness, the only other brightness coming from a thin stretch of the moon outside the front window of Colin's house.

The master bedroom in Colin's house in Vermont isn't all that large. The bedroom of his penthouse apartment in Manhattan is at least twice this size. But somehow, when the two of us stay here, it never feels small. We always sleep in Colin's room together, and the space is always just the perfect size for the two of us. The right size for me to hand Colin coffee from the other side of the sheets in the morning while he's still in bed. The right size for the two of us to bump elbows as we trade places in the bathroom.

But right now, this space feels smaller than an ill-designed closet. The walls seem to be closing in against me as I stare at Colin, watching his chest rise and fall as he keeps his eyes locked on the bedspread and away from me.

"I'm worried about him," I add in a whisper.

I've dreamed of a night like last night for so long. A night of seeing Colin on near full display, losing himself to passion and pleasure. I'd so often fall asleep masturbating to visions of that scene when I was younger. But now it's really happened, and I'm left sitting in the aftermath. Because not only has Gabe disappeared into the night (or afternoon; who knows exactly when he left), but I have to reconcile the hard truth that Colin didn't have that night with *me*.

He had it with another man. A man I also have feelings for. And I chose to watch. In fact, I wanted very desperately to watch.

The walls are getting closer and closer now, the gray walls and off-white trim heading closer to me with every second. I need to leave this room; that's the only thing I'm certain of. I jump from the bed, stuffing my feet into slippers and grabbing a fleece jacket from the back of the large wing-backed chair in the corner of the room, and I rush out of the front door and down the stairs.

Out on Colin's wraparound porch, the cool fall air hits me with force, and I shiver against its rush. The world is startlingly still, the only sound from nearby cicadas dotting the woods surrounding the backside of the cottage. Lake Devon in front of me is smooth as glass, its surface shining gently with the reflection of the moon's simple light.

All around me is peace and calm, but I feel so full to the brim with nervous energy that I worry I might burst. I feel like I felt right before I left Hollywood for the last time.

"Why? Why all of it?" I ask the universe.

"Talking to the sky?" I turn with a jolt at the sound of Colin's voice. He's standing behind me, holding a blue wool beanie. Or tuque, as some people call them around here, on the edges of the Quebec border. "I was worried you might get cold," he says softly.

I don't comment on the fact that he's wearing a t-shirt. Colin is never either too hot nor too cold, regardless of the temperature. He once raced in one-hundred-and-ten-degree cockpit temperatures in the desert for hours while other racers were forced off the track as they nearly passed out while driving at two hundred miles per hour speeds. Colin won the race, vomited, and then announced to the paddock he was fine.

I, on the other hand, begin to sweat at seventy-seven degrees and freeze at fifty-five. When we're in Vermont, Colin seems to carry a constant supply of jackets and hats and handheld fans with him, ready to hand me something the moment I start to feel even the slightest bit uncomfortable.

"I'm just worrying about Gabe," I tell him.

He raises an eyebrow and puts on the face that says he knows I'm lying. He rocks back on his heels and crosses his arms. "Are you having regrets about last night?" he asks me.

I can't imagine how I would ever answer that question. In some ways, I have so very, very many regrets about last night. Regrets that Colin can never return the feelings I have for him. Regrets that the world has sentenced me to a lifetime of unrequited love for my favorite person on the planet.

But in other ways, I could never for a single moment regret last night. Every moment I spent with Gabe was spectacular, special. Big and bright. And having Colin there by my side, as I always want him to be, only made it brighter.

"No," I finally tell him, because that seems like the simplest answer.

Colin purses his lips tightly and sinks in against himself. I haven't seen him look so small since the day I had to tell him about Christian's accident.

He nods. "I can tell you're really into Gabe," he says softly. "And whatever the fuck is going on between me and him right now, I sure as hell don't want to get in the way of that." He swallows. "So, uh, just know that I can still step away or whatever. Last night never has to happen again."

I don't know whether to burst out laughing or howl with frustration. So instead I just stare at him for a long moment. "You're serious right now?" I finally ask him.

He blinks and wrings his hands together. "Of course. I'd never want to get in the way of you falling in love, Tom. You deserve love. You deserve it more than anyone I know."

I can only stare at him again, startled into stillness. I stare at him and I remember.

"Where do you think we'll all be in twenty years?"

Colin twists the four-leaf clover he's holding around in his hands, frowning as he studies it closely. I've got my eyes trained on his fingers, watching as they trail lightly over the delicate greenery between them. Colin's fingers have gotten longer. The calluses on the end, reminders of all the hours he's spent behind the wheel of go karts, stand out against his lightly tanned skin.

I turn away quickly, moving my gaze back to the cloudless sky above me. Don't stare at your best friend's fingers, Tom. You can't do that.

I sigh as I wiggle in the grass. I haven't told Colin about all the confusing dreams I've been having lately. They started out as dreams of Jenny Safforing and Emily Pierce, but last week I had one of Albie Kent, a boy in my music class. And then there's what happened last night.

Don't think about it, Tom, I scold myself. This is the worst possible place to be reliving that dream—nightmare? In some ways, the dream feels more like a nightmare. Colin and I are spending the weekend at a cottage in Vermont that our parents rented for our two families. It sits right on a little lake, and it's surrounded by fields and woods and dirt walking paths. Colin and his twin brother Christian and my brother Sam and I have spent the last three days kayaking and paddleboarding and playing frisbee golf and laying in this field, staring at the sky and picking four-leaf clovers. Perfect final summer days before school starts again in a few weeks and I walk into a high school for the first time as a student.

Colin will be off somewhere else, studying with tutors while he trains to become the next big sensation in open wheel racing. These might be the final days we spend together for a long time. I can't ruin them by telling him.

Not that I'm sure exactly what I'd be telling him. I might not be straight, Colin. But I don't think I'm gay, either. Google says I could be bi or pansexual. I need to do more research.

I might be in love with you.

Definitely can't say that one out loud. Last night my moms dropped us off at the movie theater in town and Colin ended up making out with a redheaded girl we met while we were buying popcorn. Less than seven hours later, I woke up in a cold sweat, visions of a slipping dream dancing across my subconscious that were just clear enough to torture me: I'd become the redhead. I was in her place, lips dancing across Colin's and hands brushing against his as cars exploded on screens in front of us.

And it felt like everything I'd ever wanted.

Hence: nightmare.

"That's easy," I tell Colin. "You'll be racing cars all over the world. I'll be starring in blockbuster movies. Sam will be—"

"Bossing people around," Colin says, and we both laugh. He doesn't mean it in a bad way. Sam's the one in charge of our little group of four. He always has been. "Christian will still be doing boneheaded shit. And Sam will still be trying to stop him," he adds with a slight smile and he turns to look over at the lake, where Sam's spent the better part of three days trying to keep Christian safe whenever he decides to try some new dive or jump. Yesterday Christian was talking about finding a place where we could go cliff diving, and for a minute I thought Sam might finally just lock him up in his bedroom.

"Which is good," Colin adds. "If he's keeping Christian from getting killed, you and I can travel all around the world whenever we're not working. Have adventures." He flips back onto his side to face me. "You better not get any better friends than me this year," he tells me. The teasing note in his voice is underlined with something that rings of fear, a fear I know all too well. A fear I understand.

"Same thing, man," I tell him. "But that won't happen. It can't. We're going to be best friends forever. Right?"

Colin nods, his face a block of stone as he drops the four-leaf clover into the grass between us. Behind us there are shouts of

*laughter and then splashing as something hits the water. "Christ-
ian!" Sam's exasperated voice echoes through the trees.*

*Colin's lips turn upward in a smile. "Forever," he whispers.
"Nothing's ever going to change." He reaches out a pinky to me,
a gesture I'm so familiar with that it feels like walking into my
mothers' kitchen while Mom makes homemade pasta and Mama
sings.*

*Colin and I have been sharing pinky swears since before I can
even remember. Since his parents moved into the house next door
to my mothers' house and our parents became best friends. Since
before he started racing go karts and I decided I wanted to be in
all the school plays. Since before the world, I sometimes think.*

"Ever," I promise, as I link my pinky with his.

"Do you remember," I finally say hoarsely. "When our parents
rented that cottage in southern Vermont? By the lake? It was a
much bigger lake than this one," I add, though I'm not sure why that
feels so important right now. "And we picked four-leaf clovers, and
high school was about to start, and you were leaving for Europe.
And." I swallow. "We promised nothing would ever change. We
swore we'd be friends forever, bestie."

Colin takes a step closer to me, and the cicadas sing in time with
his movements. "I remember," he says. "You always found more
four-leafers than I did. Used to piss me off. But not as much as it
did when you started calling me *bestie*. Or when you refused to
stop."

I half-snort, half-choke on a laugh. I breathe in and then out
again. I'm holding in so many words these days, so many unspoken
secrets. Some new, some old. They're choking me alive, piece by
piece, like the algae that I've recently learned infected the lake
where our families used to stay. A side effect of chemicals used
on nearby land, as I learned when I looked into renting the place
again. I thought about taking Colin there after Christian died, but
when I discovered the algae problem, I knew I couldn't. I could

never take my best friend, the first love of my life, to watch a place we both loved be swallowed whole by its own environment.

I've spent years protecting Colin wherever I could, sacrificing enormous parts of myself for him. It's the only way I know how to exist with him. I'm sure of that now. This afternoon made that all so very clear.

I shake my head. "I have no regrets," I finally say. My voice feels high and tight and foreign to me, but Colin doesn't seem to notice. I've always found it fascinating that someone who can feel a curve in a road a hundred yards before they see it can also be so oblivious to what's in front of him. "I'm just worried that Gabe left so suddenly," I add. "That's all this is. Let's go find him."

I turn and start a slow walk back inside the house. Away from Colin. Away from this lake in front of us, which is still sparking and beautiful, without a hint of algae in sight.

Chapter 15

31 Days to the Devon Falls Leaf Festival

This all has to be another dream, right? —Gabe Gomez

"Well, little fox. Arc you ready to see all of us?"

Tom and Colin stand before me, both abnormally tall in the dark light of Dave's bedroom, which is where I've been sleeping since he left. Their perfect forms look odd against Dave's decor of posters for heavy metal bands and one mounted deer head. I gulp back a breath and arch up off the bed as they both slowly begin to unbutton their pants, dropping cloth centimeter by centimeter as my cock grows within my jeans.

"Yes," I whisper. "Want this. Want all of you."

And just like that, my jeans magically disappear, along with the rest of my clothes. They both lose their clothes less than a second later, and now they're standing completely nude above me, hard and strong and soft all at the same time.

I gulp. "What are we going to... do?" I ask.

Tom leans over to trace a hand over my knee and down my ankle. "Whatever you want, little one," he says softly. "But first, there's something I need to do." He straightens up and turns to

Colin. "I've been in love with you for a long time," he whispers. "And it's time I showed you that."

He leans over to kiss Colin, and I—

"Gabe? Gabe!"

The voice that's pushing against my ears is high and light. Definitely not Tom or Colin. *Shoot.* That's Lou. I sit up fast on the couch as I force my eyes open and grab for him. "What's wrong? Are you okay?"

Lou rubs at his eyes with the corners of his hands. Butterfly eyes, my mom used to say, whenever I did that. He's wearing the My Little Pony pajamas we recently found at the secondhand store, and his hair is sticking up in tufts across his head. Real life comes back into focus: I fell asleep at Colin's house and woke up just in time to pick up Lou from school. I had to rush there and then back here to make him dinner... and then I, apparently, fell asleep on the couch and Lou put himself to bed.

I've been told that's not a thing most kids do. But Lou's always been one-of-a-kind.

"Oh, shoot." I drop my head into my hands. "I fell asleep, didn't I? We didn't even read stories!"

"It's okay, Gabe." Lou hops up onto the couch and snuggles up against me. "I read a story and locked the door and everything, just like you do! But now someone's knocking on the door, and I'm not sure who it is." He frowns and studies the front hallway of the house like it's a mystery ready to be solved. "Maybe ghosts are here?"

I pick my cell phone off my table and nearly choke when I see the time; it's after eleven o'clock. And then I nearly choke again when I see my notifications: nine missed calls and texts.

I can't help the smile that spreads across my face. "Not a ghost, kiddo," I tell him. "Just some friends of ours." I stand up and lean over to kiss the top of his head. "Can you go back to bed for me? I'll come check on you after I get the door."

"Do I have to?" Lou whines the words more than says them. "I want to see who's here!"

There's a sharp rap at the door again. "Coming!" I call. "Okay," I tell Lou. "Tell you what. If you go back to bed now, we'll get donuts before school tomorrow morning."

"Okay!" Lou easily accepts the bribe and races off down the hallway. "But we're getting chocolate!"

"Obviously!" I call back. Here's hoping I have enough money in my bank account for donuts from Marion's bakery tomorrow.

There's another rap at the door as I pull myself up off the couch and start down the hallway. "Don't knock so loudly," I hear someone say. "The mayor lives next door. If we wake her up, we'll be on the front page of the *Devon Falls Register* tomorrow morning."

"For knocking on a door?"

"Well, I don't think people knock on doors in the middle of the night in Devon Falls." There's a sigh. "Maybe we should go. He's still not answering his phone."

"Fuck. We scared him off." That's Colin's voice. I'm sure of it.

"Maybe we did." That's Tom. "I know it was probably a lot to take in. That was his first time with anyone, as we know all too well from last year's picnic debacle."

I stop with my hand against the knob. Tom's right. This afternoon was a whole lot of firsts for me. And those firsts were beautiful. Perfect. So much more than I ever could have imagined.

I never knew that being close to someone—two people, in this case—could feel like that. Like being enveloped in care and comfort and lights of happiness. Everything about what happened just felt so *right.*

My mind snaps back to that dream I just woke up from, the one where Tom wanted to kiss Colin. Does Tom have feelings for Colin? I can't seem to shake that idea from my brain, for some reason, even though Tom's never said that out loud.

"What if something's wrong? Maybe I should break the door open." That's Colin's voice, and the words would be funny if I didn't know he's totally capable of doing exactly that. I'm trying not to laugh as I finally pull the door open and take in the two of them. They're standing on the front step, bathed in the soft porch light. Tom's wearing a hat and coat, and Colin's only got a t-shirt on.

"Hey there. Want to come in for some hot chocolate?"

We end up in Dave's bedroom, which I'm trying hard not to think about as the setting for my most recent dream. I pass out hot chocolate I made with a cheap mix before I close the door. I sink down onto the sagging mattress that my back does not love, as Tom settles into the old armchair in the corner. Colin sits on the floor next to his feet as he cradles his mug.

I take in a deep breath. "I'm sorry I took off after what happened. I wasn't planning to just disappear like that. I had to go get Lou, and after we got home I crashed out on the couch. I guess you two tired me out." I shrug, and Tom laughs. He stands up and crosses the room to sit down next to me.

"Well, little fox," he says. "You absolutely did scare the hell out of us. We worried we might have driven you away."

I grin. "Getting off while I kissed two guys I've always dreamed about? Yeah, it was a little intense. But definitely in a good way." I shake my head and sigh. "I mean, that all must have been a lot for Colin too."

But Colin just shrugs. "It's like we said. You're dangerous, little fox." He smiles slightly. "It was a lot, yeah. But not in a bad way. Definitely not." He looks over at Tom, but Tom doesn't seem to notice. Huh. I've gotten used to watching them communicate back and forth without a single word. This is the first time I've ever seen one of those messages go unreceived.

Tom clears his throat. "You are dangerous, little fox," he says softly. "In the best possible way." He leans over to take my hands in his. "I'm just relieved you're okay."

"More than okay," I tell him. "But... and I'm sorry to say it like this." I sigh. "You two probably shouldn't come over here anymore. Dave might hear about it." Colin's eyes narrow. "We can still, like, keep doing this until you both leave town or whatever," I add quickly. "But we should probably stick to your house, Colin."

"Until we leave town or whatever." Tom repeats my words slowly.

"Well, yeah." I blink as I look back and forth between them. "Bethany said you two were only planning on staying until the leaf festival. Right?"

Neither of them say anything, and my heart starts to pound just a little louder in my chest as I realize I might be wrong. Tom said he's not working on *The Good Sword* anymore, and Colin definitely put a lot of work into that house. Is there a chance one or both of them might stay here longer than the next month?

My heart's a hammer now in my chest. I want that. I want that so much: for them to stay in Devon Falls, for us to keep exploring whatever this is together for so much longer than the next month.

If they're still here when it's time for Dave to come back... none of that can happen. Once Dave's back in town, everything has to change. Just like Lou's Mary Janes getting packed into the closet when Dave comes home.

And that's assuming I'm not packing up Lou and running with him into the night.

"I'm not ashamed of being with you two," I add quickly, because I need them to know that. "I hope you get that. Like, it's so cool. The fact that you two want to spend time with me." The corners of Tom's mouth peak up slightly. "But...yeah." I trail off, because I can't finish the sentence.

"But sometimes what other people think matters more than we'd like," Tom mutters. There's bitterness in his voice.

"Yeah. Exactly." He's got it perfectly. What Dave thinks has to matter to me, however much I don't want it to. Because he's still Lou's father, and unless we eventually reach the dire point of me having to kidnap my own little brother, what Dave hears and knows and thinks about what I do absolutely matters.

Colin clears his throat. "I was going to leave after the festival. Now I'm not so sure." He shrugs. And then he steps slowly across the room to sit on the other side of me. He runs a hand up and down my thigh, slowly. I bring my gaze over to him.

"All I know," he says, "is that I've never fucking felt this way before in my life." He looks back and forth between me and Tom. "So," he goes on. "I'm all in for what we're trying here. Even if it only lasts a few more weeks. Even if we have to hide the hell out of it. Whatever you both need, or want, I can do it. I'm in."

A picture of that dream I woke up in the middle of floats across my vision, and I look to Tom next. Maybe I'm way off-track thinking he might have feelings for Colin. But if I'm right, there's no way I'm getting in the middle of those feelings.

But Tom just cocks an eyebrow and leans farther over to press his lips against mine. "Me too."

I let myself fall down against the bed, grabbing to take them with me. When we've landed in a pile against the lumpy mattress, I pull them both against me. Around me. This all has to be another dream, right? I smile as I remember the words that have started every one of Colin's races I've ever watched.

"Okay then," I murmur to the room. "Lights out and away we go."

Chapter 16

30 Days to the Devon Falls Leaf Festival

He's never called me that before. —Colin Templegate

Plenty of things have happened in my life that I never saw coming. Hooking up with some guy in northern Vermont while my best friend watched is definitely high on that list. Also high on that list is carrying around a giant pedestal sink with the same guy the next morning while Tom directs us like he's racing control.

"A little to the left. No, your other left. Oh, I meant right."

"You're really bad at this," I tell Tom.

"Blasphemy, bestie. I'm just distracted." He frowns at a wall with five different paint swatches stuck to it. All of them look like exactly the same shade of green to me, but he swears there's a difference between them. "I'm trying to decide if this wall wants Midnight Evergreen or Pistachio Pine."

"Pistachio Pine is a color?" Gabe frowns as he juggles the right side of the sink, and a small bead of sweat makes its way across his forehead.

"Tom!" I bark out. "Gabe needs help. Paint colors later!"

The words jumpstart him into action. He darts across the room to grab onto Gabe's side of the sink while Gabe smiles and rolls his eyes.

"I was doing fine. But thanks for the help."

"You could have dropped this sucker on your foot," I tell him. "Don't be afraid to ask for help when you need it, Gabe."

Gabe opens up his mouth like he might argue with me, but he quickly closes it. He, Tom, and I manage to get the monstrous sink over to the corner of the room where it's about to live out the rest of its days.

"Wonderful." Tom steps back, hands on his hips. "That's going to really complement the lighting fixture. Team, I think we might actually be on track to finish this project on schedule!"

"Agreed." I survey the room around me. We've already fully finished renovating one of the others, which means we've only got two left after this, plus the event space. That space had less damage than the bedrooms, so we're right on schedule to have all this done before the masses descend on Devon Falls.

"This is amazing." Gabe beams and claps his hands together. "You guys, seriously. I can't tell you how much it means to me that you wanted to try and save the inn like this. Now if Lou and I do get to stay in Devon Falls after the festival, I can—"

He stops suddenly, clamping his mouth shut.

Tom and I glance at each other. "What do you mean *if* you stay?" Tom asks. "That's the second time you've mentioned that. Why wouldn't you stay in Devon Falls, little fox? If we finish the project, you'll still have a job you love here."

"Yup, of course!" Gabe waves an arm above his head. "Yup, that's what I meant. *If* we finish the project, and I get to stay. Because I, you know. Keep my job."

And just like that, unspoken words are hanging in the air. Air that we still haven't completely cleared from last night. The three of us were all so tired that we fell asleep together on Gabe's lumpy mattress after we talked, and then we woke up in a tangled flurry when Gabe's alarm went off and he had to help Lou get ready for school. Tom and I haven't said a word to each other about the night before. We spent an entire pancake breakfast at Luis' Cafe talking about the changing weather and all-season tires, even though I don't think Tom's ever even set foot in a tire shop before.

"Okay." Gabe frowns as he studies the pedestal. "Should we install this bad boy or have lunch first? I brought some peanut butter, and I—"

"Okay, that's enough." Tom interrupts Gabe as he shakes his head. "Listen, loves, I've tried to go along with this strange 'everything is fine and exactly the same' game the two of you seem to be playing. But frankly, it's exhausting, and I can only talk about paint swatch colors and lighting fixtures and *tires*, of all things, for so long before my brain starts to atrophy. So. Can we please discuss how we'd all like to proceed following last night's conversation?"

I should've seen this coming. Tom's got no patience. Me? I can drive the same race track for hours while I wait for conditions to go my way. But Tom, if he ever raced, would be the type of driver who took himself off every curve trying to make a new opportunity.

I glance over at Gabe, who's wringing his hands together and looking back and forth between us expectantly.

"Okay, sure," I finally say. "What do you want to happen next, little fox?"

Gabe gulps as he sets one foot on top of the other and balances in front of us. "I think," he finally says quietly, "that I want more of what we've... been doing. You know. Trying things out. You both know I've never really been... with anyone before. So all of this is new to me. And I guess I just want to, well, explore." He looks over at me, his expression suddenly wild. "But not if Colin doesn't want to!" he adds quickly. "I know this is all kind of new to you too, and I really don't want to pressure you."

Geez. The sweet kindness, the total and complete empathy, of this man will never stop impressing me. I step around the sink to rub my palm across his cheek. "I promise, Gabe. No one here is pressuring me to do anything I don't want to."

I mean those words, too. Every single damn one of them. All of these feelings I'm having for the first time are confusing as hell, that's for sure. But nothing about this situation I'm in scares me. I don't scare all that easily.

I *am* getting more and more damned worried about whatever's going on between Gabe and Lou's father. But that's a different problem to solve.

"Coaching!" Tom beams as he claps his hands together.

"Excuse me?" I all but choke on the words.

He rolls his eyes. "You're an athlete, Colin; you know what coaching is." He shrugs. "It's all very simple, really. Gabe's feeling slightly out of his depth because sexual experiences are new to him. You're feeling slightly out of your depth because, well... the same reason, actually, generally speaking. So! You both just need practice and coaching. Enter me: a man with plenty of experience in these areas." He beams and takes an exaggerated bow.

Gabe stares at him. "Um, wait. You mean you're going to coach me and Colin on how to..."

"How to derive maximum pleasure from relationships and sexual experiences. Yes, that's exactly right." Tom whips his t-shirt up over his head while Gabe and I keep gaping at him.

"We're at *work*," Gabe whispers.

"Bethany and Evelyn know we take lunch breaks. I'm sure this is all very OSHA approved. Now." Tom points a finger at both of us. "If anyone wants anything to stop, just say the word red. If anyone wants anything to slow down, say yellow. Green means go. Got it?"

"Lights out and away we go," I mumble, as I remember what Gabe said right before we all fell asleep last night.

Tom beams. "Exactly right! Gabe, do you understand?"

Gabe's eyes are locked against Tom's chest so hard that I don't think he could look away from him if he tried. He seems almost enraptured by Tom's body. I wonder if he ever looks at me that way. "Um, yeah," he finally whispers.

"Fantastic! Then let's get started. First lesson: learning what you enjoy." He draws Gabe back against his chest, pulling him against his own body as he begins to lick and nibble up Gabe's neck until he reaches his ear. Gabe gasps with each movement, and the sound sinks into my skin, tightening every nerve in my body. My eyes are glued to Gabe's expression, to the way he closes his eyes and purses his lips tightly as Tom starts teasing his earlobe.

"Very good, little fox," Tom murmurs. "Colin," he adds, "I think we can add that area of the body to Gabe's sensitive erogenous zones. Now you try." He takes me by the arm and pulls me toward him, then slides Gabe in and against my body as he steps away.

I stand there for a moment, frozen. It's still new, this feeling of desperate *want* that seems to come over me when Gabe's close like this. But then Tom slides one of my hands up under the hem of Gabe's t-shirt, and Gabe shivers as my fingers hit the skin of his stomach. "Don't overthink it, Colin," Tom says quietly. "Just feel. Like you do on the track."

That's a direction I understand.

I fall into the moment as I let my fingers explore the soft skin and patches of hair all way across Gabe's abdomen, over his belly button. At the same time, I pick up where Tom left off with exploring Gabe's earlobe with my mouth, and Gabe's gasps grow louder and stronger and turn into something like a moan.

"Wonderful," Tom says. "Let's keep exploring, then, shall we?" And just like that, he sinks to his knees on the brand-new tile floor we laid down a few days ago, tugs down Gabe's jeans and underwear in one quick movement, and swallows Gabe's cock.

Gabe makes a jumbled, mewling noise that has me grasping to hold him against me as my cock tents against his ass. I'm not sure if I'm relieved or pissed that I'm still wearing my jeans. All I know is that I can't look away from Tom's mouth and the motion it's making as he moves up and down, back and forth, across Gabe's hard length.

"Oh wow. Holy shit. Wow." Gabe's muttering and mumbling now, and Tom laughs lightly as he pulls his mouth off Gabe's cock with a pop. "Let's add blow jobs to the list as well," he says. He stands up slowly, and the two of us manage to pull Gabe's t-shirt up and over his head while he makes noises that might be trying to be words. Then Tom pulls Gabe's naked torso back against his own body again. "Colin," he says quietly. "Are you ready to try?"

I mean, yeah. Fuck yeah. Watching Tom take Gabe in his mouth was one of the hottest things I've ever seen in my life, and all I want right now is to see what it feels like to swallow him down like that. But as Gabe leans back against Tom, sighing and whimpering slightly, all I can feel is the power and responsibility of this moment. I want to make Gabe feel good so damn badly. But I can't fuck this up. I can't hurt him somehow, or make him regret what he's sharing with us right now.

Tom reaches over to take my hand. "Trust yourself, Colin. Feel it. I'll be right here," he says. "Just like the first time you climbed into a go-kart."

The memory makes me smile: a tiny Tom standing at the edge of the go-kart track as I slid in front of the wheel for the first time. And as he laces his hand around mine and takes hold of it tightly, my entire body fills with a sensation of power and comfort.

I look to Gabe, who's watching both of us with wide eyes. His cock stands at attention still, above the jeans and underwear that hang around his ankles. I pivot slightly so that I'm in front of him while Tom stays wrapped around the back of his body. I brush a hand from the edge of Gabe's right hip, down across his body, toward the area just under his belly button. Gabe lets out another strangled mewl. And that sound gives me the last bit of confidence

I need to sink all the way down to my knees in front of him, still fully clothed. I grip tightly to Tom's hand as I open my mouth wide and take Gabe inside of me.

At first, the sensation is so big and bold that it's almost all-encompassing. I've gone down on women before. It was always fine. Those experiences always created the right responses to lead to a conclusion. But that was all that ever happened for me, and I could never have ever imagined that it might feel this arousing, this momentous, to have another person's dick inside of my mouth.

I take my time, licking and sucking, following the lead of Gabe's guttural noises and Tom's easy cues. "Take him a little deeper now," Tom whispers in my ear. "Yes, just to there." Gabe yelps. "Now," Tom goes on, "Colin, take your hand and stroke him, down behind his balls."

Gabe lets out a loud cry, and Tom laughs. "Keep the volume down, little one, or Bethany's going to come charging in here wondering what's going on."

Gabe gulps and nods as he runs one hand through my hair. "Wish we were lying down." He says the words in something like a gasp. "Wish I could hold you both right now. Have you hold me."

"Oh, little one." Tom brushes his lips against Gabe's neck. "Are we a little touch-starved? We're just going to have to fix that, aren't we?" I watch as he wraps his arms even more tightly around Gabe's torso and rests his cheek against Gabe's. It's somehow incredibly sweet and incredibly damn hot all at the same time. I let go of Tom's hand so I can reach around to pull Gabe more tightly against me and take him further into my mouth.

"That's it, bestie," Tom murmurs. "Don't think. Just feel. You're doing so well, honey."

Honey? He's never called me that before. That thought registers quickly and fleetingly, but I hardly have time to study it. Because the words he's using have my cock growing even harder than it already was, and it's nearly cement-like in my jeans now.

"Look how hard Gabe is in your mouth," Tom adds, his voice calm and confident. He lets go of my hand. "Unzip your jeans, Colin. Show yourself to Gabe. Let him see you touch yourself."

Gabe lets out another strangled cry, and Tom leans over to kiss him on the neck. "See, Colin? He wants it. Don't you want to give our Gabe what he wants?"

Our Gabe. Another phrase that rings and echoes in my eardrums. But he's right: that's all I want in the world right now, to give the man above me everything. I drop my other hand to my crotch and unzip my jeans, then help my cock pop through the hole in my boxer briefs.

Gabe lets out another moan, and Tom makes a sound I don't quite recognize. "Very good," he finally says in a high voice. "Very good job. Now, don't stop what you're giving to Gabe. But reach down and stroke yourself at the same time. Do whatever feels good."

It takes a moment for me to find a rhythm. The whole process feels like how some people describe walking and chewing gum at the same time, which I've never actually found all that tough to do. But this combination of movement takes some concentration. I don't masturbate all that often, and I have to try a few things out before I find a rhythm that makes my dick stand even higher at attention as blood rushes through it. Then I have to set that rhythm against the one I'm using as I move my mouth up and down Gabe's cock.

"Very, very good," Tom whispers. His voice is low and breathy, and when I look over I see that he's got his own hand down his pants now, moving it quickly back and forth.

And for some reason, that's all it takes: I cry out against Gabe's cock as I come in my own hand. The release feels so much bigger than usual, and I find myself thrusting against the waves of my orgasm just as Gabe cries out. He says something, something to warn me, but I don't listen. I don't want to listen. I stay there, mouth wrapped tightly around him, as he loses himself inside of me.

He tastes sweet and salty and like so many other flavors I've never tasted before, all at once.

Another high noise echoes through the room, and I realize the noise is coming from Tom. He's gotten his cock out of his boxers too. I've seen his cock plenty of times over the years—Tom and I have been sharing rooms on and off since we were six—but I've never seen it like this before. It's so hard it's purple and red at the tip, so much larger than I've ever seen it, so giant in his hand.

He grips tightly to Gabe as he lets go.

"Holy crud," Gabe whispers as I slowly release him from my mouth. He grabs for me as I stand up. "Please," he whispers.

I know what he needs. I don't need to hear it. I move to wrap my body around one side of him. Tom stays firmly wrapped to his other side.

One of my arms brushes against Tom, and we both pull away like we've been shocked—but that makes no sense. This is just Tom. We've hugged like a hundred million times in our lives. Our eyes lock, and he looks away.

It's one of those very rare and always terrifying moments where I have no idea what my best friend is thinking.

Chapter 17

28 Days to the Devon Falls Leaf Festival

Not every relationship has to look like two people. —Tom Evers

"Tom! Tom! I want that one!"

"Yes, yes. I'm coming." I laugh as I follow the tiny ball of energy in front of me through a row of bright orange pumpkins. In my entire life, I don't think I ever imagined myself spending a Saturday morning in a pumpkin patch following a six-year-old around while he picks out the "most perfect pumpkins ever" for an afternoon of carving. But here I am, at the Stock Tree Farm pumpkin patch, surrounded by shouting children and the sounds of "Monster Mash" echoing out of large, portable speakers.

It's a scene right out of some family-friendly movie. The kind of movie role I always took when it was offered, because those roles gifted me long weeks of daydreaming about what it would be like to live in a place just like this one. In those daydreams, Colin loved me just as much as I loved him. We frolicked through pumpkin patches together, sometimes with children by our side.

And then the movie would finish filming, and I'd go back to a harsh reality.

"Tom? Oh, there you are." Gabe rushes up to me, breathless. Because we're in public, I quickly remind myself not to pull him in for a hug. Since we began his and Colin's coaching a few days ago, one thing has become perfectly clear: Gabe loves touch. I'm not sure exactly how deprived of it he's been over the years, but I'm determined to make up for it, and Colin appears to feel the same way. I've lost count of the number of large and small hugs we've given him recently, and it feels very disquieting not to give him one right now. "Hello there, little fox." I take a quick glance around to see who might be watching. But no one's anywhere nearby. Lou's leaning over some pumpkins singing to himself, Colin's off getting hot chocolate for Lou at the farm's stand, and all the other families at the patch are happily cavorting by themselves. So I decide it's safe to lean over and take him against my body for a fast squeeze and a quick but explorative kiss.

"Wow." Gabe's blushing slightly when we finally pull apart. I run a hand over his cheek. "I, um, just wanted to see if you thought we should get a pumpkin for Malachai and Sam. For their porch? Lou would love to carve an extra one. And maybe we could get one for Jack and Benson too."

This man. He's always thinking of others and putting them first. I glance back at Lou, who's still humming to himself. I can't even imagine all the sacrifices Gabe has made for his little brother. Not for the first time, I wonder what Lou's father is really like. I'm starting to think the man may be a mirage as well as an asshole. I've still yet to meet him.

That's probably just as well. I'm not sure I can be held responsible for the actions I take when I finally come face-to-face with the man who abandoned sweet Gabriel Gomez after his mother passed.

I keep my hand on Gabe's cheek. "That's a lovely idea. How many pumpkins has Lou picked so far?"

"Lou?" Gabe calls out. "How many pumpkins have you picked?"

"I've got three!" Lou stands triumphantly so he can turn around to face us as he holds up three fingers.

"Do you want to find a few more?" Gabe asks him. "One for Mr. Benson and Dr. Jack, and another one for Mr. Malachai and Dr. Sam?"

"I can do that!" Lou rushes off down the row of pumpkins, tapping at each one. Gabe smiles.

"Thanks for coming with us today," he says. "You and Colin really didn't need to. I mean, it is Saturday. I'm sure you both had better things to do."

I glance around at the scene in front of me: the scene I used to hope and dream for. Of course, this isn't the man I always imagined holding in my arms with this scenery in front of me. But Gabe feels so *right* when he's this close to me. So perfect in every way. And the man who used to appear in my dreams?

He's somehow, against every odd, still in the picture itself. In fact, he's currently walking over the hill toward us, holding hot chocolate in one hand and his phone against his ear with his other.

I feel the same strangled sensation I often have in my stomach when Colin comes near. But this time, the sensation is a little less sharp. Since our first "lesson" together, Colin and Gabe and I have tried out a few more of our coaching experiences. I talked Gabe through administering one of the best blow jobs I've ever had in my life, and all three of us enjoyed some very intimate hand action together. And the more things have progressed, the more I've begun to believe that whatever the three of us are trying could really work. Long-term.

Not every relationship has to look like two people. I've always known that. For goodness' sake, I'm standing in the middle of a farm owned by one of several throuples right in this valley. Perhaps Colin and I can both have Gabe as a lover and stay as close as we've ever been. And if we can make that work, Colin never needs to know my real feelings.

Maybe. Just maybe. Maybe this could work.

I take a long breath in and wrap my arm more closely against Gabe as Colin hangs up the phone and comes to meet us. "Who was that?" I ask him.

Colin frowns at the phone. "Claire," he says.

I can't help the cough that escapes my chest. "Claire Bismark? Claire Bismark the driver?"

"The one and only." Colin shrugs. "She's coming to the opening event for the winery's new event space, so I thought she was calling about that. But she wanted to know something else, actually." He frowns again and stares off into the distance.

Oh, for crying out loud. He always *does* this: drops a lede and then waits five beats too long to share the punchline, despite the fact that he knows I have absolutely zero patience. "Well? What?" I demand. Gabe smiles.

Colin sighs. "People on the circuit are making noises about asking me to do some race weekend analysis. Broadcasting, all that shit. And Claire thinks I should do it."

"Colin, that's great!" Gabe moves forward like he's about to run to Colin for a hug. He must remember that we're standing in the middle of a very not-private pumpkin patch, because he quickly stops where he's standing.

"I don't know if I'm going to do it," Colin says. "I shut the door on racing when I left. That was the right choice for me, and I don't regret it. And it's not like I need any more money than I've already made in my career." He shrugs. "So I'm not sure. I have to think about this."

"Of course." Gabe nods. "That totally makes sense."

There have been moments in my life when I've bristled at someone else offering Colin comfort or caring. In those moments, so much jealousy, stirred by unsaid words, has boiled within me. But right now, I only feel grateful that Gabe's words raise a wide smile from Colin.

Whatever feelings Colin has for Gabe, they're bringing up more smiles and laughter in him than I've seen since Christian died. Possibly even before that. And when I look over at Gabe's bright expression, I can't feel anything but utter joy and gratitude to be here with them both.

Maybe this could work.

We spend the afternoon on Colin's porch, elbow-deep in pumpkin guts as Lou darts around us shouting out carving directions. We finish up with three faces made mostly of triangles, one barely recognizable cat created by me and a stencil, and a stunning night display of a witch flying over the moon. Which Colin created. Because the man truly is somehow excellent at everything he tries.

"Is there anything you're not good at, bestie?" I tease him as we set aside pumpkins to bring to friends and help Lou light one of his favorites on Colin's front step.

"My Swedish is abominable," he says, deadpan. Gabe laughs out loud.

The three of us cook dinner together in Colin's kitchen while Lou tells us all about his school's Halloween parade and what his costume will be. "And the leaf festival is before that," he adds excitedly. "I already have my outfits picked out! I'm going to wear my blue tutu with my green jeans." He frowns. "I think. Maybe. I might wear something else if Daddy comes home for the festival."

I jerk my head up from where I've been chopping tomatoes. Colin gives me a sharp look. Gabe's in the pantry fetching some cooking oil, and I sense we're treading over some ground he wouldn't want the two of us standing on.

But I'm a nosey bastard. I can't help myself.

"Why wouldn't your dad want you to wear that, Lou?" I ask.

He frowns and taps his chin as though he's deep in thought. "I'm not sure. But my dresses make his face all sad. Especially my favorite tutu." Lou shrugs. "Once I heard him yell about it, and then I got scared and went back to my room. I think that's why he went away again, like he always does." Lou's eyes go suddenly wide, and he winces. "I'm not supposed to talk about that," he whispers.

"Hey, guys? Is extra virgin okay for this pasta?" Gabe calls from the pantry.

Colin looks at me. The conversation we have with our eyes is quick and one built on years of practice.

Let's not make a big deal of this now.

Agreed. We'll ask more questions later.

Colin nods. "Let me come look," he calls back to Gabe. He heads toward the pantry, and I kneel down in front of Lou.

"You didn't say anything wrong, okay?" I tell him. "Please don't worry about that."

Lou scrunches his face slightly. "Okay, if you're sure. I don't like making Dad sad or mad." He glances toward the pantry. "But I really, *really,* don't like it when Gabe is sad."

Laughter drifts out of the pantry and into the wide kitchen. Everything in my body feels like it lifts at that sound. "I understand completely," I tell Lou.

But I spend the first half of dinner looking back and forth between Gabe and Lou. I know better than most what it looks like to keep a secret.

I just never thought I'd meet someone with secrets wrapped up even more tightly than mine.

Chapter 18
28 Days to the Devon Falls Leaf Festival

You can ask for things you want. —*Gabe Gomez*

I wonder if this is what family feels like.

The sentence whirls through my brain as Tom plates up pasta and Colin dishes up salad and the three of us laugh and talk about Devon Falls gossip and the possibility of Benson Lewis wearing leaf costumes. Lou hops onto Colin's lap at one point to show him something on his tablet, and Colin doesn't even blink. The whole scene feels like something out of one of the family sitcoms I'd always watch as a kid. There's a twinge in my stomach as I realize that it also feels a lot like how my house used to feel before my mom got sick. She loved making big dinners, and when it was just the two of us, before she met Dave, she'd lean across the table with excitement as she ate, staring at me as though everything I was about to say might be the most important or interesting thing in the world.

I've always hated that Lou didn't know our mother, and that he never got to feel that kind of vibrant, all-encompassing love from her. I know that Dave makes Lou dinner when he's home, and I hope he listens while Lou talks. But when it's the three of us together, I'm always the one leaning across the table, nodding and making him the center of attention. Dave's eyes are somewhere else, usually his phone, and he only looks up at Lou when something he doesn't want to hear catches his brain.

But Lou's got a fully captive audience right now, and I can't stop smiling as Colin asks earnest questions about the brightly colored game Lou's showing him. Because I'm sitting here, in this perfectly decorated dining room with its just-right pastel colors and its shiny silverware, between two men I used to actively think about while I jerked off, and they're both making my little brother the king of the universe. I mean, come on. Pinch me, right?

And that's probably why I say what I say while we're doing the dishes.

"Can I sleep over tonight?" I blurt out. The words are forward and pushy and not the kind of thing I'd usually ever say. But you have to ask the universe for what you want, right? "I mean," I add quickly, "if it's not too big of a problem for you. And if Lou could stay in a guest room or something? But maybe that's a terrible idea and we should go home."

Tom slides behind me in front of the refrigerator and wraps his arms around me. He drops his lips down to my neck and starts slowly kissing around the back of it. "Are you asking to spend the night with the two of us, little fox?"

Colin drops the dishcloth he's holding and raises his eyebrows.

"Yes?" I say. But somehow it comes out like a question. "I mean, yes! Yes."

You can ask for things you want. It's an affirmation I don't use very often, but this seems like the right time.

Colin slides in front of me so that I'm basically a Gabe sandwich between the two of them. It's a position they both seem to like, and I'm sure as heck not complaining about that. He tucks a strand of hair behind my ear. "If you stay the night," he says, "would you like more coaching?"

"Um, yeah!" I all but yell the words. Tom hasn't stopped kissing my neck, and Colin's got his hands set loosely on my hips now, and my brain is heading in some *very* awkward directions for the middle of a kitchen when your little brother is in the next room.

Colin grins. "What do you think, Tom?"

Tom nibbles at my earlobe, and my cock tents my jeans. He nips at the skin there one last time before he pulls away. "I think the two of you are making excellent progress. And I am happy to offer continued coaching wherever it's necessary." He looks down at my pants. "And I'm guessing we need to get this kitchen cleaned up and some little ears off to bed as quickly as possible."

I don't think I've ever gotten a dishwasher filled that quickly in my life. I probably set a world record.

By the time I've gotten Lou bathed in one of Colin's four guestrooms—in the room's ensuite, of course—and fast asleep, I am more than primed for whatever's coming next. I may be new to this whole physical relationship thing, but Tom says I'm a quick learner. And isn't that what matters?

I practically sprint back down the hall to Colin's giant master bedroom. And when I open the door, every cell in my body stands at attention.

Colin and Tom are both standing, stark naked, on either side of the bed. They've placed candles all around the room, dropped the light low, and some kind of soft classical music is playing nearby.

"Lights out and away we go," I whisper. Colin laughs and holds a hand out for me. "Take your clothes off, little fox," he says.

I probably also set a world record for undressing.

Colin draws me over to the bed and he and Tom sandwich me again from either side. They seem to love cuddling and snuggling, these two, and I let myself fall into the calming sensation of their skin against mine. Tom's lips drift against my neck again and Colin's hands travel up and down, across my skin. My cock's growing harder and harder with every stroke, and when Colin finally ghosts a finger over my cockhead, I yelp and rut against him. He laughs.

You can ask for things you want.

"I want to do something," I blurt out. Since some kind of ghost of empowerment has taken over me today, I figure I may as well lean into it.

"Always," Tom says against my ear. The words tickle, and I giggle.

"Um, okay. Well, sometimes? When I'm alone? I like to touch myself... um, behind. And I was wondering if we could try that today. With fingers. And maybe more."

Colin's eyebrows go up, and Tom runs a hand across my hip. "Are you asking us about assplay, little one?"

Just hearing him use the term sends more blood straight to my cock. "Yes!"

And then they both do that thing where they look at each other over my head and have a conversation with their eyes. But maybe I'm getting better at their language, because I can translate it this time.

Do you think he's ready?

Yes.

Do you think we're ready?

Yes.

Okay.

Tom starts circling a finger gently around my hole. I'm not sure if I'm more or less sensitive there than most people, but every part of my body goes tense at just how damn good that feels. I grab hold of Colin, and he drops his head down to mine.

"Remember the colors," he says. "Red, yellow, green."

I nod, and he captures my mouth in a kiss.

He holds me there, teasing and playing, while Tom dances his finger back and forth. "Nightstand, Colin?" he asks. I'm not sure what he means at first, and I can't really be bothered to care. I'm too busy seeing stars as Colin presses our cocks together. I rut up and down against him, because holy hell I don't think I'll ever get over how good it feels to have his body against mine.

Then something wet and just a little cold hits my hole, and I know what Tom was getting from the nightstand.

It all washes over me, then. The reality. I've never had anything but my own fingers back there, and I honestly had no idea what to do with them. I just knew what seemed to feel good. But now I'm going to have Tom's fingers there, and maybe Colin's, and maybe... maybe even more.

Some kind of strangled noise fills the room. Tom laughs, and I realize it's me.

Tom draws circles with the liquid, teasing every nerve there until I'm thrashing up against Colin. "Don't forget your colors, little one," he says into my ear. "And push back when you feel me."

And then his finger is inside of me, moving up just toward the knuckle.

I bear back against him, against the slight pain and pressure that dances with sensation and shocks of pleasure. Colin pulls me more tightly against him, and I feel him drop lube against our cocks before he takes us both in his hand and begins jerking us together, hard and fast. I wrap my arms around his neck and hang on for the ride.

And then Tom pushes in deeper. I lose myself in sensation as he adds another finger.

"I'm touching myself too, little one," Tom whispers in my ear. "I've got one hand on my cock, and the other is inside of you.

You're a masterpiece, do you know that? The way you move against both of us. The way you respond to every little touch."

I *think* I whimper. It's not entirely clear.

Colin presses his forehead to mine. "You have no idea what it's like," he whispers, "to watch Tom play with you like this. Hottest fucking thing I've ever seen."

Tom presses his fingers in farther, and I feel another finger dancing around the edge of my hole. "Do you think you could take more?" he asks softly. "Would you like to try that, Gabe? Would you like me to go deeper?"

Words are *very* hard to find right now, so I don't try for many of them. "Green!" I yelp. "Green! Green! Green!"

Tom and Colin both laugh, and Tom lifts one of my legs up in the air as he presses in more deeply. The pressure is full and somehow not nearly enough, and I'm on the edge of begging for more when he presses a third finger into me.

"Hell, yes," I whisper.

Colin's still jerking our cocks together, setting a rhythm that perfectly matches the rhythm Tom's using to move in and out of me. He's pushing in farther than I've gone; farther than I've ever even dared to go myself. "I'm wondering," he says, "if you've ever felt this..."

And then he moves inside of me hard and fast, and something *happens.* He hits something in me, and it's like every nerve in my body explodes at once. "More!" I scream. "More! More! More! More!"

I'm panting hard as Tom nibbles at my earlobe and then whispers against it. "Just imagine," he says, "if this were my cock. Filling you all the way. So very deep inside of you. I'm about to come all over my hand, little one. Can you imagine what it would be like, having me come inside you? Is that something you think you might want one day?"

"Yes! Heck, yes!" The words sound strangled in my own ears, and I latch onto Colin, holding him hard, as he dips his head down again and brings our lips back together. I fall into the rush of constant sensation: his mouth against mine, his cock and hand against mine, Tom's fingers whirling and swirling and dipping in and out of me. Colin nips at my lower lip with his teeth as he pulls his mouth away from mine. "You're so perfect, little fox," he whispers.

I close my eyes and get lost for a moment in the haze of pure sensation running through me. When I open them again and glance above me, I realize something: Tom's eyes are locked on Colin's, and Colin's back on Tom's, and Tom's leaning farther over my body toward Colin, and Colin's shifting toward him—

But then Colin moves his hand across the top of my cock, and suddenly I'm holding onto him for dear life as every single muscle in my body tightens and then releases. I come apart across Colin's hand, over and over and over again while I clutch him against my body and Tom whispers into my ear.

"That's it, little fox. Dammit, you're beautiful to watch. Isn't he beautiful to watch?"

Colin presses another kiss to my lips and pulls back. He brushes the hair off my forehead and smiles. "So damn beautiful."

I look up between the two of them, searching. Looking to see if what I thought I saw between them before is still there.

But they're both looking away from each other now. I collapse against the bed, just a messy mass of feeling and sensation. I don't try to fight the sleep that comes next.

I wake up hours later, tangled between Colin and Tom. Tom's snoring softly, one leg over my ankle, and Colin's face is pressed into my chest. I'm not sure I've ever had to pee so badly in my life, but the urge to stay right here, locked between the two of them, is strong.

Sadly, my bladder eventually beats what my brain wants. I make my way out from between them, careful not to wake either one of them. They must have cleaned us up, but neither of them closed the curtains before they fell asleep. It's not like there's a lot of need for that. Colin's closest neighbor is the winery, which is all the way across the lake.

I stop at the edge of the bed and stand for a minute, admiring the perfect sky outside. Clear, no clouds in sight. The stars pop light everywhere, and moonbeams are falling through the window and onto the carpet.

It's been so long since I felt peace like this, I think as I finally make it to the bathroom. I take care of my business, and I wonder: have I felt this way since my mother died? This calm? This *right*? And I still have no idea exactly what we're doing here, Tom and Colin and I, or what's going to happen with Lou the next time Dave reappears in our lives. But I do know one thing: I don't want to ever stop feeling like this.

I pull on shorts and a t-shirt and check on Lou, who's sleeping soundly down the hall. I'm ready to hop back into bed and keep living every moment of this fever dream I'm in, when I notice my phone on Colin's desk. I've got a new text.

I swallow hard when I see who it's from.

Dave

> I forgot to tell you. Make sure you get Lou a good Halloween costume this year. Iron Man or something. No more of that princess shit.

One feeling I don't spend a lot of time with is anger. I don't have much use for it. I've never quite understood the point of it:

all it does is make you miserable when you feel it *and* make other people miserable. So why bother?

But right now, there's no doubt that seeping, vicious anger is moving through my body, coming up from my toes and lacing its way through my stomach. So. Much. Anger.

This man has the best kid in the *world,* and he's so wrapped up in himself that all he cares about are the clothes Lou wants to wear and the toys he wants to play with. As if any of that should make him love his own child less or more. And the fact that he keeps walking away from Lou so easily, without a backward glance, just like he did with me all those years ago—what kind of father does that?

Lou deserves so, so much better. And the fact that I have almost no control in this situation is sending fire through my entire soul.

For once, I don't try to fight that anger. Not at all. I let it sit, stewing.

You can ask for things you want.

I start typing out a text.

I hit send and take three deep breaths. I force every single thought from my mind, the way one of my former foster mothers used to teach me to do when I meditated with her.

And then I climb back in between Tom and Colin. I carefully place Tom's leg back over my ankle and pull Colin's head against my chest.

Sleep comes quickly and easily.

Chapter 19

27 Days to the Devon Falls Leaf Festival

No risk, no loss. —Colin Templegate

"Hey, loser."

The sound of Claire's cheerful voice over the phone brings an immediate smile to my face, the way it always does. Even when she's calling me names. We were bitter rivals on the track, but we were good at leaving the rivalry there. We could go from worst enemies to best friends with the lift of a checkered flag, and I've always appreciated that about my relationships with Claire. The consistency. The certainty.

"Hey yourself," I tell her gruffly as I make my way down to one of the Adirondack chairs I put by the lake when I first started work on the farmhouse. I figured that everyone else in Vermont had an Adirondack chair, so why shouldn't I? Turns out the fuckers are pretty comfortable. I like that they sort of force you to lie down halfway whenever you sit in one of them. "What's up? Didn't you just call me? I haven't heard from you this often in months."

"Well, some of us are not retired," she reminds me. I expect the words to sting just that little tiny bit, the same sting that usually runs through me when someone reminds me I'm not a race car driver anymore, but today I find that they... don't. Instead, they just sit there in my ears as truth. Christian died, and I left the sport that had once been my entire life. Claire didn't. That's what happened.

Huh. Not sure I've ever had that exact thought without getting so antsy I had to fix a broken carburetor or run a few miles. I'm going to have to think about this later.

"So," I say. "Why the hell are you calling me twice on one of your rare weekends off?" She's in Brazil next weekend. I still pay enough attention to racing to know that.

Claire sighs. "I just felt like I sort of dropped a weight on you yesterday. I didn't want to leave things like that. And listen, Colin, if you don't want to come back to the racing world, I get that. Okay? I wanted to make sure you know that. I'm not trying to force your hand just because I miss the hell out of you. You know?"

I smile as I drop farther down into the chair, letting it take my weight just a few inches from the ground. The lake's soft and glistening today, and I can hear the distant chatter and laughter of Tom, Gabe, and Lou. They're back in the kitchen, making pancakes. I told them I'd take this phone call outside when I saw it was Claire, but I'll admit, it was hard to leave the tranquility of that kitchen on this perfect Sunday morning.

Especially after what happened last night.

Not that I'm sure exactly what the hell *did* happen last night. Well, theoretically I know. I had the hardest orgasm I've ever had in my life—who knew that scale could keep tipping up—while I watched my best friend finger the guy I'm dating. And then, at the very end of it all, just as I was coming my fucking skull out and pulling my lips apart from Gabe's, I had the weirdest urge: to lean over and kiss Tom too.

Like: *what the fuck.* I've had plenty of feelings for Tom in my life, but they've never stretched anywhere near wanting to kiss him.

"You know how I never dated a lot when I was driving?" I blurt out. Because what the hell. I can't exactly talk to Gabe or Tom about this problem. Telling Sam is out of bounds right now, because no one knows that Tom or I are dating Gabe. But Claire's at her house in London, probably, thousands of miles away. Who better to ask for advice, I figure. She knows me about as well as anyone else.

Claire fakes a gasp. "You mean we didn't get married after that last race when we hugged on the podium?"

I snort. "Fucking funny."

"Yes, Colin. I know you were the monk of the paddock back in the day. Does that have something to do with you deciding whether or not you want to come back to the racing world?"

I pull at a patch of clover just under the front right leg of the chair. Then I smile as I think about the four-leaf clover hunting Tom and I used to do. "Not exactly. But sort of. Here's the thing. I always figured I was straight, right? And just not into relationships the way other people are. Now I'm wondering if maybe I'm actually demisexual or something, but I'm definitely not straight. Because... I kind of caught feelings for this guy who works at the winery I own part of. And we're dating now."

Claire lets out a noise between a choke and a snort. "Really? You're dating someone?"

It's definitely not the gender of my partner that's surprised her, but the fact that I'm dating at all. This doesn't shock me. I really was known as the monk of the paddock when I was at the height of my career. My fellow drivers all assumed that I just wanted to keep my focus on racing, and I never bothered to correct them.

"Um, yeah," I tell Claire. "Like I said, I'm still figuring it all out. But I'm pretty into this guy. He's sweet and smart and funny, and he's helping out with raising his little brother, which is cute as hell for some reason. And... yeah, I'm having a good time, I guess." I sigh. "Just not sure where it's going."

"Okay. Well, cool." I can almost hear Claire's smile over the phone. "Listen, Colin. If that's why you're thinking of not coming back, I get that. Truly."

If only it were that simple. I clear my throat. "Honestly, things are a little more complicated than that, actually. Because Tom's dating him too."

There's a long pause, and I imagine Claire whisper-screaming into the air in her London loft. She's got a flair for the dramatic, something the fans love about her. "Does that mean you're dating Tom too?" she finally asks, her voice incredulous.

"Um, no." Shit, how am I going to explain this all and still get back to the house in time for pancakes? I may have bitten off more than I can chew, pun not intended. But I can't stop now, or Claire will be blowing up my phone all day. "So, Tom's dating him. And I'm dating him. We're sort of dating him... together. But *we're* not together. If that makes sense."

Another long pause. I've got no idea what Claire might be thinking right now. I wonder if she's pacing around her island countertop, the way she always used to do when she was running racing simulations in her head.

"Okay," Claire finally says. "Sorry, I just needed to wrap my brain around all of this for a minute. And now that I'm fully up to speed, I have to say: I think that arrangement makes a lot of sense. I always worried about how the two of you were going to detach from each other's hips when Tom finally found a serious relationship. Solution found! No need to detach. I'm happy for you, mate."

I close my eyes and think about last night: about Gabe wrapped around my neck, about Tom, behind him. He stared at me, right in the eyes, as he wrecked Gabe, and I felt myself leaning closer and closer toward him, drawn to him in a way I've never been before. I mean, I've always been drawn to Tom's presence. His passion. His energy.

But last night? That was different. I've never been drawn to Tom *physically*. I've never wanted to see what it would be like to press my lips against his, to kiss him soundly and softly.

Fuck. I barely wanted to kiss anyone at all until I met Gabe.

"So, see." I clear my throat. "That's sort of, um, what I need help with. Because I was kind of feeling the same way. Like maybe this was all working out, you know? But then last night, the three of us were all fooling around."

"Hot," Claire teases.

"You have no fucking idea, Claire. Anyway, it got pretty intense. And at one point, I wanted—fuck, Claire. For a minute there, I really wanted to kiss Tom. I've never felt like that before."

"Oh, honey." There's the sound of a mug clinking against the counter. She's drinking tea, I'm sure, because Claire lives on that stuff. I once saw her drink eight cups in one sitting. She tried for years to get me into it, but I've never gotten the appeal of leaves in water. "I imagine that was confusing as hell."

"It was something. That's for sure." At the time, I was so wrapped up in sensation, nothing more than a raw nerve ending, and I didn't really have time to analyze it all. I fell asleep fast. But when I woke up this morning and watched Tom walking around my bedroom, half-naked as he picked up clothing and talked about breakfast options, I knew. I knew that moment last night was a hell of a lot more than just *a moment.*

"I don't know what to do," I tell Claire. "I mean, what we're doing here with Gabe is all pretty new as it is. We haven't even told anyone yet. I should keep this to myself, right? See if it goes away?"

"Hmmm." Claire lets out a soft sigh, and I imagine her dropping into her favorite white recliner. That thing is so fucking impractical, but she loves it. "You could do that. Or you could tell them both. Put it all out there and see what happens."

I draw in a breath so fast I almost choke on it. "Yeah, right," I finally say.

"I had a feeling you'd have that reaction. So let's get into it. Why does telling Tom feel like such a wild idea to you?"

My pancakes are definitely going to get cold soon, but this is why I told Claire, isn't it? I knew she'd make me talk through things. I knew she wouldn't let me off the hook. "Okay." I study a duck making its way across the calm water. "I never really told you exactly why I left racing, right?"

"No. Not exactly. We knew it had to do with Christian, of course." And she's nudged me for more information, but she's never pushed me too hard. Because Claire is good people like that.

I sigh. "Christian's death just made me reevaluate some things. It was like I suddenly realized that I had no idea what I even cared about besides winning. I was never like you, Claire. I never loved being behind that wheel or the feel of the engine underneath me. I just loved..."

"Winning," Claire says simply. "And to be fair, you were very good at it."

I bark out a laugh. "Yeah. But when Christian passed, I realized winning isn't what I wanted to live for anymore. And ever since then, I feel like I've been trying to figure out what I *do* want to live for. You know?"

Claire swallows. "I do," she says softly. And I think she means it. There are whole parts of herself she keeps locked away from the world. The girlfriend she had in her early twenties who only a select few people know about. The man she met at a Barcelona race and once thought she might marry. The house she owns in the lake district in England that she hides out in once a year, going out in disguise at times so no one can ever find her there.

"The thing is," I tell Claire, "I've never been sure of much in my life except racing. Tom is one of the few parts of my world I've always been sure about. If I take that risk with him, and it doesn't work out." I swallow hard. "If he disappears on me, then I'm not sure I ever will figure it out. What all this is really supposed to be about."

"Oh, Colin." Claire sighs. "I get that. I do."

We're both quiet for a long moment. The duck peeps his head out of his breast, looks around, and then takes a dive underwater before Claire speaks again.

"Colin, do you remember the Montreal race from the year before you retired?"

I run back through years of mental tapes of races until I find the one I'm looking for. I won, I remember. Claire took second. I overtook her in the Driver's Championship that weekend; she came back with a vengeance the next weekend in Italy and knocked me back into second again. That was a hell of a competition year for us. "I do."

"Third to last lap, right? I was in front. You had newer tires, so we both knew if you managed to get around me you had the race. But it was raining that day. Every pass was dangerous as hell, and both of us almost went into the wall like a hundred times."

"Sure did," I say. I remember how driving into a wall at absurdly high speeds barely registered as a concern for me, then. At least compared to concerns over winning.

"And then, on that turn with the sharp corner, you took an inside line no one would ever imagine taking. You came on my right and pulled off a pass so impossible and dangerous that sports networks played it on repeat for days afterward. I was so pissed."

I laugh. "You made me pay when you took first the next week."

"Well, I couldn't let you have all the fun. My point is that after the race, I asked you where you got the balls to make a move like that. You know what you told me?"

I do. I said the phrase that was Christian's favorite, the one he liked to throw out just before he did something like jump off a cliff or throw a hundred dollar bill down on a fifteen on a Blackjack table. "No risk, no reward," I say softly.

"We both know better than most what the cost of high risks can be. But just remember: you knew what you were doing when you made that pass, Colin. You'd calculated the risks. You'd done the math. You made that turn with no fear. And you made the right choice."

When we hang up the phone a few minutes later, I'm still running the replay of that corner in my mind. I made that decision in a split second, I'm sure I did. It's hard to even remember a time when I was that sure of myself. That self-confident.

Because the flipside of the no risk, no reward statement? That's the phrase I've lived by since I got the call about Christian.

No risk, no loss.

Chapter 20
19 Days to the Devon Falls Leaf Festival

It's all driving me a little batshit, if I'm being honest. —Tom Evers

"Wow. I can't believe this is the last bedroom." Gabe puts his hands on his hips and steps back as he studies the crown molding we just installed—well, he and Colin did most of the installation, to be fair, but I provided important direction—throughout the room. "It looks amazing!"

Colin pulls him in for a side hug. "Just the event room work after this, and that's mostly cosmetic. We should be done with plenty of time before the festival. Enough time for Bethany and Evelyn to prepare, and for us to hold that big event to show off the new space."

"It's really stunning. You two have a lot to be proud of." I give Gabe a kiss on the cheek, and he blushes.

"Hey, you did a lot of the work too," he tells me.

I have worked hard, he's right. But ever since the incident with the pipe, where I nearly flooded the entire inn, I've been all too happy to take on the role of oversight. Colin and Gabe have done a lot of the heavy lifting together, and they deserve to be proud of all that they've accomplished. "Just wait until you're checking people into this room," I tell him. "You can say that you installed that molding, and painted those walls, and put in that toilet." He beams, and I pull him in for a hug. "You did fantastic work here, little fox."

"We were a good team. All three of us." Colin says the words softly, and I swear he's staring at me when he says them. He's been doing that a lot lately, I've noticed: watching me carefully in moments when he, Gabe, and I are together.

It's all driving me a little batshit, if I'm being honest. Mostly because I have no idea why I'm suddenly noticing these small changes in Colin. And also because something happened last week when Colin, Gabe, and I were together in bed. Something that happened right after I fingered Gabe to the point of wrecking him. Colin was staring at me so very hard in that moment. He leaned toward me, at one point. And I wondered—just for a moment—

If he was going to kiss me.

It was a ridiculous idea, of course. I know that. Colin's never been interested in anyone until Gabe, and Gabe's got the entirety of his attention. I'm beginning to worry that this inadvertent threesome I've gotten myself into might be wreaking havoc on my thinking skills.

Since that night, the three of us have enjoyed ourselves together a bit here and there. But we've all been busy with the renovations, and Gabe's been busy with Lou's after-school activities and his other responsibilities at the inn. We've had some stolen moments, but the three of us haven't been together in the same kind of way. So I haven't had a moment to test whether I'm going to start imagining horribly dangerous things about Colin every single time the three of us are together that intimately.

"You know," Gabe says. "We're ahead of schedule. Which means that we could take an hour and a half off for lunch. If we wanted to."

My eyebrows go up. "Are you suggesting a long, leisurely lunch at the diner?" I tease. Because I know, of course, exactly what he's suggesting. I can see it in the way he's shifting back and forth from his right leg to his left as he looks back and forth between me and Colin.

Gabe gulps, and then grins. "Could you show me how to have anal sex?" he blurts out.

Colin lets out a long cough. I stand there, frozen. But not for very long; I do pride myself on being a man of action, after all.

What on earth does it matter whether or not I'm losing my mind? I've been losing my mind over Colin Templegate for years now. Certainly my constitution can take a little more stress.

"I'll see you both in Colin's bedroom," I tell Gabe and Colin. "Underwear will be optional, and it is not encouraged."

Gabe laughs so loudly I wonder if they can hear him from the other half of the inn.

"Let's take a moment to talk about this."

The three of us are in bed, clothes gone except for our boxers, and Gabe is lying between Colin and me on Colin's behemoth of a mattress. "First of all, I want you to remember the lights, little fox." I brush a finger down across Gabe's hip, and he shivers. "If there's anything you're not enjoying, anything that makes you uncomfortable, all you need to do is say the word. Red. We stop."

Colin nods. He leans over to kiss Gabe gently on the cheek. "We don't want to do a single thing you're not comfortable with. Say the word."

Gabe looks back and forth between me and Colin. "I think I'm ready." His words are low and breathy, but I believe him. "Um. Will one of you...? Or... both of you?"

Colin smiles. "You know what? I'd really love to see you with Tom. To watch the two of you." He leans over slightly and nibbles on Gabe's earlobe. "Maybe with some additional support with my mouth." And on that note, he bends himself in half, pushes Gabe's boxers down, and swallows him.

I go instantly hard as I try not to dwell too hard on the words *I'd love to see you with Tom.* That doesn't mean anything, of course. Just that he likes watching Gabe get off. Who wouldn't, honestly? There's nothing more sensual than the way Gabe reacts to intimate touch. His body acts like every stroke has set his entire nerve bank on fire.

Which is how I'm starting to feel right now, as Gabe clutches slightly at the top of my boxer shorts while Colin moves up and down on his cock. "Are you ready?" I whisper in his ear.

"Yes, yes, yes. Please, yes," he answers.

I try not to laugh as I move him farther onto his side and Colin adjusts his own body position to Gabe's movements. I pop open the lube bottle I've got at the ready, and I slide my own boxers down. Colin, I noticed, has at some point made Gabe's boxers disappear completely from his body.

I start slowly, gently, determined to make this experience everything that Gabe deserves it to be. I tease around the sensitive nerves at his entrance, studying each small section of him with my fingers. I pay close attention to every single touch that makes him startle or gasp or thrust deeper into Colin's mouth. My eyes drift down, and I see that Colin has one hand down his boxers as he's sucking and teasing Gabe.

That sight alone makes me so very hard that it's difficult to stop, slow down, or have all the patience I need at this moment. But patience is what I must keep hold of right now. I cannot rush this.

Gabe has given Colin and me so many gifts already, and this one must be treated with all the reverence that we've given every other first moment he's shared with us. So I take a breath, and I take my time.

Eventually, we reach a point where I feel confident enough in Gabe's reactions to slide one finger just slightly into him, and then another. I'm careful to remember and repeat everything that brought the best reactions out of him the last time we did this. I lean over to nibble at his ear the way I know he likes, and I kiss down his neck as I pull him closer against me with my other hand.

"You're so beautiful, little fox," I tell him. "Beautiful in every way. The way you're reacting to me right now? You're like a stunning work of art, spread out on display for us." He whimpers again, and below us, I hear Colin let out a grunt that sounds like agreement.

Colin's eyes are locked fully on Gabe's body; I don't think he's looked up toward me once since he took Gabe into his mouth. I take a moment to wonder if I really did hallucinate that moment between us the last time we were in this room—but there's not time to think about that now. I need to focus on Gabe.

"Just your fingers make me feel so full," Gabe says. "It's going to hurt a little, isn't it?"

"Yes," I tell him honestly. "And that's why you have to be honest with us. You have to tell us to stop if everything gets to be too much."

"I know. I promise. Please? I want this," he whispers.

I kiss his ear again, and then his cheek. I look for Colin's gaze one more time, and this time I manage to catch it. His eyes are dark and bright all at the same time, somehow. I'm not sure I've seen them look like that since the last time he walked onto a track on race day.

I swallow hard and thrust another finger into Gabe's body.

"Very good. You're doing so well, little fox. Keep pushing back. Bear down now."

I feel it when he pushes back against me. He takes in a long breath, breathes out, and the pressure against my finger intensifies as I push in a little bit harder, searching for that spot. I can't wait to hit that bundle of nerves that I know will light him on fire.

When I first find it, he lets out a squeal and juts his hips upward so quickly that I worry he might have injured Colin. But Colin just laughs below us, and that sound feels heavy in my ears.

"Oh, my God, Tom," Gabe whispers. "Tom, please don't stop. Feels so good. Feels so, so good."

"Am I hurting you at all?" I ask him.

He swallows. "Like, a little. But please don't stop."

I know what he's feeling right now. I know that edge of pleasure and pain, when it all blurs together so quickly that the sensations become mixed in your body, driving forward nothing but endorphins and adrenaline. "Don't forget your colors," I remind him. He nods. I see him reach down and grip against Colin's hair, and Colin rubs a hand up and down his thigh.

"I promise," Gabe whispers.

I stretch him carefully, moving my fingers back and forth inside of him, listening for every single nuance of sensation. His yelps grow higher, his whimpers a little deeper. I'm pleased to realize that I know his body well enough now to know when he's ready for more.

And only then do I kiss him carefully on the cheek and say, "Let's move."

It's a little bit of a strange adjustment. I want Gabe on his back so I can watch him, so I can be sure of his facial expressions as we do this. Colin pulls off Gabe's cock, and we shift him carefully so that I can lift his hips up onto a pillow as I kneel in front of him.

Colin curls around him and gets his mouth immediately back on Gabe's dick, as though it was painful for him to be away from it for so long.

I'm so very ready to feel what it's going to be like to be inside of him. "Are you sure you're ready for this, little one?" I ask him as I lift his ankles up and place them on top of my shoulders. I can see how hard he is inside of Colin's mouth, and watching the reddish purple head of his cock go in and out of Colin's lips has to be the strongest aphrodisiac I've ever experienced in my life.

"Yes." He nods quickly. "I want you... want you inside of me. Tom, please."

I rip open the condom I've got nearby and slide it on. I've just finished covering it in lube when I hear Colin whisper, "I can't wait to see this, babe."

At first, I'm sure he must be talking to Gabe. But when I look down at him, I see that his eyes are on me. He's staring at me hard again, the way I remember from the other day. And he's not looking away.

I close my eyes against a rush of emotion just as I push inside of Gabe.

He lets out a quick gasp as I settle partially inside of him. "Push back," I remind him, and he does with a quick nod. I'm fairly versatile, and I've been fucked well enough and often enough to know that this part is always an adjustment for me, no matter how many times I have someone's cock, or a dildo, pushed into me. There's always that moment of push and stretch as your body finds its new footing.

"Color?" I ask Gabe.

"Yellow," he whispers. I nod and stay still for a long moment before I finally start moving back and forth slightly within him while I drag a finger around his hole. It looks like his erection has flagged just slightly in Colin's mouth. But then Colin does something with his tongue, teasing at the end of Gabe's cock, and Gabe ruts against him with a quick shout. "More!" he calls out. "Green, green, green!"

"Okay," I say with a laugh. Then I push just a little bit farther toward that bundle, searching for it again.

We catch a rhythm fairly quickly. As Gabe juts back and forth between me and Colin, he reaches out a hand like he's desperate to find mine. I grab his hand and hold it, just as I see that he's latched his other hand to Colin's shoulder.

Colin looks at me, staring hard, again. I don't look away. And then he reaches out to me with his other hand.

I grab hold of it.

It's like we're a circle now, completely connected all the way around. We all let go quickly, because the positions we're in don't allow for lengthy hand holding, but then I press my hands against Gabe's legs and Colin pushes his hand up against my hip, and it's like we're connected again, our circle still intact.

I'm moving inside of Gabe as slowly as I can, but it's so fucking hard not to lose myself inside of him. He's so warm, so tight, and it takes everything I have to hold on each time his body clenches around my cock. I hold on to his body for dear life as we all fuck in the same rhythm, with Gabe moving steadily back and forth between my cock and Colin's mouth. Except this doesn't feel like fucking, not at all. I'm making love to Gabe, I'm sure of that. And Gabe is making love to Colin. And even though Colin and I are only touching one another, somehow, we're making love too.

I suck in a long, deep breath and try not to panic that I'm in too far over my head.

"Oh," Gabe whispers. "Please don't stop. Please don't stop, Tom. Colin. Please!"

He has no idea what he's doing to me right now. I'm not going to be able to hold on much longer.

"Gabe," I whisper, "tell me when you—"

Just then, he lets out a cry and screams as he thrusts hard up into Colin's mouth. I watch him as he comes inside of Colin, shaking and shouting and whimpering all at once, somehow. At the same time, Colin makes a movement, and I realize he's losing himself in his boxers, his other hand still on his cock. That's all it takes for me to go over the edge, and I swear I see stars as I come inside of Gabe.

And then everything stops. I stop. Colin stops. Gabe stops. The room stops. Gabriel's ankles are still on my shoulders, and Colin's mouth is still wrapped around Gabe's cock. I'm still planted firmly inside of him.

"Wow," Gabe whispers.

Colin lets out a laugh as he gently pulls his mouth off of Gabe, stopping to leave a long, lingering lick across the head of his cock. Gabe shivers.

I should pull out of him. I know I should, but I don't right away. I'm not ready to leave just yet.

I'm not ready to leave this beautiful, perfect space where these two perfect men feel almost as though they could both belong to me.

We don't talk much as we clean up.

I make it a point not to say anything to Colin about the connection between us while we both made love to Gabe. What's the point? Surely he was just caught up in the moment, and there will be nothing but danger for me if I read anything else into what just happened. I'm puttering around in the kitchen, making us sandwiches to help us get our energy back, when my phone buzzes with a text from my agent.

Melody

Hey, we need to talk. Rumors are starting to spread out here about why you left The Good Sword. I think we need to get out in front of them. It's time for you to take another role, don't you think? Let's get you out here for some auditions.

A lump lodges in my throat. Nothing sounds more horrific right now than heading back to Hollywood, back into the lion's den and away from this beautiful bubble. The only thing I'd like to do less is stick my head in an oven.

The Glorious Thomas of House Evers

Hi. I'm finishing up a project here. I wouldn't be able to come out any earlier than late October.

I hit send, but my thumbs stay poised over the keyboard. Maybe it's time I really thought about taking Max up on his offer and getting my side of the *Good Sword* story out into the world. I'm so tired of living in other people's projections.

The Glorious Thomas of House Evers

Maybe it's time for me to be honest and tell everyone what really happened on that set.

Melody

Tom, please tell me you're not really considering that. You want to keep your career, right? That means no one can know what really happened between you and that director. Once you get another role, all the noise from this last project will go away. You've got this! I promise.

I slide down the kitchen island to sit on the floor against it. Because I absolutely do not "got this." I do not have the power or the energy to go back to Hollywood and deal with everything I left behind there. I simply don't.

Especially when I have so much more to look forward to here. Particularly if I could just figure out how to look deeply into my best friend's eyes while I have the best sex of my life with another man I care deeply about—one who can't even be seen with me publicly.

And am I really ready to give up the career I worked so hard to build? Could I actually walk away from acting without a backward glance?

I swallow and put my thumbs back on the keyboard.

The Glorious Thomas of House Evers

I need some time to think. I'll text you soon.

Chapter 21

12 Days to the Devon Falls Leaf Festival

Optimism has gotten me a long way in my life. —Gabe Gomez

I was sixteen years old when I was placed into foster care.

I remember so many small details about that day.

My mother died at 11:53 a.m. I remember thinking that seemed like a strange time to die. I'd always thought people died in the middle of the night, but here was my mother, fading away from the world while the sun shone brightly outside her hospital room window.

I remember she took my face in her hands and stared at me for a long time. "My beautiful boy," she said softly. "My beloved boy. I'll love you forever. I hope you know that."

I remember her holding tightly to Lou, who was still just a baby at the time. I remember wondering if he'd remember anything about her at all, even glimpses of her face. Probably not, I figured.

I remember Dave shouting angrily at doctors and nurses, blaming them and threatening lawsuits.

And then I remember the social worker. I remember overhearing their conversation with Dave.

"He's not my kid anyway." The words washed through me like hot oil, all of them true but still hard to hear from a man I'd lived with for so many years of my childhood. "I've got a job lined up in Vermont, and I'm not taking him with me. He's nothing like me. I didn't mind being his stepdad, but I ain't ever going to be his dad. We never had much of anything in common except for his mom."

I remember sitting on a bed in a group home, flipping back and forth on my phone between pictures of Lou and my mother and desperately holding back every tear building up inside me. I remember making a vow to myself: I would get back to Lou. I would make sure I stayed in his life. I would be certain he always had unconditional love. I would be by his side the entire time he was growing up to tell him that he was perfect and lovable and wonderful exactly the way he was.

I'm thinking of that day now as I scan through my last text messages to Dave. My fingers stop on the last message I sent. It's still on Read, all these days after I sent it.

You don't have to come home at all, you know. We're fine here without you.

I want to be Lou's guardian.

I don't regret texting a single one of those words. I meant them with my whole body, because Lou is thriving right now. He puts on whatever clothes he wants in the morning. Tom and Colin dote on him every time they see him. Every night when I tuck him into bed I ask him if he's had a good day. He doesn't say yes every day, of course. Last Monday there was an incident at school with George Ryker and a truck they both wanted to play with. Apparently, that day was *kind of stinky.* But most days he gives me the same answer.

"It was the best day I've ever had."

He's his own personal positive affirmation, my brother. And he deserves to stay that way, no matter what.

I study the message again. I still think Dave loves Lou. He loved him enough to bring him to Vermont after our mom died, to try to give him a home here. But then again, once upon a time I thought Dave loved me.

There are so many things about this world I just don't understand. Like how someone can leave a child they fed and clothed for years inside the walls of a group home two weeks after their mother dies of cancer. Or how someone can look at the child they brought into the world and only see the clothes they like to wear.

"Everything okay?"

Colin's voice jolts me out of my thought spiral. "Huh. Oh, yeah. Just checking on something."

He smiles as I slide the phone into my pocket. He takes hold of one of my belt loops and pulls me a little more closely toward him. "Hard to believe this is the last reno project left," he says softly.

I look around at the event space, the last part of the inn left that needs to be renovated. It's probably a miracle this area sustained so little damage. When the professional cleaners came through after the fire to clean the smoke and water damage, they didn't even have to do much in this space. It's an old building that was attached to the large Victorian house Evelyn converted into an inn. A shed, Bethany calls it, but I think it was originally a horse barn, and it's always seemed just a little more fragile to me than all the other buildings on this property. I wonder if it would have survived any kind of massive damage.

Luckily, it didn't need to. The fire didn't do nearly as much damage here as it did to the rest of the rooms, and Tom and Colin and I have made a lot of progress here in the last few days. We replaced a section of the floor that had scorch marks, repaired some damaged paneling along the walls, and now all that's left is the fun part: making this space shine and sparkle for the star-studded event Evelyn's hosting here to kick off the leaf festival this year.

And that event's going to be in less than two weeks. In just twelve days the festival arrives, and Dave will either come home or he won't. And either way, I know I'm probably going to have to make some very, very hard choices.

I can't look at Colin right now, so instead I let my eyes do more traveling around the space. It's long and wide, and the large beams of wood that stand proud above us, reminders of the hayloft that I think used to lay above them, give it warmth and character. "We should hang fairy lights across all the beams," I tell Colin. "Wouldn't that look great for the big event? I know Evelyn has a whole bunch she keeps in storage."

Colin frowns as he studies the beams. "Yeah, probably would." He sighs. "But fuck, those beams are way up there. I'll get some ladders."

"Thanks, babe!" I call out as he walks away. And then I quickly clasp my hand over my mouth, because did I just call him *babe*?

I have very, very definitely never done that before.

But Colin just turns slightly and looks back over his shoulder. The right corner of his mouth moves upward, just a notch, until he's half-smiling. "No problem, little fox. Be right back," he says easily.

My heart rises like a bird in my chest. Like hope. Maybe Dave won't come back. Maybe I can have Colin forever, and Tom too. In my mind I can see it: the three of us out to lunch together, in public, eating all the empanadas we want without anyone ever looking over our shoulders. My shoulder.

Tom comes jogging into the barn. "Great news!" he shouts. "The hardware store had the perfect sconces for this space. I've got four of them out in the Jeep, and we can—"

Before he can finish, I launch myself at him, wrapping myself around him like a spider and attaching our lips together. He holds onto me like a vice, and we both lean hard into the kiss.

"Well," he says, when we finally break apart and he sets me down. "I'm not entirely sure I deserved that hug just for picking up some light fixtures, but I'll take it."

I shrug and grab hold of his hand as I look around the room, thinking about everything we've already accomplished. Tom, Colin, and I have done so much together. I've never been happier than I am with the two of them. And in moments like these, I can almost convince myself that maybe what we have together could really last. Past the festival, through whatever happens with Dave, through whatever Tom and Colin still have to figure out. Through all of this.

We can do hard things.

Maybe.

Optimism has gotten me a long way in my life. I hold onto that thought as my other hand brushes up against my phone, still warm in my pocket.

I squeeze Tom's hand a little more tightly. "You've done a lot more than find some fixtures," I tell him.

He opens his mouth, and I brace myself for a classic Tom Evers witty retort. But then he closes his mouth again, and nods. He leans over to kiss me.

"Thank you, little fox."

The bird in my chest rises again.

"Be careful up there," Colin calls up to me.

"It's just a ladder," I call back. "I haven't exactly climbed into the cockpit of a car that goes two hundred miles an hour, Colin."

Colin snorts and goes back to frowning at the sconces he and Tom are unpacking from their boxes.

"I'm fine," I tell them as I reach one hand up to secure another section of lights around a beam. "I've only got one beam left and then I'm done." There's a buzzing in my pocket, and my heart rate immediately goes up. Not too many people text me. The usual suspects are Lou's school, Dave, Evelyn, Bethany, and the two men standing in this room with me.

So: either my boss needs something, Lou's in trouble, or Dave's finally texted me back. I rush to grab my phone, but I can't get it out with one hand. It's stuck in the cloth of my pockets. "Gabe?" Tom says. "What are you doing up there?"

"Just trying to get my phone!" I take my other hand off the ladder, ignoring Colin's calls for me to be careful, and manage to get my pocket untangled and get the phone out of it. I click into the messages app, and my brain feels like it comes to a full and complete stop when I see the message there.

Dave

> What the hell are you talking about? Lou's my kid. Look, I'm done with you acting like you know more about him than I do. When I get back to Devon Falls, I want you out of both of our lives.

There's a humming noise in my skull now, and it's getting louder and louder. It's drowning out the voices of Tom and Colin, who are bickering about sconce placement and lighting angles. The room suddenly looks dark and blurry around the edges, and I realize I can't seem to catch my breath. *Why can't I breathe?* I hear shouting now, ringing against the edge of the humming, and I grab for air, but it won't come. My hands and feet are going numb, and I can't move, I can't breathe, I can't move, I can't breathe—

There's another shout, and I realize my feet are going out from under me.

And then I'm racing down toward the floor. I catch a glimpse of Colin and Tom, see terror etched across their foreheads and their mouths lifted in screams.

That's the last thing I know before everything goes black.

Chapter 22

12 Days to the Devon Falls Leaf Festival

Of all the people I could imagine might ever say those words to me, Gabriel Gomez is at the bottom of the list. —Colin Templegate

"He never, ever should have been up on that ladder."

Tom paces the waiting room, barely looking at me, barely looking at anything. I close my eyes and then quickly open them again.

Because every time I try to close my eyes, I see it again in my mind: Gabe losing his grip, falling from the ladder, catching his head and leg against the metal on his way down.

"Do you have any news?" Benson comes rushing into the room in a dress shirt and khakis. "I got over here from the office as fast as I could. Jack went to Devon Falls Elementary to pick up Lou. Is Gabe okay?"

Tom crosses his arms over his chest as he shakes his head. "No updates. The paramedics thought it was a broken leg and a concussion, but they're looking at him now. The doctors removed us from the exam room," he adds.

Benson snorts. "I can't imagine why. You two look like the picture of calm right now." Tom glares at him, and Benson holds up his hands in surrender. "Hey, I get it. You must have been terrified when he fell. But a broken leg and a concussion are both treatable. I'm sure he's going to be fine."

Tom sighs as he sinks down into the chair next to me. His hand creeps toward mine across the fabric of his jeans, and I have to fight the urge to grab hold of it. I just want to feel his hand against mine, to hold onto him tightly, to promise him that everything's going to be okay. Not long ago I wouldn't have hesitated to grab my best friend's hand for comfort, and it's pissing me off that whatever weirdness I've been feeling around Tom has me pausing now. I start to inch my hand toward his.

Sam and Malachai appear in the doorway, with Bethany right behind them. I pull my hand back.

There's a rush of conversation, but it all goes over my head—both literally and figuratively—as I sit in the hard plastic-backed chair breathing in and out, over and over again. Anything to stop seeing the image in my head of Gabe, so still and so very silent, laid out on that backboard as paramedics wrapped a collar around his neck and shouted orders about pulses and breath sounds.

"Hey." Sam's standing above me now, frowning. "I just talked to the nurses at the station; they know Jack and me. They said he's stable and his injuries look relatively minor. He's going to be okay, Colin."

Everyone keeps saying that. Paramedics. Doctors. Nurses.

But my brain fucking refuses to believe it.

Then Jack's in the doorway, and Tom and I both stand up, ready to rush over and comfort Lou. Except—

Jack's alone.

"We have a problem," he says.

"I'm afraid I still don't understand."

Tom says the words softly, and they seem to drift through the room where Gabe lies between us. Not the way he usually does, though. Not all sated and soft and melting in between our touches. Right now, he's wrapped in bandages and a large, long cast, stretched out across a hospital bed with plastic lines weaving in and out and around his body. But Tom's holding one of his hands, and I'm holding the other, and we're told he should wake up soon. He's only sleeping because of the concussion, everyone says.

Jack and Benson had to have seen the way we both rushed to Gabe's side and grabbed his hands when the four of us got to this room, but they haven't asked any questions about how close either of us are with Gabe these days. I wonder how that conversation will go if they ever do ask. I wonder what they'd say if they knew about the arrangement the three of us have. I wonder what Sam and Malachai and Bethany would say.

But those wouldn't even be the most important conversations we'd have to have today. No. First we have to have a much, much harder one.

One of Gabe's eyes slowly starts to flutter open. Then the other. He blinks and looks around, getting his bearings, as Tom brushes a hand against his cheek. "You're finally awake, little one," he whispers.

Gabe's eyes go wide as they travel around the room. "I'm still in the hospital," he finally manages to say.

I nod. "You are. You're in the hospital over in Fairlington. You're a little drugged up, and you managed to knock your head and your leg on that ladder pretty good when you fell off of it. But you're going to be okay."

Gabe blinks. "Lou!" He says the word in a rush and tries to sit up, but Tom and I manage to gently keep him on the bed.

"Lou's okay," I assure him. "He's safe. But. There is something we have to tell you."

Gabe closes his eyes. "No. No... no... no," he whispers.

He knows. He knows what we're about to tell him—or some version of it, anyway. Every muscle in my body aches with pain for him as I listen to the words Jack starts to say to him.

"I went to the school to pick Lou up," he says. "But I'm not on his pick-up list, of course, and you know how seriously any school has to take a child's pick-up list. So they called Dave to get his permission for me to take Lou."

Gabe lets out a low, small noise, like that of a wounded animal. Tom squeezes his hand tightly, and I bring my other hand up to rest on his uninjured leg.

Jack sighs. "I'm not sure exactly what Dave said to them. But I know he wouldn't give them permission to release him to me." He shakes his head. "And Gabe. I know they told him not to let me bring Lou to you in the hospital. I'm not sure where Dave is or when he's coming back to Devon Falls, but Gabe... I think the school may decide to call social services and let them sort all of this out."

The noise Gabe lets out then is so guttural, so laced with pain, that Tom and I both grab hold of him from either side and cling to his body as he sobs. "Lou," he whispers through the tears. "Lou. I screwed up. I lost him."

"You haven't." Benson shakes his head. "That's why I'm here. Gabe, I know you feel like shit right now, but you have to tell us the whole story. I need to know why Dave wouldn't let Jack bring Lou to you today. Everyone in town knows you're basically Lou's second caretaker. What the hell is going on?"

Gabe makes a strangled noise. I squeeze his hand and rub my thumb against his palm.

Benson takes a step closer to Gabe's bed. "Listen, Gabe. I know there has to be a good reason you don't want to talk about all of this. But I hope you will. Because if you do, maybe there's a chance we can help keep you and Lou together."

Gabe blinks, and I move to brush back the tears that are falling down his face now. "Okay," he finally says softly. "Okay."

The story comes out slowly, in pieces, because Gabe's on strong drugs and the words aren't flowing well for him. But we get there. Some of it, I already know. Some of it, I've never heard before.

He tells us how his mom got sick right after Lou was born and how Dave went downhill from there. He tells us about being left behind in foster care after his mom died and about Dave taking Lou to Vermont. He tells us how he came to Vermont after he aged out of the system and did everything he could to be part of Lou's life again. I grit my teeth and manage not to punch the wall whenever his asshole stepfather's name comes up in a sentence.

And then he tells us more.

He tells us how he started to worry more and more about the kind of dad Dave was. He tells us all about Dave disappearing for weeks and months at a time. He tells us about the things Dave's been saying to Lou. Comments about his clothes, his favorite toys, his favorite games. It's an absolute miracle I don't put three or four holes into the wall of the Fairlington hospital when he gets to that part.

He tells us about Dave leaving for Rochester, and about Dave's threats to take Lou out of Gabe's life.

"Little fox, I don't understand why you kept so much of this a secret," Tom finally says to him. "Why didn't you want to tell anyone how bad things had gotten? This is Devon Falls. The people here love Lou. They love you, Gabe." I hear the unspoken part of that sentence on his lips.

We love you, Gabe.

Gabe purses his lips and shakes his head. "Because I was worried the state would never, ever give me custody of Lou if they found out I was acting as his primary caretaker." He sinks down into the bed, into himself. "I have a record," he says quietly.

"Excuse me?" I blurt out. "You?" Because of all the people I could imagine might ever say those words to me, Gabriel Gomez is at the bottom of the list.

Gabe gulps. "It happened after I aged out of the system. Money was really tight," he goes on. "I was trying to save up to come to Vermont, so I ended up moving in with this guy because the rent was cheap. What I didn't realize was that he was dealing out of the apartment. And he was working with some pretty nasty stuff."

I see Benson's got his phone out now, taking notes. Good. If anyone can help us fix this mess, it's him.

Gabe shakes his head. "I didn't even know what he was doing until the cops busted him. But he'd hidden a bunch of illegal stuff in our apartment, in my room, and he said it was mine to keep his charges lower or whatever. The lawyer the court assigned me said it would be too hard to prove I didn't even know what was going on in the apartment, and he pushed me to take a misdemeanor charge."

"Fucker," I mutter.

"What an absolute travesty of an attorney," Tom adds.

Gabe shrugs. "I figured I had to listen and do what he said. It's not like I had money for another lawyer. And the court only gave me community service." He lets out a small laugh. "The judge really liked me. She said I smiled more than anyone else she'd ever seen in a courtroom."

"Okay," Benson says. "Well, a misdemeanor drug charge isn't the end of the world, Gabe. I've seen a hell of a lot worse. We can work with this. Especially given that you're Lou's brother and there's a serious case to be made here against Dave for child neglect." He types something else out on his phone before he locks it and drops back into his pocket. "I've already got Ellie working on this; she knows people at the state offices. Jack, should we tell them?"

Jack looks at the three of us and hesitates. Then he nods.

"Tell us what?" Tom asks.

"Gabe," Benson says, "I'm going to assume that part of the reason you've tried to keep the peace with Dave is that you had a lot of fears about Lou being placed in foster care if he was removed from Dave's custody. Am I right about that?"

"I mean, yes?" Gabe blinks. "Yeah. Definitely."

Benson looks at Jack, who gives us a weak smile. "Benson and I," Jack says, "recently became licensed foster parents in the state of Vermont."

We all stare at them. "You never thought to mention this to anyone?" Tom finally says.

Jack shrugs. "We weren't sure if or when we'd be ready to take on placements."

"And we knew if we told anyone it would be the first story on the town message board," Benson adds drily.

"But Gabe," Jack goes on, "it seems like things are escalating with Dave, and with it looking like a possibility that Lou will be placed in care... would you be comfortable with me and Benson requesting that he stay with us?"

Tears are running down Gabe's face right now, fast, and it's all I can do not to wrap his injured body and soul up in my arms and hold him as close to me as I can. "Please," he whispers. "Please."

Benson nods. "Okay," he says. "Jack, let's go. We need to get moving here, fast. We'll text you all as soon as we have any news, okay?"

The three of us nod, and Jack and Benson disappear from the room. "Little fox," Tom whispers. "I'm so sorry that—"

But Gabe pulls his hands away from both of ours, and mine feels suddenly empty and cold. "Please," he whispers. "I need a minute, okay?" He closes his eyes as he wraps his arms around his chest. Tom and I hesitate as we look across at each other.

Should we?

I'm not sure. He needs us.

"Please," Gabe goes on. "I just... I don't know what all of this means. I don't know what any of this means." He shakes his head. "I'm used to doing things on my own. I've had to do them on my own for a long time. And right now, I just need a minute to try and figure all this out on my own."

Those are the words that echo through my ears as I step through the doorway of his room, with Tom in front of me, and shut it behind me. The metal closes against its frame with a long click that echoes in my ears for hours.

Chapter 23

11 Days to the Devon Falls Leaf Festival

I cry harder than I cried at Christian's funeral. —*Tom Evers*

"What do you think the sheriff's going to say?"

Colin's words are edged with the same tension that hums through my body. In the eighteen hours since Jack and Benson left Gabe's hospital room, Gabe's barely said a word to either of us or anyone else. He has been sleeping quite a lot, to be fair, but when he does wake up it's only to stare at the ceiling, eyes despondent and dark. Colin got him to nibble at a pudding cup this morning, and he'll drink water when we place the straw in front of his face, but most of the time he keeps his eyes closed off or locked on the white tiles above him, his gaze empty and bleak.

And that's why Colin and I are standing guard at his doorway right now, waiting for the sheriff and the county social worker who are coming over to the hospital to talk to Gabe. He's due to be released from the hospital in a few hours, but it sounds as though they want to talk with him immediately.

Neither of us know whether this visit is a good or bad development in Gabe and Lou's situation. And neither of us will let anyone into this room who's going to do Gabe more harm than good right now.

"I just don't know what to think, bestie," I tell Colin. I shake my head as I run one hand through my hair. It feels greasy and wild, another reminder that I've barely slept in the last twenty-four hours. Colin and I took turns staying awake in case Gabe needed us, but the barely-padded wooden chairs in his hospital room didn't make for very good resting conditions. "But Benson's coming with them. And at least we both know Benson doesn't put up with nonsense from anyone."

Colin snorts. "Yeah. There is that."

A tall woman in a sheriff's uniform rounds the corner with a younger man wearing a bow tie and carrying a briefcase. They both look much more serious than I would like, and I can feel the tension in me start humming at a new level of speed. Benson's walking behind them. It's clear from the wrinkled button-up he's wearing, the same one he had on yesterday, and the dark circles under his eyes, that he hasn't gotten much sleep either.

The sheriff arrives in front of us. "Hi. Maggie Sefferson," she says as she holds out a hand for us to each shake. "You must be Colin and Tom. It's not often we get famous people hanging around Devon Falls. This is Mario Ramirez, the county social worker."

"Where's Lou?" Colin demands.

"With Jack," Benson says. "They're outside playing on the hospital swings." He glances over at Mario. "Mario may let Lou see Gabe for a few minutes."

"Just a few minutes?" I blurt out. "Gabe's losing his mind in there. Lou must be too."

Mario nods. "I understand. Yes, Lou's upset. But please understand that every step Maggie and I are taking right now is for Lou's safety. Do you both believe me when I say that?"

Colin looks over at me.

Do we?

I think we have to.

Colin sighs, then nods. "Okay, let's go in. But just know that Gabe's still on some pretty intense painkillers, and he's really upset about Lou. Just... remember that. Okay?"

The *or I will personally destroy you* goes unspoken.

Mario nods. "Of course. We both understand."

Gabe's awake when we walk inside, the bed propping him up from behind and his broken leg resting on a pile of pillows. "Is Lou here?" he says. The desperation in his voice circles the room.

Benson walks to the side of his bed and pats him on the shoulder. "Jack and I were granted temporary custody. He's safe, Gabe. He's outside with Jack."

Gabe falls back against the bed, sighing. "Okay," he whispers. "Okay." He opens his eyes back up again. "I'll tell you everything you need to know," he says. "Please, please just don't take Lou away from me. He's all I have."

Colin sends the sheriff and the social worker the same look he used to give reporters when they asked him stupid questions in the media pen after a race. I pity them both if this conversation goes poorly.

Maggie opens up a notebook. "Listen, Gabe. Everyone in Devon Falls knows you and Dave and Lou, so I'll skip right to the down and dirty here. Dave's saying that he left Lou in your care in good faith, but he believes you've been emotionally abusing Lou while he's been away."

"Excuse me?" I can't help the volume my voice rises toward. "What on earth is wrong with that man?"

"Stay calm there, cowboy." The sheriff sends me a quick half smile. She's got miles of freckles across her face, I notice. "Lou's teachers were also surprised by that accusation."

Mario nods. "Dave had some things to say about the time he knows you've been spending with Tom and Colin, Gabe. He was particularly worried about Lou being influenced by the 'Hollywood lifestyle.'"

I sigh. "Which in this case is code for 'queer lifestyle,' of course."

"That's all some homophobic bullshit," Colin growls.

"Sure is," Benson mutters.

"I wish I could say I thought you were wrong," Mario says. "But the fact is that Dave is Lou's legal guardian, not Gabe. He has the right to make decisions for his son. However," he adds, "Lou's teachers tell us that you often seem to act as Lou's primary caregiver, Gabe. Is that true? If it is, we need to look at this as a possible situation of neglect on Dave's part. We'd need to know everything you can tell us about Dave's absences and how you're really spending your time with Lou while Dave's gone."

Gabe opens his mouth and closes it again. He looks over at me, and then Colin, and then Benson. "I'm not sure what I'm supposed to say," he finally says quietly.

I hear what he's asking me and Colin. He wants to make sure we're comfortable with whatever he tells the sheriff and the social worker about us. And I hear what he's asking Benson: is it safe to tell the truth?

I look over at Colin. *Do you care who knows about you? Us?*

Not right fucking now I sure don't. And I know you don't either.

"The truth, love," I tell him. "Just tell everyone the truth." Benson and Colin both nod in agreement.

"Okay." Gabe gulps. "Just... uh, sorry. My head's still sort of pounding. It's hard to get the words together." Colin and I rush to get him more pillows and water, and I see Benson raise an eyebrow. "Don't you start now," I whisper to him.

"I said nothing."

Gabe takes in a long breath and hands his water cup back to Colin. "The thing is, Dave is gone a lot. And he's been leaving more and more over this past year. But this last time he left, I was actually relieved." He sighs. "For a while Dave had been saying things that really worried me. Things about Lou needing to 'man up,' whatever that means for a six-year-old. He hated certain clothes and shoes Lou liked and the toys he wanted, and he was starting to say some things about Lou's favorite TV shows and movies. Things that weren't very kind, I guess is how I'd put it."

Mario's typing something into a tablet. "I see."

Gabe swallows. "He said some stuff about me, too. Pretty homophobic stuff. So I was worried about what would happen if... if he found out I was dating Colin and Tom."

"Oh, you are? Huh." Maggie nods. "And here I thought La Fierte had filled the county quota on throuples."

Except we're not exactly a throuple. I don't bother to correct her, though. That's certainly the easiest way to explain things right now, and Gabe and Colin don't correct her either.

"Lou adores Tom and Colin," Benson adds. "Jack and I can vouch for that."

Mario nods as he takes some more notes on the tablet. "Okay. Well. Dave says he's on his way back to town and should be here in a few days. Once we talk to him, we can move forward." He sighs. "Gabe, I know you don't want to hear this, but for now, we need to leave Lou in Jack and Benson's custody." Gabe makes a strangled noise, and Mario sighs again. "I know that's hard to hear. But Dave also made some... he hinted at accusations of impropriety."

"Excuse me?" Colin hisses the words.

"After talking to Lou and Lou's teachers, I'm not concerned about that," Mario adds quickly. "But we still have to act by the book here. I'll let Jack bring Lou into the room to say hello because he's worried about you, but after that I'll have to ask you to go no-contact with Lou for a few days while we get things figured out."

I see something shift in Gabe's face just then. Something dark and heavy that I've never seen before. "I want full custody," he blurts out.

"I wondered if you might ask for that," Benson says easily.

Gabe nods. "Dave's not a safe parent for Lou. And if he's making accusations like that, his judgment really hasn't gotten any better since he left. He's angry at the world. He's been angry since my mother died, and he's letting that anger cloud everything. It's clouding how he sees me and his son. Lou shouldn't be with him."

Mario adds something to his notes. "We're aware of your drug charge in Connecticut. You do know a judge will take that into consideration if you're asking for custody, right?"

Gabe frowns, and I grip his hand a little tighter. He needs to remember that he's not alone in this fight. He won't be. "You can do this, little fox," I whisper. Colin nods from the other side of the bed.

"I was barely out of foster care," Gabe says. "The drugs weren't mine, and I should have fought that charge. But I was young, with no money and no support, and I did what I had to do then. And you know what? I'm never, ever going to let my brother get stuck in a situation where he's got no support. I'll die before I let that happen to him." He looks over at Benson. "We have a case, right?"

"Ellie's taking it," Benson tells him. "So I can focus on helping Jack with Lou. But yeah, you do have a case. And you know Ellie. She fights to the death for her clients. She even puts on clothes when she goes to court."

Mario sends him a strange look, but he keeps writing notes. "Clearly, this situation is all going to take some time to unravel." He puts his tablet under his arm and nods to Benson. "You can have Jack bring Lou in so he and Gabe can have a moment together. But after that, Gabe, I'm going to have to ask you to keep your distance from Lou until you hear from me again. I'm not trying to be a jerk about this. Believe me when I say that it will be better for any legal case you want to start if a judge sees that you took this investigation seriously."

Gabe closes his eyes, and I grip his hand a little harder. It's going to cost him so much, saying goodbye to Lou like this. "We're here for you and Lou," I hear Colin whisper.

"Okay," Gabe finally says. "Whatever you tell me to do, I'll do it. Just give me a few minutes with my brother, okay?"

When Lou bursts into the room a moment later, dropping Jack's hand to run to his brother's side and wrap his arms tightly around Gabe's stomach, I cry harder than I ever have in my life.

Harder than I cried at Christian's funeral, quite possibly.

A few hours later, we're helping Gabe get dressed into some clothes Sam and Malachai brought over. It's time for him to check out, and I know Colin and I are both looking forward to getting him far away from this hospital.

"Thanks for the help," he says to us. He's back to hardly saying a word, and he's barely looked at either of us since Maggie and Mario left and Benson and Jack took Lou home with them. I can't even imagine how much emotional energy it cost him to watch Lou walk out of this room, his hand in Jack's. "Listen," Gabe adds as Colin and I help him negotiate a giant pair of sweatpants around his cast. "I talked to Malachai while you guys were outside waiting for the sheriff. He says I can come stay with him and Sam for a few days. So if one of you can just take me there after we leave, that would be awesome. There's no way I'm going to keep staying at Dave's place, and I gave up my apartment a while ago."

I straighten up so fast I drop the sneaker I'm holding. What in goodness gracious is he talking about? "Why on earth would you go to Malachai's, little fox?"

"I figured you'd come to my house," Colin adds.

Gabe looks away, toward the maple tree outside his hospital room window. It's lost a few more leaves, I notice, since the last time I saw it. More yellow and orange hues dot the ground below it. "Look," Gabe says. "Everything we've tried together, it's been great. I care about you both so much. But I don't think we ever should have done this." He blinks, and I watch, frozen, as more tears run from the corner of his eyes. "It's just too big a risk for all of us, you know? If I'm going to show a judge that I can give Lou a stable home, being halfway in two relationships with guys who may or may not be in Devon Falls much longer probably isn't going to look great. And if Dave does keep full custody of Lou, there's no way he'll *ever* let me see him again if I'm in a relationship with two men."

Colin looks as shocked as I probably do. I swallow and do my best to order the swirl of thoughts in my head.

Gabe shrugs. "And let's be honest, okay? We don't even know what we're doing here. Tom, you've got a movie career to get back to. Colin, you're still figuring out what you want your life to be after racing, and then there's the fact that you two are best friends, and Tom has all those feel—"

He stops, suddenly, clamping his mouth shut. But I know precisely what he was going to say. My heart wrenches inside of my chest.

"Tom has what?" Colin asks.

Gabe shakes his head. "Never mind, nothing. Painkillers are just messing with me. Can you help me with this shirt?" He holds out a t-shirt to Colin, but Colin's looking back and forth between us, and he doesn't take the shirt.

"What the hell am I missing here?" he asks.

"Nothing!" Gabe says quickly. "I don't even know what I'm talking about, okay? Like I said, it's just the painkillers."

Except he does know exactly what he's talking about. Gabe's figured out what no one else in my life, or Colin's, ever has. He's dug up the secret I buried a hundred miles deep.

Everything happening around me seems to have stopped in time, and the smell of some kind of antiseptic is stinking my nostrils.

It's my gut instinct to keep this secret. To hold onto it tightly, the way I always have. The way I'm still holding onto everything that happened on the set of *The Good Sword.*

But I stood in this hospital room today and watched how quickly secrets can unravel a person. I saw firsthand how they can destroy a world one thread at a time until the fabric of that entire world is lying in pieces on the floor.

I draw in a deep breath and stand up tall, next to Gabe's bed. "He knows exactly what he's talking about." I send Gabe a quick smile and squeeze his hand as his eyebrows go up in alarm. "It's okay, little fox. It's time, I think. Time to air out some secrets for good."

Colin's face is wrinkled in confusion as I smile at him. This is one conversation we won't be able to have with our eyes, so I say my words loud and clearly for Colin. For Gabe.

"I was let go from *The Good Sword.* Fired. That's why I'm not filming right now. And Colin, I've been in love with you since we were twelve." I smile brightly at them both. "Now, if you two will give me a moment, I need to compose myself. Colin, can you help Gabe out to the car? I'll be waiting there."

The silence that echoes through the room as I walk out the door is so loud I'm absolutely certain they can hear it in the Devon Falls town square.

Chapter 24
11 Days to the Devon Falls Leaf Festival

I want an escape. —*Gabe Gomez*

The drive away from the hospital reminds me of my first trip to a group home.

My mom had just passed. Then Dave disappeared down the road, his truck loaded up and Lou in a car seat in the back. The whole world felt fogged, gray around the edges. The social worker he'd handed me off to made small talk about school and what I wanted to be when I grew up. I must have answered the questions, but I've got absolutely no idea what I said.

And then we started driving down roads I didn't recognize, in unfamiliar neighborhoods, and for the first time I gave myself permission to wonder where I was going to end up. Would I get to keep going to the same school? What kind of food would be there? How quickly would I be able to get a job near the place so I could start saving up money and get myself back to Lou?

Everything felt so uncertain. And I always thought I was pretty good at uncertainty, especially after my mother got sick. I was good at looking forward to what might be possible rather than always being terrified of the bad things that might be coming. But that day, in the car, the uncertainty felt so big that it started to make my skin itch. I scratched and scratched, blaming the sweater I was wearing, and I remember I scratched so much that I turned my right arm red.

That's how I arrived at my new group home: with a bright red arm in need of calamine lotion, skin crawling with uncertainty.

Now, as Colin easily guides Tom's Jeep down a long road away from the hospital, I feel the same kind of uncertainty moving across my skin. Colin hardly said a word after I spilled Tom's secret. He said about four words while he helped me out to the car, and now it's like the Jeep is filled to the roof with silence.

I swallow hard and search for an affirmation. But every single one that moved through my mind feels wrong. Impossible. Silly.

I can do hard things.

Maybe I can't.

I will accomplish everything I need to today.

Well, things aren't looking so good on that front right now.

And then Colin takes a sharp turn off the main road toward Devon Falls, onto a road that leads toward the defunct Devon Falls ski area.

I scratch lightly at my wrist. "Uh, where are we going?" I ask. Colin and Tom helped me lay out across the back seat, but my broken leg, with the cast up to the ankle, is already not feeling that great. I'm not in the mood to take the scenic route to Malachai and Sam's house.

"I'm kidnapping the two of you," Colin says easily as he focuses on the road.

"Excuse me?" I say at the same time Tom says "What does that mean?"

"It means," Colin says, "that I'm taking a risk. And you two are coming with me. And you have to, because I'm driving. So I make the rules."

I'll admit, that makes me smile. I pull my fingers away from my wrist.

"Seriously, though," Colin adds. "I made a decision while Gabe was finishing packing up his things. After you left the hospital room, Tom. We're going to a cabin my friend Claire found when she was planning her trip to the winery's leaf festival event. She hates staying in hotels, and she says inns give her hives, so she found this place near the ski area—the one that I guess isn't running anymore?" Tom nods. "Anyway, she booked it for that weekend. I looked at the booking page, and it's available right now. I snagged it."

I can't even imagine having enough money to just decide on a whim to rent a ski cabin for a few days. I know what the cabins up in the hills of Devon Falls go for during leaf season. They are hella *not* cheap. "But why?" I ask. "You could have just kidnapped us back to your place."

Colin frowns and focuses on the road for a minute. "Because I think we all need a break," he finally says. "It's going to be tough enough for you to be away from Lou right now, and being right in Devon Falls staring at everything that reminds you of Lou isn't going to help. And it's pretty obvious there are some things we need to get out in the open here. I thought it might be easier to do that in a place where everyone is on an even footing." He glances back at my cast. "So to speak."

"Very funny," I tell him. But I smile. Because I know that I could tell him no. I could tell him to turn this car around and take me to Malachai's house. He'd do it in a heartbeat, I'm sure of that, even though he probably already spent a non-refundable fortune on this cabin.

But honestly? I don't want to do any of that. I want an escape. I don't want to sit on Sam and Malachai's front porch, cast in front of me, spending every single second of the day wondering what

Lou's doing with Jack and Benson. What he's eating. Whether he misses me.

Not to mention that whole giant can of worms I opened up on Tom and Colin back at the hospital. I probably owe them more than throwing that thing out in front of them and running.

"Okay," I finally say. "I'm game if Tom is."

Tom's been quiet—well, for him anyway—since we left the hospital. Right now, he stares out the window as he answers, not looking at either of us. "I suppose that's fine," he finally agrees.

The cabin is one of the most beautiful places I've ever seen.

I mean, I'm sure it's beautiful all year round, but it's hard to imagine it gets much more perfect than it looks like now. It's a large A-frame, made up of brown logs and windows and doors painted in a green trim, and the wraparound porch has a large swing and a bunch of chairs set across it. But the best part about the place is definitely the giant forest of maple and birch trees surrounding the whole area. They've only got about three-quarters of their leaves right now, with the rest already on the ground, and the leaves on and off the trees are a painting of pure color: every shade of maroon, red, orange, yellow, and gold imaginable stretches across branches and against the skyline.

"Okay," Tom tells Colin as he steps out of the car. "Points for scenery, I suppose, Colin."

I notice he doesn't call him *bestie.*

He and Colin fuss over me as they take my crutches out of the back of the Jeep and help me out of the vehicle. The cast is awkward and bulky, and I'm already worried about how I'm going to go back to work with it. Bethany visited me in the hospital to tell me that I didn't need to worry about the winery while I healed. Tom, Colin, and I were so close to finishing the event space when I fell off that ladder, and she said she was sure she and Evelyn could finish it. She made a joke about putting the damn fairy lights back in their box, though. And she did promise to teach me how to properly operate a wheelchair when I get back to the winery so I can get around more easily while I'm recovering.

None of that seems like it matters very much now. Everything's a mess, and winery's event space is the last thing I can bring myself to care about right now.

Tom and Colin watch me like hawks as I use my crutches to make my way up the few steps to the porch. My leg throbs in time with my head, but the painkillers the hospital left me with are doing their job, and both throbs are pretty gentle, all things considered. When Colin opens the front door to a wide-open space with bright mahogany floors, a fireplace, carved furniture, and an open kitchen that rivals his for shine, I feel no pain at all. All I can think about is how perfect this cabin is. Lou would love it here.

Well, I feel that pain. But it's a very different kind. Much, much harsher than the broken leg.

"There's a hot tub on the back deck too," Colin says. He frowns down at my cast. "We might not be able to get you in there right away. But I do have an idea."

I don't ask for details. I'm getting tired already, and I let the two of them fuss as they settle me onto the couch. I notice that they barely look at each other as they make tea and soup and sandwiches and Colin goes through the packed bags that some-one—I'm guessing Sam and Malachai—have left here for us.

I nibble at the tomato soup and a turkey sandwich. They both taste good, I guess, but I can't focus on food right now. My mind is spinning around social workers and Dave's accusations and questions about whether Benson and Jack got all of Lou's favorite outfits and toys from Dave's place. Oh, and then there's the giant secret I accidentally spilled in the hospital room that's now sitting between me, Tom, and Colin like a live grenade. I set the food down on the coffee table next to me while Colin and Tom eat in silence.

"I visited a place like this once," I finally say. Well, I whisper the words, really. Colin and Tom look up at me, glance at each other, and then look away. I realize this might be the first time they've ever heard me talk about my childhood in any kind of detail.

"It was right after my mom married Dave. He really was different then, before she got sick," I add as Colin's eyes narrow. "He was really nice to me. Honestly, I loved having him as a stepdad. He went to all my soccer games and baseball games and my plays." I shrug. "Anyway, some friends of his rented this house in the Connecticut mountains. The leaves there aren't as good as here," I go on, and Tom nods in agreement, "but they're still pretty." I smile. "They had two boys around my age. We ran all over that cabin and swam in some indoor pool that was part of the bigger property. We had scavenger hunts and made s'mores over a fire. My mom played the guitar, and played every night we were there while everyone sat around the firepit and sang. It was one of the best weekends of my life."

"It sounds absolutely lovely," Tom says quietly.

"Yeah. It was." I can hear my voice break. "I don't remember much about my father. He died when I was really young, and when my mom met Dave, I remember how excited I was that I finally had a new father. I loved my mother, and we were always really close, but I liked it when it wasn't just the two of us anymore." I sigh. "For a while, things were really good. Lou was born, and I thought things would get even better. But then she got sick. And in one sentence from a doctor, everything changed. Dave changed. And sometimes, in the middle of the night, I get so mad at her for getting sick. And I hate that I ever, ever feel that way." I bury my face in my hands.

"Oh, little fox." Colin's fingers brush their way across my good ankle, and I sigh.

"I kept thinking," I whisper, "that the Dave I remembered from back then would just show up again. Like someone could just push a button and that would erase all the years he's spent getting so angry and hateful. I'm such an idiot."

And then I let myself cry, tears spilling down my cheeks as Tom whispers soothing words and Colin keeps rubbing my uninjured ankle gently. "You're most certainly not an idiot, Gabe," Tom finally says. "You're a true gift to the world, little fox. You see light in places where other people only see darkness. You have hope in a world filled with despair." He gently brushes a tear from one of my cheeks. "You've had every single reason to have given up on the world, on people, the way it sounds like Dave has given up on so much. But you've never let yourself do that. You're so very special."

"You really fucking are," Colin agrees, and I feel more tears rise to the corners of my eyes.

Tom sighs. "Not to mention, Gabe, that you see things in people others don't." He laughs, but the sound is hollow in my ears. "Colin, I've been in love with you since I first knew what love was. You *are* love, for me. Every time I look at you, I see my entire world. I can't imagine my life without you. But somehow, no one's ever noticed that before. And I can't blame you for missing any of this, bestie—I hid that love from you with every single tool I had at my disposal." He looks back over at me. "But you, Gabe. You saw it all. You saw into my soul."

Colin sucks in a long breath then. He looks over at me, and for the first time, I understand: I understand how he holds those silent conversations with Tom. Because right now Colin's only looking at me, but it's like he's loudly shouting at me into the large space of this room.

I'm going to tell him how I feel. Are you okay with that?

I know exactly how to answer him, and I don't have to say a word.

Yes.

Colin sits up and takes a few steps, until he's standing in front of Tom. He sinks slowly to his knees and takes one of Tom's hands in his.

"I'm sorry I've been so quiet since we left the hospital. But you know I'm not great with feelings. It takes me a minute to think through them before I can say them out loud."

Tom scoffs. "A minute? Try eighty-four years, sometimes."

Colin grins. "Fair enough. Listen Tom. I spent years thinking I just didn't love like other people did," he says. "But I've never been able to imagine my life without you. Now I wonder. Maybe it's not that I was ever wired to love differently than other people. Maybe it's that I was always wired to love some very, very specific people." And then he leans over... and Tom doesn't lean away.

Colin presses his lips to Tom's, and my heart fills with hope. Hope for them, and for the future they deserve to have together.

And just a little pinch of hope that maybe, against all odds, I'll get to have that future with them.

Chapter 25

11 Days to the Devon Falls Leaf Festival

Somehow, that's even hotter than if he was completely naked.
—Colin Templegate

There was always a moment, right after the start of a race, when I'd lose time.

It was always right after the clusterfuck mess that happens when you get off the blocks and fight for placement. When the proverbial dust settled and I found my spot and sank into the rhythm of the drive, into the feel of the track below me and the steering wheel in my hands. When time and space seemed to meld with me, and my whole world felt peaceful. Right.

Kissing Tom feels like that.

I knew the risk I was taking when I pressed my lips to his. *What the fuck am I going to do if this doesn't work?* My brain was shouting at me. *You'll lose your best friend. He's your whole damn life, Colin! You can't afford to lose anything else!*

But a thought came to me then, like a fever dream: if Tom's been in love with me our whole lives and never told me, I've never really had him at all. Not all the way. Not every single part of him. He's kept such massive secrets from me, the person who was supposed to be his very best friend in life, for decades. And these weeks with Gabe have opened up possibilities for my relationship with Tom that I just never saw in front of me before. It's like Gabe's put a brand-new car in front of me, one I didn't even know had been manufactured, and handed me the keys.

So I shut off my fucking brain and leaned over to start the car. And now, as my lips meld with his and sparks of color and light fly across my brain while it goes into that autopilot, perfectly peaceful space, I feel alive. Whole.

Right up until Tom pulls away from me, abruptly, and gets to his feet. "This can't be really happening," he mutters to himself. "Surely I'm dreaming this. You're not pulling some sort of joke on me, are you, universe?" He says the words to the ceiling.

Gabe lets out a strangled noise. "You think this is some kind of joke? I haven't seen a kiss like that since the last time I watched porn. And I watch really good porn!" he adds.

Tom puts his hands on his hips and starts pacing, his frame small under the tall, beamed ceiling of the cabin. "No. This cannot be right. This simply isn't how things work. Dreams don't just come true like this!" He throws up his hands. "The best friend you've loved since puberty *who's never loved you back* doesn't just decide in a span of weeks that he's changed his mind and kiss you like that!"

I open my mouth to answer him, but he keeps going.

"I landed the dream role of my life," he says. "*The Good Sword* was the job of a lifetime. Everything I wanted, there on a platter in front of me. But then *he* came for me." He shakes his head. "*He* ruined it all, and I lost everything I'd worked so hard for." He drops his head into his hands and falls back onto a chair. "It can't be like that with us," he finally whispers into his hands. "I want this so badly. But Colin, you're so much of my world. I can't lose you too. We can't try this and let it fail. We can't..."

I so badly want to know who this *he* is—because I will find and destroy anyone who's done harm to Tom Evers—but it feels like I've got some other things I need to clear up with Tom before I ask that question. I glance over at Gabe again, and I read his thoughts with my eyes.

Tell him. He needs to hear it.

I walk on my knees to the space in front of Tom and stay kneeling before him as I take his hands and clasp them with mine. "I understand," I whisper. "I get it, Tom. I've been pretty stuck since Christian died and I left my career behind. Not quite sure how to look back at that world again, and not quite sure of my path forward. Maybe I've been a little afraid to actually give a fuck about anything real again, I guess."

Tom looks down at me, finally, and I trace the tears from the corners of his eyes with my fingers. He sighs. "I thought you were feeling that way. Even though you never said so. Not exactly," he adds.

He knows every single part of me. How have I never fucking realized that?

"I understand," I tell him, my voice low. "I understand how damn terrifying it must feel for you to put yourself out here with me. Especially after all these years." I reach one hand up to take Tom's chin between my fingers and lift it until he's looking me in the eye. "I think it's time," I say softly, "that all of us—all *three of us*—started trusting ourselves a little more, and I think it's time we started trusting each other. I know you remember what Christian used to say all the time, Tom."

He sighs and shakes his head. "No risk, no reward," he finally says softly.

I look back over at Gabe again, then back at Tom. "We've got a few days here, you know. A few days while we wait for that dumbass investigation, and a few days before anyone in Devon Falls expects to see us again. So. Let's take this time, okay? Let's use it to take some calculated risks in trust. And let's see what happens."

Gabe swallows. "You're not just talking about risks like me trying out new sex positions, are you?"

I laugh. "No, little one. Not just new positions. Although," I add quickly, "there should definitely be some of those."

Gabe laughs, and even Tom cracks a smile. But he's still looking away from me. I can tell he still doesn't quite trust that I mean what I say.

So I guess I'm just going to have to rebuild some trust with my best friend in the whole damn world.

"Okay then," I say. "No risk, no reward. Everyone remembers our safe words, right? Green, yellow, red. We all know the rules."

Tom nods tentatively. Gabe's nod is definitely more eager.

"Then let me show you," I say to Tom. "Let me show you exactly how much I mean what I'm saying right now. Let me show you exactly how happy I want to make you for as long as you'll let me. Let me show you how I feel."

I watch Tom's wide-eyed expression carefully as I zip open his fly, pull his cock out of his boxers, and wrap my lips around it.

Tom lets out a long, sharp gasp as he feels my mouth against him for the first time. I know I let out some kind of noise myself, and that leads Tom to grind harder against my tongue. His cock is still soft, but he's hardening. I lick the salt I taste on his skin and curve my tongue around his length as I adjust to the feeling of his body inside my mouth. I've seen Tom's dick so many times over the years, in locker rooms and bedrooms we've shared and during late night skinny dips in pools and lakes around the world. I've memorized most of his body across the decades we've spent together, but right now it's like I'm learning him all over again for the first time.

I want to map every inch of his skin. I want to memorize the way every single part of his dick feels against my tongue, against the insides of my cheeks.

The sensations are strange and heady, and I hold onto them as I bring Tom farther inside of me and let the tip of his cock nudge closer and closer to the back of my throat. He's almost fully hard now, and he lets out a long gasp. "Oh, bestie," he whispers.

Holy hell, that's hot.

I pull off of Tom's cock with a quick pop. "Do you believe me now?" I say to Tom as I stand to take his face in my hands. "Do you believe that I'm all in for whatever comes next with us?"

Tom sets a hand on my waist. "You have no idea how much I want to believe this is real. I'm trying so very hard, bestie." He smiles softly. "But you're up against decades of your own history right now, darling."

Well, that's a fair statement. And it only makes me even more certain of what we need to do next.

"Then I think I need to keep showing you." I bring his lips to mine and spend a few moments teasing, playing, practicing what it feels like to kiss this person who knows me better than anyone else. Every sensation is new, and somehow familiar, at the same time. Like sliding into a car that's had all kinds of new updates and comes with so much promise for the future.

But I'm all too aware that Tom isn't the only one in this room who's blown my world wide open recently. I don't want Gabe to be left out of this moment. He needs to be a part of this, part of Tom's and my first experience together. Gabe's been there for every single small shift that's brought the two of us together like this, and Tom's been there for every one of my first moments with Gabe. It isn't right for anyone to be left out of this magic.

But I need to make sure a bigger, deeper magic between the three of us is what Tom and Gabe want too. I sure as hell know it's what I want.

I end the kiss and guide Tom over to the couch where Gabe's lying down, so we're standing together just above him. "I just want to make something clear," I tell them both. "I mean it when I say I'm all in here. But I'm all in with both of you." I look to Tom. "Tom Evers, I know I took a different route to get to a place where you've always been, but I'm here now. And I'm not leaving. And Gabe," I say as I look down into his bright, earnest expression, "I want to make sure you know that you're so much more than a stop on the journey I've been on. You're the destination too. I can't imagine having one of you and not the other, and I'm hoping you both feel the same way."

Tom's eyes are filling with tears, I realize. "As if I could ever leave our little fox." He looks down at Gabe as he smiles, and I realize what he's just said. *Our* little fox. *Our.*

Gabe's blushing now, and I think he's fighting back tears of his own. "This doesn't feel real to me either," he finally says. "And I don't know what my future holds, you know?" He blinks hard and fast. "I just know that I want to fight to have the two of you in it."

Tom kneels down then, and I follow him, until we're both face-to-face with Gabe. "Then we fight together, little fox," he says softly.

I nod. "What Tom said. We fight together."

Tom and I lean in then, and we try something completely new: a kiss with all three of us. Honestly? It's a little awkward and weird for a moment, and I can't quite figure out right away where to put my lips or my tongue. Just like the start of a race, I guess. But then I let myself settle into the sensations, the feeling of just being this close, this connected, to Tom and Gabe. And then?

Then it's lights out and away we go, and all I feel is the thrill and the excitement and the hope of what this race has in store for us. All three of us.

At some point, we all come up for air.

"I want to watch you," Gabe whispers. "You two. Together. I want to see you both."

Tom lets out a choked sound, and I immediately go into planning mode. *Must make Tom and Gabe happy,* my brain orders. But I also know Gabe shouldn't be moving around much right now. He's just barely out of the hospital.

Good thing I'm a problem solver. In less than thirty seconds, I have a plan.

"Okay," I announce. "Here's what we're going to do. Gabe, you're staying on the couch. Pull those sweat pants down just enough that you can take your dick out. But don't touch it after that."

Gabe's eyes go wide and he starts to slowly pull at his waistband.

"Tom," I order. "Stand up and get naked."

Tom arches an eyebrow.

"Yup," I go on. "Tom, I know you're used to bossing the two of us around, but I'm giving the orders around here right now. For at least the next thirty minutes, you two belong to me. Whatever I tell you to do, it's happening. Unless you want to bring in some colors and change that."

"Look who's gone into racing mode," Tom mutters, and I know he's thinking about the way I used to talk over the radio when I was trying to tell my engineer I wanted something. Tom probably hasn't heard me talk like this since the last time I was on a track.

"You know it," I tell him. "So get to work." He stands and starts stripping, and I check in with Gabe as I stand up too and pull my own shirt over my head. Gabe's got his sweatpants pulled just slightly down his waist, and the head of his cock is peeking out of the top of the waistband. Somehow, that's even hotter than if he was completely naked. Don't ask me how. One of his hands is inching toward his dick. "No touching yet," I order him. "Soon, though. I promise."

I get my clothes off in record time, and soon after that Tom's got his clothes off and in a pile next to a chair. I pull Tom toward me, drop us both down gently onto the large, shag rug below us, and I wrap him up in my arms as tightly as I can.

"Wow. That's so hot," Gabe whispers above us.

"No touching yourself yet," I order him. "All you're allowed to do right now is watch." And then I take Tom's cock in my hand, pull it toward mine, and wrap them together within my palm.

Tom gasps again. Our bodies are braided together now, our cocks entwined, and the skin-to-skin contact feels almost as magical as it does unbelievable. I never once imagined that I might have Tom's body pressed against mine like this. I've never imagined the feel of the hairs on his chest rubbing into mine or feel the weight of his ankles moving between mine as I slowly lean in to kiss him again.

I stop only millimeters from his lips. "Gabe," I say. "You can touch yourself now. But here's the rule: you have to ask before you can come. Do you understand?"

"I do," Gabe says in a small voice.

"Good, little fox." Then I move in the rest of the way and take Tom's lips in a long, hard, exploratory kiss. And we're off to the races again, re-learning the familiar and finding new curves in the track. My brain and body are on fire, and every inch of me craves more of Tom. It's like I have to map every part of his body with mine. His mouth, his dick, everything. I let one hand tread up and down his ass, studying the curves and dips there, while my other hand holds tightly to the two of our cocks, stroking them together. "Do you like this?" I manage to murmur against his tongue. "Do you like feeling us together like this?" There's no lube, and the harsh friction of our dicks together creates as much pain as it does pleasure. I pull some of the liquid at the top of our cocks together and coat both of us with it, and Tom lets out a long sigh.

"This isn't real," he whispers. "This can't be real."

His words hit my heart dead-center, and suddenly I'm twelve years old again, lying in a field of clover with Tom next to me. But this time, when I remember the way he turned to look at me while we hunted for four-leaf victories together, I see something I never saw back then.

I see longing. Loneliness. Hopelessness.

There's not much point in regretting the past; I learned that long ago. But one of the best lessons I ever learned from racing is not to regret the past, but to *use* it. Take all the lessons the past offers you, one of my trainers used to say, and use those lessons to build your future.

And right now, building my future means showing both Tom and Gabe exactly how much I'm all in with both of them.

Chapter 26
11 Days to the Devon Falls Leaf Festival

And that's when I burst into tears. —Tom Evers

"Can't believe how perfect you feel against me," Colin says.

His lips are at my neck, my ear, my other ear. So many places I only ever imagined I'd feel them. This is a dream, I'm still sure of it: me and Colin, my best friend in life, locked together on a rug, while he strokes our cocks together in time. I look up to see Gabe lying on the couch, wide-eyed, his hands down his lowered sweatpants and a thin sheen of sweat across his forehead. I hope he's not exerting himself too much. He is still healing, after all. We'll have to make sure he gets in a nap after this.

Colin brushes a finger across the top of my dick, pulling me fully back into the moment and reminding me I don't want to miss *any* of what's happening in front of me. Who knows what the future holds when our time at this cabin is over? What if this grand experiment doesn't work? I can say with one hundred percent certainty that it's going to work for *me.*

But Colin. He's quite another story. He always has been.

So I focus. I focus on his face, his hair, his eyes. He's staring at me so very intensely right now. I fight with my memory. Has he ever looked at me so deeply?

"Now, here's what's going to happen, sweetheart." And he's definitely never called me *sweetheart* before; I'm certain of that. Despite the fact that he gifted Gabe the title "little one" and now uses "little fox" with him just as often as I do, Colin is not normally one for nicknames. That's half the reason I so enjoy calling him "bestie." This new moniker he's attached to me sends shockwaves of pleasure through my body. "You're going to tell Gabe how this feels. Describe exactly how it feels to have our cocks together like this, to feel my hand around you. You're going to tell him everything you're thinking and feeling right now, until Gabe's so turned on that he comes all over those sweatpants and we have to find him new ones."

Gabe makes a noise somewhere between a laugh and a yelp.

"Just remember," Colin adds. "You have to ask before you come, Gabe."

And why is this dark, demanding voice he's using right now so incredibly attractive? Maybe I have some kind of unexplored domination fetish. I make a note to look into that as Colin keeps staring, his eyes clear and direct and fully focused on me.

I swallow hard. I can never ignore anything Colin wants from me, but right now it might just take the entire town of Devon Falls to keep me from obeying his orders. And I'm not even sure they'd be successful. "His cock is so big, Gabe," I manage to get out.

"Good start, sweetheart," Colin murmurs as he kisses my neck. Another shock of pleasure moves through me as he says the words, and I blurt more of them out.

"His hand is big, too. You probably know that, Gabe," I add. "So big that it's like my dick is swimming with him in his giant hand." I swallow hard. "It hurts a little, sometimes, when his hand and his cock rub just so. But in a good way," I add quickly as Colin's eyes go up. "I want more of it, I think. More speed. I want to feel his hand on every part of me, all the time."

Colin's lips turn up in a smile, and then he starts to move ever so slightly faster.

I push myself farther into Colin's hand. "I've always loved watching his giant body swallow yours up when he wraps around you, Gabe. It's such a beautiful sight, the way he just folds you up into him."

Gabe makes another slightly strangled noise. I look up just enough to see that he's panting a little more now, his face red, and his hand is moving more quickly within his sweats.

"But feeling it," I go on. "Feeling him around me... that's more than I've ever imagined." I rest my head into his neck, smelling the familiar scent of his salty skin and his cologne. Scents I've smelled probably one million times before. But they're different now. So much more deep and intense as I breathe them in. "My whole body feels like it's going to explode at any moment," I murmur against Colin's skin. "Especially when he—" Colin draws another finger across top of my cock. "Does that!" I call out loudly.

Colin's pumping us a little harder together now, a little faster. "Goodness, this cock of his," I tell Gabe. "It's perfect, isn't it, little fox? I want to feel it against me forever. I wonder what it would feel like to have this inside of me, to be—"

"I need to come!" Gabe shouts the words out loudly, desperately, and Colin smiles.

"Excellent. You look so fucking hot right now, little fox. So perfect for us. Here's a new rule: you can come when Tom comes."

Gabe whimpers. "Please, Tom?" he whispers.

Colin brushes my sensitive tip again, and I'm already riding a wave so high I know it's only a matter of time before I lose myself. Knowing that Colin wants to choreograph this so that Gabe and I come together...

It's official: this is going to be the hardest orgasm of my life to date. I already know it.

I sink into the moment, letting myself lean hard into Colin's body as I focus on nothing but the sensations of his dick and hand against mine. More of the liquid there, our liquid, is mixing together in his hand. And then I feel it—his other hand, his finger, moving slowly along my ass until his fingers are brushing, just teasing, against the sensitive nerves of my entrance—

"Colin!" I yell as I thrust upward, so hard it hurts, and Colin teases and turns his finger, nudging it just slightly inside of me. Another wave of pure pleasure washes over me, and I scream again as I lose myself, rocking and shaking against Colin as I fall apart against him.

"Tom! Colin!" Gabe shouts our names, and I look over to watch as he thrusts upward off the couch slightly, into his own hand. Liquid dribbles from the tip, down against his sweatpants, and the sight of him, knowing he's coming just from watching the two of us, is so incredibly heady and powerful. I keep jutting against Colin, keep letting go against him in a wave of pleasure that never seems to end, and it isn't long before I feel him coming too, hugging me harder against his body as he spills against my cock and liquid mixes across the two of them, dripping down between our two bodies.

I cling to him, desperate and needy. I need proof that all of this is just as real as the come and sweat clinging between our bodies, as real as the hard, panting sounds Gabe's still making in this room. I need to be sure—certain—that I haven't dreamed all of this.

Then Colin lets out a long sigh and pulls my body against his. He moves two fingers through the liquid covering both of us now, draws it back up between our bodies, and holds it out.

"That's us," he whispers. "You and me, sweetheart. Together as one. Just like we've always been. Just like we were meant to be."

And that's when I burst into tears.

The world is blurry for the next hour or so. I know I cry against Colin's shoulder while he soothes and comforts me. I know he finds washcloths and cleans up all three of us gently, helps Gabe take more painkillers and eventually moves us all into a gigantic bed—a California king, I suspect—in the room right off of the living room. I know he lights a fire and helps both of us change into warm pajamas from the magic bags that appeared in this house, and that he changes into a pair of his own.

They're covered with race cars. I laugh. "Sam packed those, I suppose?" I ask.

"Or Malachai," Gabe says softly next to me. "He's got a pretty wicked sense of humor, that guy. When he lets it out." He nuzzles into my side, and I readjust the pile of pillows his leg is resting on. "This is nice," he mumbles. "You're all soft and cuddly."

"Perhaps it's the giant crying fest I just indulged in," I mumble. I appreciate that neither of them pushed me or pressured me to explain my tears right away; I'm not sure I could have explained them in the moment. It was as if some kind of pressure point burst within me, and those tears were all of that pressure releasing, like water from a valve that's just been opened.

Gabe sits up and narrows his eyebrows. "Don't talk about you crying like it's a bad thing," he tells me as Colin sits on the edge of the bed. "Like crying is something you should be ashamed of. That's how people like Dave think. And it's not true."

He falls back against the bed, and Colin rubs a hand down his spine. "Good reminder, little fox," he says. He smiles over at me. "Sweetheart, you've never worried about crying in front of me before. Or anyone else for that matter. Why now?"

I try to parse the words, to express the muddled feelings rolling through my brain right now. There are things they still don't know; things about what happened when we were shooting *The Good Sword.* Stories I think I owe to them both. But not right now. "This was different crying," I finally say. "It wasn't crying because I'd lost someone I love, or found out I didn't get a part I wanted. It was as if... I suddenly had everything I wanted in the world right in front of me." I shake my head. "And that probably doesn't make any sense at all."

"No," Gabe says. "It makes perfect sense, actually." He sighs. "That's how I've sort of felt these last few weeks, I think. Like I had everything I ever wanted right in front of me. You two. Lou. A job I love. Devon Falls. And I don't think I've ever felt more anxious, you know? More stressed. It's like when you have everything you've ever wanted right in front of you, it just feels like..."

I hear the words he doesn't finish saying echo through the room

It just feels like the only thing left is to lose it all.

I swallow hard and take his hand. A few moments later, I feel Colin settle in next to me. I've felt the warm weight of his body in bed next to me so many, many times over the years. But now it feels different. Especially when he wraps his arms around me and reaches over to carefully pull Gabe closer against my other side.

"I get it, sweetheart," he says softly. "I know. But we're all here. Together. Tom, you don't have to keep any more damn secrets from me." He nuzzles his face into my neck. "I'm finally ready to see every part of you."

"Me too," Gabe whispers. "Well, I mean, we didn't meet that long ago, so I don't think it's really the same, but—"

"Oh, little fox." I laugh and pull him into a hug, mindful of the pillow his leg is elevated on. "I always knew you were going to be trouble."

Gabe smiles, and Colin kisses the back of my neck. I let myself fall back against him, my body against his.

And for the first time in a very long time, probably since my final days on *The Good Sword,* I let all my muscles relax.

Chapter 27

10 Days to the Devon Falls Leaf Festival

My whole brain shut down as he took control, and I felt totally and completely at peace. —Gabe Gomez

Watching Tom and Colin realize how they really feel about each other is like watching the plot of a book unfold in front of you, page by page.

It starts with breakfast, and Colin cooking for Tom while Tom makes snarky comments about how many chives he's putting in the eggs. It's a scene you can tell is comfortable and familiar for them, even in this strange place. All their usual patterns are there: the way Tom pokes a spatula against the eggs in the pan and jokes about color ratios, the way Colin nudges him with a hip while he takes down plates and hands Tom a cup of coffee. I watch from the recliner they've pulled into the kitchen for me, my leg raised and my own cup of coffee on the little TV tray next to me that Tom set up, and I laugh at how well they know every moment of each other's patterns

Right up until Colin turns around from the stove to lean down and kiss Tom on the lips. He stands slightly and runs a hand back through Tom's hair, and Tom's eyes go wide. His body stops and tenses for a moment, and he blinks and stares at Colin.

Like he still can't believe this is real.

But Colin just keeps adding more moments like that into their routine. He hugs me around the neck gently after he sets down my eggs, and then he does the same for Tom. As we all eat together, he stops every now and then to gently trace a hand up and down Tom's thigh. The third time he does it, Tom stops looking so surprised.

My two caretakers are obsessed with making sure I get my painkillers in the proper dosage, and that I get plenty of rest, so after breakfast I'm relocated to the couch with my leg raised on a stack of pillows while they do the dishes. I look around the room, then down at the TV remote Tom placed in my hand before he kissed me on the forehead and lined water and tea cups around me. The ache for Lou that's lived in my chest since we left the hospital pings gently in the silence of the room. I imagine my brother in this space, begging Colin to do puzzles and asking Tom to play tag outside. I wonder what he's doing right now. My phone says it's nine o'clock, so he should be at school. I wonder if he's even going this week, or if he's too upset. I wish I could text Benson and tell him how much Lou likes chocolate chip pancakes when he's sad, but the social worker said I shouldn't even text Benson and Jack during this waiting hell he's putting me through. He said it might be seen as me "impeding the investigation" if I reach out to Lou's caretakers.

My phone rings in my hand, and hope rises in my belly, then sinks when I see who it is. I answer. "Hi, Bethany."

"Don't you sound thrilled to hear from me."

I wince. "Oh, sorry. I was just hoping the social worker was calling. With, you know. News."

Bethany sighs. "Oh, hon. Yeah, that sucks. No, just me, calling to check on you. But it's only been like a day, right? I know it's hard to have patience right now, but this will all work out. That dude will see how much you and Lou mean to each other. He'll see through Dave. I'm sure of it."

I glance through the living doorway into the kitchen, where Tom and Colin are hip to hip again, laughing lightly as they hand dishes back and forth to each other over the sink. Seeing them together like that, so full and free in every way, makes my heart soar. Maybe I'm supposed to be jealous of the two of them together or something, but how could I be? All I see when I look at them together is pure happiness.

"I hate Dave," I burst out in a low voice.

"Okay. Well, I'd say that's more than reasonable," Bethany says.

"I mean," I go on, "I just don't understand, you know?" I study Tom and Colin through the doorway. I try to imagine looking at them and seeing what Dave sees: something different from how he falls in love. Something that doesn't make sense to *him,* personally. Therefore, it must be wrong. It must be hated and fought against.

Just like little boys wearing princess dresses.

None of it makes any sense. "How can he look at people living in love and be angry at them for it? How can he see the way Lou's face lights up when he sees a dress or a toy he likes and feel anything but thrilled that he's happy?" I let my voice drop again. "I almost texted Dave last night," I whisper into the phone.

"Oh no." I can practically hear Bethany groan over the phone. "Please tell me you didn't, Gabe."

"I didn't," I assure her. "But it was really close. I woke up in the middle of the night, and Tom and Colin were both asleep. I couldn't stop thinking about how messed up everything's gotten since my mother died. Dave was so different before she got sick, you know? I kept thinking, maybe I could text him and make him change his mind. Remind him how happy he and my mom were when Lou was born." I poke at the fringe on the blanket covering me. "I even thought," I whisper again, "about just... lying. Telling him I'm not dating Tom and Colin and he's got it all wrong. Maybe I could ask him if we could just go back to the way things were."

Bethany's quiet for a moment. "Is that what you want?" she finally asks.

I try to imagine that for a moment. Lou and Dave living together again, in the small blue house. Me in my old, tiny apartment back in Dairy Corners, where I had more rats than heat. Me begging Dave for space in Lou's life, always wondering and worrying what Lou might try to wear or say around Dave.

No more Tom. No more Colin. No more of this bubble of happiness that wraps around me when I'm with them. I close my eyes against the tears that start to well up there. "No," I whisper. "I don't. I really, really don't. But Bethany, I told you about that stupid drug charge they have against me. And Dave is Lou's dad, and I—"

"And you're his brother," Bethany interrupts in an even tone. "And, hon, I've never seen anyone who loves their brother more than you do. So be honest with me. Could you really live a life with Lou where you're constantly showing him that people don't get to be fully, totally themselves because of what other people think? Could you live with yourself if you let him be raised believing there's something wrong with him just because he likes certain clothes or toys? Could you really do that, Gabe?"

It all feels so obvious when she puts it like that. "No. I couldn't."

"I don't think you could either." Bethany sighs. "I can't even imagine how hard this must be for you right now, playing this waiting game while you can't even talk to Lou and you have no idea what's going on with Dave. And I know you've had to be in control and be the person who takes care of everything and fixes everything for a really, really long time."

I let out a strangled laugh. "Yeah. That's pretty true."

"So maybe you just need to give yourself permission to let go of that control, just for a little bit. Trust Jack and Benson. Trust Ellie.

And trust those hotties of yours to take care of you. For now, okay? Just... let go, Gabe. Let some other people be in control, just this once."

Those directions are so exactly opposite to what I'm used to doing that my whole body clenches as I'm listening to her. But then I remember how it felt yesterday, to lie in one place while Colin ordered me to do exactly as he asked. My whole brain shut down as he took control, and I felt totally and completely at peace. Just for those few minutes.

I can do hard things, I think to myself. *All by myself.*

But maybe I don't have to all the time. "I'll see what I can do," I tell Bethany.

"I guess I'll have to accept that answer for now. Oh hell, did I tell you what happened with the guests who checked into the red room last night? So they tried to take a shower together, but they were using these handcuffs..."

Bethany unwinds a story involving another visit from our favorite La Fierte firefighters, but I'm only half-listening as my eyes stay on the men in the kitchen. I watch as Tom slowly reaches across a counter, gently rests his hand on Colin's, then pulls it away quickly, like he's touched a live burner. But Colin grabs hold of Tom's hand and wraps it up in his. He grins at Tom. "Trust me, sweetheart," he whispers.

I can do hard things.

Still, even as Bethany's talking, my thumb itches toward the contacts list on my phone. And it keeps landing right back on Dave's number.

Chapter 28

9 Days to the Devon Falls Leaf Festival

And then I know I'm ready. They're ready. We're all ready for more.
—Colin Templegate

"This is really nice."

Gabe leans his head back against the padded headrest of the hot tub and sinks lower into the water. Tom beams at me from the other side of the tub, where he's keeping watch on the large plastic cast wrap we all but welded to Gabe's leg before we propped it up on the edge of the tub. "This was a wonderful idea, bestie," Tom murmurs to me.

I shrug. "I figured if anyone knew how to get a broken leg into a hot tub, it would be one of the doctors in town." Sam came through with that cast wrap, that's for sure. Gabe looks the most relaxed he's been since the hospital, his eyes fluttering open and closed as his dark hair floats down against the water.

Gabe peeks one eye open. "Thanks for this," he whispers.

I can almost let myself fully relax into the water. This is only our second full day at the cabin, and I know we all have plenty of shit itching against the backs of our brains. Especially Gabe. He jumps every single time one of our phones goes off, his eyes lighting up, then falling when he sees it isn't the social worker or the sheriff or Jack or Benson calling. It's like taking Christmas morning away from a little kid. Every. Damn. Time.

And there's something else itching against the back of my brain right now too. Tom. He's finally leaning further into what he and I are finally trying together. He's not second guessing my touches anymore, and he's looking a lot less wide-eyed when I kiss him now. But.

But.

He still hasn't told us what the hell happened at *The Good Sword.* Tom getting fired? From any job? That doesn't compute. Tom's moms may be well-off, but he was never some Hollywood nepo baby. He worked his ass off to get every single role he ever had, moving all the way from commercials to the franchise role of his dreams across many, many years. He's good at what he does, and he's got incredible drive and perseverance. Something fucked up happened to him out there, I'm sure of it.

I can't push him to tell us, though. I'm also sure of that. Tom's the kind of guy who puts so much of himself out to the world that when there's something he wants to keep hidden, he wraps it up *tight.* Over the years I've learned that getting the hardest truths out of him requires time. And patience. So for now, I'll just keep pushing him toward relaxing hot tubs, working him closer and closer to trusting what we have here. I look out across the patio, at a fresh bed of leaves that have fallen to the ground overnight. Lots of reds, some oranges. A golden one here or there.

"Christian would have loved this place."

I say the words out loud without thinking about them, but I don't regret them. Especially not when Tom pushes one hand across the tub to take my left and Gabe pushes another over to take my right. I'm circled between the two of them now, and the sentence feels right as it lingers between us.

"Yes, he would have loved this place," Tom echoes.

Gabe smiles. "Tell me about him?" he asks.

Tom laughs. "Oh, he was the trouble twin. That's what Colin's mother used to call him, anyway. A total daredevil."

Gabe laughs. "And you were a perfect angel?" he asks me, his voice teasing.

"I was absolutely the fuck not." I grin. "A lot of the time I was two steps behind him."

"Like that time," Tom says, "that you both decided you wanted a dog, so you kidnapped the neighbor's and hid it in the basement."

Gabe's mouth drops open. "You did not!"

"She was always chained up outside alone, barking!" I shrug. "But yeah, we did. We definitely got up to some shit together. I had nothing on Christian, though, when it came to causing chaos. Sam spent most of his time chasing after Chris, keeping the chaos to a bare minimum."

"They sound like they were a good pair," Gabe says.

"We always thought so." I glance over at Tom. "Now we know they weren't so great together at the end, before Christian died. But when we were younger, you never saw one of them without the other." I smile at Tom. "Just like us."

Gabe sighs. "I wish I'd had someone like that," he says softly. "Someone who I knew I could always count on to be behind me, one thousand percent, no matter what." He smiles. "That was my mom for a long time, I guess. Until she got sick."

Tom and I separate to move closer to Gabe, until I'm leaning against his shoulder and Tom's pressing against his good leg under the water. "Tell us about her," Tom says.

The bubbles from the hot tub's jets seem to hum in time with Gabe's voice as he starts speaking slowly. "She was an artist," he says "A painter. Abstract stuff, mostly. I never understood it." He grins. "I remember someone told her once that all her paintings just looked like shapes, and she told him his whole face just looked like shapes."

Tom snorts. "Oh, yes, I would have liked her very much."

"You would have," Gabe agrees. He looks back and forth between us. "She would have liked you both, too. She would have loved the way you dress, Tom. All the colors and patterns you like."

"Thank you very much." Tom takes a miniature bow in the water.

"Colin, she would have loved the way you look at something like a destroyed room and see all the possibilities for it. She was like that too. She loved finding old furniture pieces at estate sales and restoring them."

"Huh." I frown. I'm not sure I ever realized that was something people actually did. It sounds... fun.

"She was loyal, and strong, and really good at asking for things she wanted. And she wanted me and Lou to be like that too." Gabe shakes his head and sighs. "She's rolling over in her grave somewhere if she can see what's happened to Dave since she died. She'd hate the way he acts around Lou."

"And around you," I remind him steadily. "You matter too, little one. I think you forget that sometimes."

"Agreed," says Tom.

Gabe frowns and then swallows. "Thank you," he finally says.

I answer by leaning over and kissing him across the lips. When I pull away, he's smiling. "Can I ask for something?" he says.

"Anything at all," Tom says before I can answer the exact same way.

Gabe takes a deep breath. He's staring down into the water now, not looking directly at either of us. "I liked it," he whispers. "Yesterday, when you took control, Colin. When you told me and Tom what to do. I liked that a lot. I was wondering if we could, you know. Do that again."

"Oh my goodness," Tom mutters. "You really are trouble, little fox. In the very best possible way. What do you say, Colin? Do you feel like bringing out that racing voice of yours again?"

I can't figure out how to answer him. I can barely speak. All I know is that my cock's rising in the water, and my entire body feels like it's thrumming as I remember how good yesterday felt... how much I liked being in charge of these two. It was like all the best parts of driving again: locking in on a goal and steering toward it, making every choice and movement with that goal in mind. But in this case, my goal gets to be about making all three of us feel good.

Fuck, yes. I would like that very much. And maybe a little more of me taking charge is exactly what Tom needs to finally trust this and open up all the way. I stand up so fast I splash water across the patio.

"Let's get out of this tub."

I can't tell if I say the words or growl them.

We end up in the bedroom, with Gabe's broken leg stacked comfortably on pillows. Both of them are naked, laid out in front of me, and every animal instinct in me wants to fall across the bed and devour them, but I stay standing. Patient. I've got my shirt off, but I'm still in jeans and boxers. I want them to remember that I'm in charge here. They won't have me until I say the word.

"Tell me," I say to them, "what your wildest fantasies are."

Because even though I've known Tom all my life, I know almost nothing about this side of him: what he likes in bed. What makes every nerve in his body stand at attention when he's touching someone else intimately. There's so much I have to learn. And Gabe... well, there are so many pieces of him neither Tom nor I know anything about, and I want to learn all of them.

Gabe's pupils seem to be a little dilated as he starts speaking

"Um," he says, "well, since I first started dating you both, there's something I've always wanted to try. But it never would have worked when the two of you weren't together." He purses his lips.

Tom sits up on one elbow and raises an eyebrow. "Tell us," I order.

Gabe gulps. "So, yeah. In this fantasy I have, Tom is, um, inside of me." He blushes. "He's making love to me. And then, Colin, you're inside of him, fucking him into me..."

He trails off, but Tom quickly starts talking. "Enough said. That's my fantasy too." He looks over at me. "Or it most certainly is now. My goodness."

I grin. "Okay." I pace back and forth in front of the bed as I study them. "We're going to make this happen, then. If we can do it safely, anyway." I frown down at Gabe's leg.

"The doctors just said no weight bearing and that I had to rest it a lot and be careful about not moving it too much," Gabe says. "I can be careful! I promise!"

Tom laughs. "We will have to be especially cautious," he tells me. "But this bed is covered in pillows, and I know I won't mind if we move very slowly." He sends me a sly smile that looks like it's from the Tom I know so well. *Yes.* Gabe and I are breaking him back out of the shell of worry he's been wrapped in. I can feel it.

"Okay, we can try," I agree. "But Gabe, you have to tell us to stop the absolute second something doesn't feel right. Stay stop, and we'll stop right away. Or use the light system if you'd rather. You both remember? Red, yellow, green?"

"Yes, love," Tom says sweetly. "I know neither Gabe nor I are internationally recognized racing champions, but we both do re-member how street lights work."

Tom Evers' snark is also a good sign.

"Very funny. Okay." I slide open the bedside table next to Tom and pull out a bottle of lube, and then I stand over the two of them. "Listen, I hate to sound like some kind of director here, but I want to make sure we all stay on the same page about what we're doing so we can make sure Gabe stays safe. Here's how we'll start. I'm going to drip some of this across both of your cocks. Tom, handjob for Gabe. Gabe, handjob for Tom. Simple. But," I add. "Neither of you get to come until I say so. No matter what." Tom makes a giggly, almost squealing sound, and I pop the lid. It's lube that warms immediately on contact, and it was already in Tom's shaving kit when we arrived. I wasn't surprised when he unpacked it into the drawer next to the bed.

I slowly drip the liquid across their cocks. I watch as they cross arms and take each other in hand. Gabe gives a little gasp.

"I love the way you feel," he says softly.

Tom smiles. "Same, little fox. Same." He's got his eyes closed now, as Gabe works his hand slowly up and down.

"Very good," I tell them. Now, for this next part. I've got something in mind, but it's very definitely something I've never done before, or even thought about doing, with any of the women I've been with. I hope I'm ready for it.

They put me in charge of Gabe's fantasy. And I'm damn sure going to make sure it's perfect. This is more than just sex we're building here. We're building connections and new pathways together, and trust. Trust more than anything, I think. I spent years working with teams in garages, and those years taught me a few lessons about what creates trust best: you show up, you do your work like you're part of a team, and you do it with respect and care. And I want everyone in this room to know just how much respect and care I have for them both.

"Gabe," I say, "you're going to keep your broken leg on the pillows and bend the knee of your good leg and pull your heel up against your ass. Tom, do that same thing with both your legs."

Tom grins and licks his lips as he closes his eyes. I think he might have a guess of what's coming. They both obey quietly as they keep their hands moving, and soon their holes are both fully on display in front of me.

I lean down at the edge of the bed, studying. It's like I'm walking a racetrack the day before a race, as I memorize the curves and opportunities in front of me. Then, when I'm sure I'm ready to drive, I drop my head down and push my mouth against Gabe's entrance.

He gasps as I slowly tease his entrance with my tongue. "Oh wow," he whispers. I knew, logically, that this would be something new for both of us, and I relax slightly as his body tenses with excitement. I follow his signals as I test and experiment, playing with how my mouth moves against the nerves there and how my tongue dips in and out of him. I don't go very deep or very far. I'm new to this, and so is Gabe, and I'm not in any hurry to push either of us past our comfort zones.

"I was hoping," says Tom softly, "that this was what you had in mind when you ordered us all into the shower together on our way from the hot tub to the bed."

To be fair, that stop had just made sense. Gabe already had the protector on over his cast, and I wanted to make sure he could safely use the shower stool Sam left here for us. Plus, helping our little fox shower definitely got me more than a little keyed up for this moment, and I know it didn't hurt Tom or Gabe either.

But I wasn't sure, when I brought us all into the shower, if I'd be ready to try this. Now I'm glad I took the risk. It's like nothing else, being this close to Gabe. His responses and reflexes are so bright against my tongue, my mouth, and our bodies might as well be melding together as he pushes back against me. I'm not sure I've ever felt closer to anyone, until I pull away slightly, move over and repeat the same pattern with Tom.

He leaps against me. His reactions are a little different, a little faster as my tongue moves against his body. "Colin," he whispers. "Oh, fuck. Colin, please don't stop. I dreamed... but I never thought... never imagined..."

And now I wonder what it would be like to have one of them do this to me. I may have to order that to happen one day, but not today. Today, we have other plans.

I pull away eventually and see that they're still following orders, although their hand movements have slowed slightly. Gabe's staring down at where my face is still next to Tom's ass. "Don't stop," I remind them both. Tom swallows, hard, as I drip lube across both of their holes. Gabe startles slightly when the liquid touches his ring, and even more when I push fingers into each of them and start prepping them simultaneously.

What's weird is that this is all such new territory for me, and I wonder if maybe it should still feel strange. But it doesn't. Maybe it's all the good coaching Tom's been giving us, or maybe it's just something about being with these two men. I can tell from their reactions when it's time to slide a second finger into Tom, and then a second one into Gabe. I wait for their reactions before I go deeper, testing for when they're ready for more. Tom gets there more quickly, which makes sense. And when I reach that certain bundle of nerves within him, he thrusts up into Gabe's hand.

"Bestie!" he yells out, making Gabe giggle.

I get there with Gabe a few moments later, and he yelps like an excited puppy, which makes Tom laugh. "No coming yet," I remind them both.

"Absolutely not. Wouldn't dream of it, sir," Tom whispers.

And then I know I'm ready. They're ready. We're all ready for more. We're going to have to be so careful about this with Gabe's leg, but I've got an idea. And I trust Gabe to use his colors and tell us if anything goes wrong.

"Take your hands off of each other," I demand. Then I move to one side of the bed and maneuver Gabe on the pillows, pushing him slightly to the side so that his broken leg is still propped and he's on his side with Tom behind him. Then I shift Tom until he's all but spooning Gabe.

"Okay," I tell Tom. "I'm going to put a condom on you now, sweetheart."

I rip the package open, and Tom moans as I wipe the lube from his cock with a washcloth I had waiting next to the bed. He gets even louder when I carefully slide the condom over it. "No coming," I whisper to him again. I drop my jeans and boxers to the floor, and then I rip another package open and slide one on myself before I kneel down on the bed behind Tom. I'm hard as a rock as I stare at these two, but I'm determined not to rush this next part.

"Gabe," I whisper, "you're going to touch yourself while Tom enters you. Tom, you're going to go so slowly that it almost hurts. Remember, we're not going to be able to do anything fast today. Gabe, we have to be careful of your leg."

"We understand, bestie," says Tom. Gabe nods.

"Good," I tell them both. "Now, Gabe. Tom is going to slowly take you apart while I take him apart. Does that sound good to you?"

Gabe makes a strangled noise, which I take as a yes, and Tom laughs.

"Okay, Tom," I say. "Give our little fox what he wants."

Tom enters him slowly at first, then a little more quickly. I watch Gabe's face change as his body moves to accept Tom's entrance. I study the way he pushes back against Tom and gets his bearings through the first sensations of pain, and then when his entire face relaxes as his body pulls Tom forward.

"Touch yourself," I tell him, and he starts moving his hand up and down his cock as I jack myself and wonder how I ever got so lucky to be in this place, this room, with these two fucking fantastic men. I drop some lube across the condom and then I slide down onto the bed and wrap my body around Tom.

"I'm about to be inside you," I whisper into his ear. He shudders, and I push.

He takes me into his body, easily, naturally, and it takes everything I have not to come the second I feel him clench around the base of my cock. This is like nothing I've ever imagined, nothing I've ever felt before. The way his body pulls at the back of my dick, holding it tight, squeezing it, is just so damn *good*. I move in and out of him, highly aware with each push that I'm inside of *Tom*, my best friend in life, and he's inside of Gabe, a man who's unlocked parts of me I never would have found on my own. I savor exploring and finding the different ways that his body reacts to mine. I close my eyes for a minute and settle into a rhythm. I push into Tom as he pushes into Gabe, who pushes back against Tom who pushes back into me.

It's like driving a car with a perfect setup, when you can just become one with the steering and go, fully trusting that every move you make will work the way you want it to. I see our checkered flag ahead of time. "Come when you're ready," I order them.

Gabe falls over the edge first, huffing and arching into his hand. Then I lose myself in Tom, pumping into the condom as I clutch him against my body. Tom's last, as I kiss his neck while Gabe turns slightly to nuzzle their faces together.

We lay together for a while, in comfortable silence for a long time. Eventually, I kiss Tom again, clutch the base of the condom and pull out of him, and Tom carefully does the same thing with Gabe. "That was amazing," Gabe whispers as Tom fluffs the pillows under his leg, frowning at his cast, while I wipe down his stomach and cock.

"You were amazing. You both were." I lean over to kiss him.

"I just don't get it," Gabe says softly. "How can Dave think people being together like this is anything to be ashamed of? This isn't shameful," he adds. "This is…"

He doesn't finish the sentence, but Tom and I look at each other, and I feel the same word I know he's thinking.

Love.

Chapter 29

8 Days to the Devon Falls Leaf Festival

I wonder if the world will ever know our real story. —Tom Evers

"This isn't shameful."

Gabe's words are echoing in my head as I pour pancake batter into a skillet, listening to it hiss and sizzle against the heat.

"Hey there," I whisper to the pancake. "What are you ashamed of?"

It doesn't answer as I drop some blueberries into it.

I'm alone in the cabin's kitchen this morning. Just me and my swirling, rabid thoughts. I left Colin and Gabe in bed, with Colin wrapped around Gabe's torso and Gabe's head nestled into Colin's neck. I stood for a moment above them, watching. And Gabe's words wouldn't leave my thoughts.

I flip the pancake and sigh. I've never been ashamed of being pansexual. I was lucky and privileged to grow up in a house with two loving mothers who taught me and my brother that love is love. I went into a career in film and television fully out and proud, and I've always been very at peace with the fact that some people stop following my career or supporting me when they learn I'm not straight, or that I enjoy wearing bright, loud outfits and putting on an occasional dab of eyeliner.

Their loss.

Then *The Good Sword* happened. And for the first time in my life, I understood how someone's hatred or fear of others has the power to destroy other humans. Gabe's spent so many years shielding huge parts of himself and his brother from his stepfather... I can't even fathom how exhausting that must be.

"No more, little fox," I whisper as I lift the pancake and add it to the plate of others that are keeping warm in the oven. "At least not as long as I have anything to say about it." I've got no idea how Colin and I are going to protect Gabe and Lou through this custody battle with Dave, but I'm determined that we will.

Shame can't win today. That's what I'm thinking as I start to pour more batter into the skillet, then stop as my phone buzzes on the counter.

Melody, the screen reads.

My stomach immediately clenches. The last person I feel like talking to right now is my agent. Melody's a lovely human and all, but this cabin has become such a safe space for me over the past few days. One where the outside, dangerous world dare not tread. And Melody is very much a part of that outside, dangerous world.

Only I've been dodging her calls, and she must know that. When I let the call go to voicemail and the phone immediately starts ringing again, I sigh and do what I must. I answer.

"Tom! There you are!" Melody's voice is high and surprised. "Finally decided to take my call?"

I turn off the stove and grab my jacket from the back of a kitchen chair as I make my way out the patio doors. I don't want to risk waking Colin and Gabe. "Well, you're quite persistent," I tell her.

"You know I am." I can hear the smile in her voice. "Listen, Tom. We *really* need to talk about setting you up for some auditions. You know what a short memory Hollywood has, hon. If their last and only memory is of you stepping away from *The Good Sword* franchise, then—"

"But I didn't step away," I say, interrupting her.

She sighs. "Babe, I know that. You know that. But that's not the story the world knows. And since they can't know the real story, we have to make sure the narrative stays strong. We said you walked away for other opportunities. So now the public needs to see you take some of those opportunities."

I turn to look through the patio doors, letting my eyes drift to the open doorway of the house where Colin and Gabe are hopefully still sleeping, still tangled in each other. They're so beautiful together, those two. One the man of my dreams, the other one who I never imagined in my wildest dreams.

I wonder if the world will ever know our real story. Will Dave's fear and hatred conspire to destroy what the three of us are building together? My stomach twists again as I try to imagine coping with that sort of loss. For all the years I spent desperate for a life of love with Colin, I know now how gray and blurry that life would be if Gabe weren't there, sharing it with us.

And suddenly, I'm overwhelmingly tired. I'm so tired of parsing truths to the world out of shame. I'm so tired of living for other people's fears and hatreds and angers.

Or maybe I'm just tired enough. Because I hear myself say, out loud, the word that I've been wanting to say to Melody for months.

"No."

"Excuse me? What do you mean, no?"

I close my eyes and imagine Colin and Gabe, limbs crossing limbs, sleepy eyes fluttering, as I pull together the words I need to say. "No, Melody. I don't want to keep the narrative strong anymore. I don't want to keep hiding what really happened to me with that movie from everyone." I sigh. "I just want to tell the truth. Being ashamed of losing that role is exhausting. And I don't want to do it anymore."

For a moment, she says nothing. I wait, in the silence, for what must be next: she'll drop me as a client, and then my career as an actor, the career I've loved and worked so very, very hard to achieve, will be gone for good. But then Melody speaks again.

"I know it cost you a lot to stand up for what you believe in on that set," she says quietly.

She's right, of course. But I regret nothing. My actions on that set cost me so little compared to the price others were already paying there.

"Okay, Tom."

I cough. "Excuse me? Did you just say *okay?*" I ask.

Melody sighs. "Do I think this is the best choice for your career? Honestly, no. But Tom, you're more than just your career. You're a human being. And it's clear what happened with that movie franchise is eating you alive." She clears her throat. "I care about you, Tom. Share what you need to share. Do what you need to do. Talk to others about what happened so you can do some healing. And just let me know when you want me to find you another audition, okay?"

Tears are at the corners of my eyes now. I watch as one lone, yellow leaf falls from a tree in front of me, surfing on a slight breeze as it drips and drops through the air before it slowly hits the ground. Released from the tree that gave birth to it, then held it hostage until it was ready for something else. Something different.

"Thank you," I whisper. "Thank you, Melody."

The three of us have eaten through most of the pancakes and half a dozen eggs before I tell them. I pour us all more coffee, check that Gabe's got his leg properly propped up and elevated on the recliner he's sitting in, and then I clear my throat.

"So," I tell them. "There's something I need to tell you both. About what really happened to me at *The Good Sword.*"

Colin's eyebrows go up. "You're finally ready? Thank fuck. Please tell us, sweetheart."

My heart soars a little at the sound of his new moniker for me. I wonder if that will be the case each and every time he says it.

I draw myself up straight in my seat. I take a deep breath, and then I start talking.

"Things were going well after the first movie," I tell them. They both nod. "Good box office sales, good critical reviews of my role. We were in the middle of filming the second movie when things hit a snag." I pause and close my eyes as the memories start to roll through me, and I feel two very different hands, one smaller and one larger, each land on my own. And then I go on.

"This film had a different director than the first," I go on. "Someone I'd never worked with before. And one of our castmates, Dellie Shephard, is non-binary."

"Oh," Gabe says. "Yeah, I love them in that sitcom about the high school." He frowns. "But wait, they're in *The Good Sword* franchise? I never heard about that."

I nod. "They had a small role, and they were playing it perfectly. We had some scenes together. But this director—Ron Valvo is his name—sometimes misgendered them or called them by a name they don't use anymore. Several of us corrected him; people do make mistakes, and we hoped that was all it was."

Colin's eyes are narrowing now, and Gabe's face is getting paler. And I keep going, because I suddenly realize that sharing this story, saying it out loud, is like emptying my body of trash that's been sitting in it for so, so long.

"But then one evening, after filming," I tell them, "he'd had too much to drink at a bar where the two of us happened to be together. And he started going on about how proud he is to be bisexual, and how lucky it is that we both have a strong LGB community in Hollywood."

"LGB?" Colin asks.

I nod. "Exactly. I pointed out he'd forgotten a few other letters there. And then he snorted at me, like a horse! He started talking about how trans and enby and intersex people aren't part of *our* community, and then he was spouting all that nonsense people like Dave like to say about how gender and biological sex have always been simple and basic to understand and how anyone who thinks differently must be dealing with mental illness. He even said something about intersex people being a myth. Any physician listening to him would have been horrified. He genuinely thought he was sharing scientific fact, I think."

Gabe makes a strangled noise.

"Exactly," I tell him. "Then he went on to say Dellie's casting was a mistake, but there was no need to worry, because they wouldn't be back for the next film."

"Holy shit," Colin murmurs.

"Indeed." I sigh. "And, well, let's just say I did not let any of that stand. I asked him what business it is of his how anyone identifies. I reminded him that people once thought anyone who identified as bi or gay or lesbian had a mental illness, and I made it clear how hard people have had to fight against that dangerous idea. I asked him how he could ever wave a pride flag with any kind of dignity, knowing full well how many people suffered and died so that *everyone* in our community could be allowed to live and love proudly and as our full selves. I told him that he needed to start respecting Dellie by using their preferred name, just as he'd call anyone else by the name they like to be called. Because that's just good, human manners."

"Wow." Gabe shakes his head. "Did you really say all that?"

"I really did." I close my eyes against the words I say next. "And then, the very next day, he started making my life miserable on the set."

Colin's eyes go dark. "What did he do?" he asks, his voice menacing.

"Nothing much to Dellie," I assure him. "Their scenes were almost over, thank goodness, so they wrapped quickly after that night. But Ron turned plenty of ire on me. He started embarrassing me in front of the cast and crew and refusing to work with me when I had ideas for takes. So I went to a producer to explain what had happened at the bar and that I felt there was retaliation involved."

"And the producers did something?" Gabe asks.

"They certainly did. They decided to kill off my character and fire me."

The room goes silent. "I will destroy them all," Colin says, and his voice is just steady enough that I believe every word. I laugh.

"Well, no murder would save my career at this point anyway." I sigh. "It was made very clear to me that some of the producers of the film, generally speaking, agree with Ron, but no one's said any of that publicly. When I mentioned what happened to a few of our colleagues, it was obvious they were hesitant to fully believe me or stand behind me." I shrug. "I couldn't bring it all up in public without creating hell for Dellie, who left the set before any of this even happened. So it's all Ron's word against mine. The PR message has become that they adjusted the storyline of the book in such a way that my character had to die. And that's what everyone will be told when the movie releases. My agent thinks it's best that we stick to that story and tell the world how I wanted to move onto new roles. She's been asking me to come back to LA for auditions."

"Oh, Tom." Gabe grabs my hand, squeezing it tightly in his. "That's... I don't even know what to say."

"Colin's murder eyes say it all," I tell them both, because this room clearly needs some light in it right now. Colin raises an eyebrow, unrepentant.

"But I don't need anyone to commit homicide on my behalf," I add. "I'm taking action on my own, bestie. Finally. I called Max, that reporter who's shacked up with those hot firefighters. He's coming over to interview me later, and I'm going to tell him all about what really happened with *The Good Sword.*" I hold up my coffee mug in a salute. "Once more into the breach, I suppose. I mean," I add, "I won't share anything Dellie doesn't want me to. I'll call them today to talk about the situation, and I absolutely won't drag them into anything they don't want to be involved with. But I'm going to make it clear that I was fired because I chose to speak up against a toxic work environment, one that did not fully include and embrace all of its employees."

Colin just stares at me. It's Gabe who speaks first.

"Wow," he says. "You're incredible, Tom."

I shake my head. "I wish I would have done more, sooner. That I'd had the courage to speak out after everything happened. There are so many things I'd do differently if I could travel through time." I sigh. "But I've been thinking about what you said last night," I say to Gabe. "About shame. I don't have anything to be ashamed of. I did my best work for that production. So did Dellie. I'm proud that I chose not to tolerate intolerance that night in the bar, and I need to start acting like it."

"Wow." Gabe shakes his head as he smiles. "Tom, that's amazing. I'm proud of you."

"Me too." Colin says the word softly. He shrugs. "Sometimes I wonder how the last few years could have been different for me if I was ready to be that open about how much I struggled with my mental health after Chris died."

"Hey." I shake my finger at him. "No beating yourself up. You needed time, and space. Just like I've needed it. There's nothing wrong with that."

"Thanks, sweetheart." My heart coils around the word as he stands to kiss me on the head and starts clearing plates. "I know, you're right. But it isn't just me, you know? Maybe I could have helped other athletes working to improve their mental health. So much of that gets hidden in the sports world. Maybe me talking about it could have made a difference for someone else."

"It still could, you know," Gabe says softly. Colin looks at him, eyebrows raised in a question.

"I just mean," says Gabe. "That there happens to be a reporter coming over today, to talk to Tom. And you'll be here too, and..."

Colin sets the plates on the counter and frowns. He picks up his coffee mug, cradling it in his hands. I don't say anything. If there's one thing I recognize after years of life with Colin, it's his *thinking, thinking,* face.

Eventually, he sets the mug down. "Yeah," he says quietly. "Yeah. I think I also want to talk to Max, Tom. You think he'd be okay with that?"

I snort. "Would a freelance reporter be okay with talking to a Hollywood star about all the sordid details of his lost career *and* also getting the scoop on an international racing driver's mental health journey? Yes, Colin, I think he'll agree." I stand up to pull him into my arms. "Good for you, love," I whisper.

"Well, that's settled then. Max is getting a banner headline, that's for sure." I wink at Gabe. "Now we just need to find a way to make sure we keep Lou protected and cared for. And we will," I add. Colin nods and grunts in agreement, his eyes narrowing. I'm quite certain Colin's spending a great deal of his time in this cabin creating custody backup plans and revenge plots against Dave that may or may not be suitable for all audiences.

Gabe frowns and fidgets in his chair. "What if we told Max even more?" he says quietly.

"Like what?" Colin takes Gabe's pain pills from the counter and shakes the right amount out for Gabe as he fills a glass of water.

Gabe looks back and forth between us. "Maybe you two aren't ready for this," he finally says. "And if you're not, I don't want to rush you, so please just say so." He draws in a long, deep breath. "But I was just thinking that you two aren't hiding anymore, and I don't want to either." He shakes his head. "And then I was thinking that if we just told Max about the three of us—that we're, um, together..." he trails off. And then he looks up, back and forth between us, and there's nothing but determination written across his face. "And then Dave would know. The whole world would. We wouldn't have to hide. And he would know I'm not ashamed of this. Not one bit. But," he adds quickly, "this isn't just about me. We don't have to do this if either of you don't want to."

Colin and I have, I estimate, held thousands and thousands of silent conversations in our lifetime together, in places all over the world. We've silently mocked bad reporters in Abu Dhabi, worried over a grieving Sam in Manhattan, speculated on my dating prospects in Sydney. But right now I have every feeling that when we look back on this moment, years from now, we'll both remember this as one of the most important silent conversations we've ever had.

I lock onto his eyes with mine. He needs to answer first, because the answer to this question means so much more for him than me. Colin's only just discovering new aspects of himself, his identity, and I'm not sure he's ready to share so much of himself with the world so quickly.

But when he looks back at me, there's a fierceness in his gaze that I haven't seen in years. Not since his last race before Christian died. I see his answer there. *Yes.*

I smile. Nod. I know he hears my response.

"We're in," I tell Gabe. "But are you sure, little fox? What about Lou and child services and custody?"

Gabe fidgets in his chair and stares down at his cast. Then he looks back up at us, lips pursed. "There are too many people in the world," he says finally, "who keep telling people like that director and Dave that they should resent anyone who's different from them. They tap into the frustration and anger Dave has and tell him to direct it at people like us and Dellie and Lou instead of dealing with what's actually wrong in his own life. They keep promising Dave that anyone who's too different from him is going to hurt the whole world." He swallows hard. "Those kinds of people are telling Dave to resent his own son. They tell him that differences make people weak, even though the things that make Lou unique are the things that make him amazing, you know? And for years, now, I've had to just live with Dave listening to those people. I was a party of one. I didn't have anyone standing behind me. And it's easier to stay silent and not speak up when you feel there's no one behind you, backing you up. Does that make sense?"

I gulp as I lean over and take one of his hands. Colin takes the other. "I do understand," I tell him softly. I think of how alone I felt the day Melody told me I'd been fired: like every person who'd ever cheered me on suddenly disappeared through a false door on my stage of life, and there I was, all by myself in the spotlight.

Gabe smiles slightly. "I thought about running, sometimes," he says quietly. "With Lou. Just taking him and disappearing." I grip his hand tightly as I try to imagine Gabe and Lou, disappearing from Devon Falls, away from me and Colin. From *this*. From whatever we're starting to build together.

Colin's eyebrows knit together fiercely. "Thank fuck you didn't," he all but growls.

Gabe nods, slowly. "Yeah. Because I've got people behind me now. Don't I?"

I laugh. "Oh, little fox. Not just behind you. In front of you. Off to the side. Wherever you need us."

Gabe purses his lips again, and I watch as a soft fierceness slowly takes over his entire face. "Then it's time," he finally says, "to stop being silent. Lou deserves better than silence." He clears his throat. "It's time," he says, "to fight for Lou. And me."

A combination of hope and excitement and something else I can't quite put a word to rushes through me as I grip Gabe's hand harder and look where I always do in moments of importance: Colin.

Colin nods, just slightly, and I hear his next words before he ever says them out loud.

"Yes," he agrees. "Now we fight. Together." He looks back over at me. "All three of us."

Chapter 30

3 Days to the Devon Falls Leaf Festival

And just like that, I know exactly where I'll be at 7:30 tonight.
—Gabe Gomez

"Hi, Gabe!"

Max's cheerful voice on the other end of the phone makes me smile. Who would have thought that spilling all your secrets to a reporter, the same secrets you've protected for years, would end up feeling like talking to an old friend? When Tom called Max and he showed up at the door of the cabin, I was so nervous I was actually shaking. But Max immediately started making jokes about signing my cast, and then he started wondering aloud why he was the one signing when I had two famous guys sitting right next to me, and the next thing I knew we were all laughing and he was telling us stories about the two giant firefighters he's dating. It turns out they first met when he accidentally sent them a *very* NSFW text, and that story's one I won't be forgetting anytime soon.

So, yeah, it wasn't long before I was shaking with laughter, not nerves. And by the time he left, I could have been saying goodbye to an old friend. He even invited me to grab a beer sometime so we could discuss the pros and cons of dating two very large, overprotective men. I said yes, of course.

I'm not so worried about what that article's going to say anymore. What the rest of my future, and Lou's, really hinges on is what Dave does when he reads this article.

But that's the risk I took, for me and Lou, when I decided to talk to Max. I'm not living in shame anymore, and I'm not going to let my little brother spend his life in it.

Now we fight, I said to Colin and Tom the day we called Max. That's been my new morning affirmation ever since that day.

I can do hard things. I can fight for the people I love.

Once or twice I've wondered whether it's time to expand that definition beyond Lou. But it's too early to even think about the word *love* when it comes to Colin and Tom... isn't it? I mean, I've been dating the two of them for about ten minutes. And they've been dating each other for about five.

"Hey," I say to Max. I'm on the lounge chair of the back patio of the cabin, next to the hot tub, sitting up with my leg stretched out across multiple pillows Colin piled under it while he makes lunch. We knew the article was coming out today, and I woke up feeling like a nervous wreck again. Colin and Tom have been plying me with food and hugs all morning. "What's up?"

"I just sent that article over." Max coughs. "And I just want to say thank you again, to you and Tom and Colin, for all the vulnerability the three of you showed me during our interview. I took that vulnerability seriously, Gabe. I promise I did. I respect the hell out of all three of you. Oh, and I ended up interviewing Dellie separately. They had plenty of their own stories to tell about that movie set. I'm writing a different article about what happened at *The Good Sword,* but it's running in the same issue as the piece I'm sending over now."

I put him on speaker while I open up my email tab and pull up the article he's sent over. And there's the headline.

THREE'S NOT A CROWD AFTER ALL

A smile slowly stretches across my face as I start reading. The most important and meaningful time period of my life to date lies across the screen in my words and Tom's and Colin's.

I can do hard things. I can fight for the people I love.

I take a deep breath, and I read on.

The article tells the story of the fire and the inn and the renovations. The story of what happened to Tom at *The Good Sword.* Tom's quoted there. *"It took these two men, and what we've found here, the three of us, for me to remember that the way we stand up for each other in society matters. I needed to remember that there's never any shame in standing in support of another human so that all of us can live our best, most productive life. The relationships we build, the way we take care of each other and show up for each other against hate and misunderstanding: those are the accomplishments I want to leave this world with."*

I blink back the tears at the corners of my eyes as I move through that paragraph and onto where Colin talks about what really happened when he left racing. *"I knew I needed to leave racing. But I wasn't ready, then, to talk about why. Explaining about all the ways my brain was fucking up as I grieved? That seemed like my own personal hell. So I ran as far as I could from the public eye and I hid. But I don't want to hide anymore."* I remember the way he looked back and forth between me and Tom as he said that, and I smile.

"What do you think," Max asks softly, "of what I wrote about you and Lou? I kept everything really general," he adds. "I wanted to make sure I respected your boundaries and Lou's and didn't cause any problems with the investigation or any future custody battles."

I keep reading.

And I keep blinking.

It's impossible to talk with Gabe Gomez without learning everything there is to learn about the younger half-brother who's influenced and changed so much of his life. "He's everything to me," says Gabe. "All I want is to be a good role model to him. But I've been afraid for a while now to show him that it's okay to love and be who you are in public. I hid that I like people of all genders, not just women, because some people don't understand that. I didn't want anyone to find out that I was dating two men, because some people most definitely wouldn't understand that." Gabe pauses, and it's written all over his face what his secrets have cost him. Then he clears his throat. "But," says Gabe, "that's not being a good role model. My little brother needs to know that people don't need to understand how he loves or what he loves to appreciate him for who he is. And it's time for me to be the role model who teaches him that."

"Oh, wow," I say. "Max. This is..."

"I know," he says. "I'm an incredibly talented writer."

I burst out laughing as I read over the paragraphs again. "You told our story exactly the way I would have wished for it to be told. I can't believe," I whisper, "that I did this. That I told the world everything."

"The publication is a pretty small one, like I told you," Max reminds me. "But since no one's seen Colin in public in years, and since *The Good Sword* is a big franchise, both pieces got picked up by some larger outlets pretty quickly. They're already going viral, Gabe. So, yeah. You told the world."

I draw in a long, deep breath and let it out. *I can do hard things.*

I glance back through the patio doors, where Colin and Tom are standing at the kitchen table spreading mayo on sandwich bread. *I can do hard things.*

And I don't have to do them alone anymore.

"You said Jack and Benson are coming?" I ask as Tom ties my bow tie. I'm still not sure how, exactly, he and Colin magicked up a suit for me to wear tonight. I've never owned one. Sort of makes me wonder if they've been measuring me in my sleep.

"Yes," Colin answers for him, as he slides a shoe onto my good foot. The suit pants didn't fit over my cast, so I'm wearing black track pants with the jacket, but Tom insists I look dapper. He slides a giant black sock onto the foot that's casted so it doesn't get cold. Both of them seem to like dressing me while I'm injured, and maybe that should make me feel weird. But it doesn't.

It just feels like they care about me.

"They were always invited to the opening of the tasting room," Tom adds as he finishes with the tie and leans over to kiss my forehead. "Most of the town will be there, plus some of Colin's racing friends."

"Because they love booze," Colin agrees as he stands up straight. "And Claire says she loves, and I quote, 'weird small town festivals that celebrate dead plants.'"

I snort.

"Anyway," Colin goes on, "yeah, Jack and Benson will be there. But I heard through our very well-connected grapevine that Malachai didn't want to come tonight, so he's watching Lou."

I can't decide if that makes the pit in my stomach bigger or smaller. It's been three days since the article came out, and the only thing I've heard from the social worker is that Dave is back in town and that their investigation is ongoing. He also told me Lou is doing well with Jack and Benson and that he misses me. I was really hoping to at least catch sight of my brother tonight, even just for a second. But that's probably not allowed.

"Are you worried?" I ask them. "About being out in public again now that the article's out?"

Colin plops down on the other side of me, and just like that I'm a Colin-and-Tom sandwich. Just the way I like it. "I guess, in a way," he says simply. "Sort of feels like the start of a race, for me, actually. Like everything in front of us is nothing more than possibilities."

I smile. *Possibilities.* I like that.

"Ah, that's a lovely way to think of it," Tom agrees. "And we're in the first place starting position."

"Pole position," Colin corrects him.

"How do you not know that?" I ask Tom. "Didn't you go to like a bazillion of Colin's races over the years?"

Tom scoffs as he leans over to kiss my cheek. "Little fox, do you know how many gorgeous and charming people are at those races? Believe me when I say that terminology was the *last* thing on my mind."

Colin snorts, but he's smiling.

My phone buzzes with a text, and I feel every inch of my stomach start to turn inside out as I read the words that have appeared on the screen.

It's a text.

From Dave.

"Holy shit," I whisper.

Colin and Tom both lean across me to look at the screen. "Is he even allowed to text you?" Colin demands.

I frown. "I bet the social worker told him not to." But there's no way in hell I'm not reading this text. I click on the notification and hold the phone out for both my—boyfriends? Still feels weird to call them that—to see.

Dave

> Saw the article. I'm tired of all this legal bullshit. Let's talk, kid.

"Oh, hell no," growls Colin. "If he thinks he's getting anywhere near you, then I—"

My phone pings with another text before Colin can tell us everything he's got planned for my ex stepfather.

Dave

> I hear you'll be at the opening of the tasting room tonight. I'll be behind the winery at 7:30. I hope to see you there. No fucking social workers or sheriffs or reporters, just us.

Colin and Tom immediately start chattering together above my head, about social workers and legal protocols and Benson and Ellie's legal proceedings, but I'm too focused on the next text that comes through.

Dave

> It's what your mother would have wanted.

And just like that, I know exactly where I'll be at 7:30 tonight.

Because I can do hard things. I can be like Tom was in that bar, standing up for what's right and for what people deserve.

I can fight for the people I love.

Chapter 31

1 Day to the Devon Falls Leaf Festival

Just to be clear, I've loathed plenty of people in my lifetime. —Colin Templegate

We get to the winery at 7:20, a few minutes before this clandestine meeting Gabe's got set up. I'm not all that into the idea of taking Gabe into any space where that fucker Dave will be, but Gabe's made it clear he wants to do this, and Tom and I had a silent convo where we agreed to support him.

Plus, I'm not afraid to take down some queerphobic motherfucker with a quick throat punch if it comes to that.

Northern Stars Winery is already bumping when we pull up to the parking lot in front of the main building and tasting room. Most of the other cars there, though, are at the other end of the lot, next to the old barn that's attached to the inn: the new event space, which is what everyone's celebrating tonight. The walkway to the space is decorated in solar lights, the trees dotting the walkway are strung up with fairy lights—I'm never touching another one of those fuckers again as long as I live—and the whole pathway looks magical, almost ethereal. My eyes drift past the walkway across the tall roof of the inn, to the windows of the rooms that Tom, Gabe, and I refurbished together after that fire.

I'm proud of a lot of things in my life. I'm proud of my championship titles. My race wins. The relationship I had with my brother, and the deep friendships I built across years of time. But I'm not sure I'll ever be prouder of anything than this inn, this place that I put back together with two people as they put me back together.

I look over at Gabe and Tom, and I find them staring at the same spot: the window of the room where Tom burst the pipe in the wall. Gabe grins. "You know why I had to run into the lake that day?"

Tom cocks an eyebrow. "Tell us."

Gabe laughs. "You two got soaked, and I was so turned on I panicked. I didn't want either of you to see. It was like I was back in seventh grade, using math books to cover my hard-on."

Tom bursts out laughing, and I just smile and shake my head. "No more hiding," I tell him softly.

Gabe looks from the inn over to the winery building and the pathway leading to the large yard space behind it. "No more hiding," he whispers. He swallows. "And actually, on that subject, there's something I need to talk to the two of you about before I see Dave."

Tom frowns. "Tell us, little fox."

"Okay. So. Maybe this thing with Dave won't go well. But if it does, and I end up getting custody of Lou or at least keeping him in my life..." He worries his lower lip with his teeth. "I mean, if the three of us keep doing what we're doing, you two would sort of become, like, parents? Kind of? And that's a lot of responsibility, and I don't want either of you to feel like—"

"Hey, stop." I put my hand on his shoulder. "Take a breath, okay? Let the two of us say something here." I look over at Tom.

Do you feel the way I do?

He gives me a short nod, just like I knew he would.

"Gabe," I say, "I know I speak for Tom when I say that neither of us ever planned to be parents."

Tom lets out a high laugh. "Definitely not. My house in LA has approximately one thousand child death traps built into it. There's a circular staircase with no handles, for goodness' sake." He smiles. "But now I'll speak for both of us." I nod, and he goes on. "Sometimes, little fox, paths appear in your life that you never saw on a map. Then you step onto one of them, and you know that path is exactly where you're supposed to be."

Gabe blinks fast. "Oh. Yeah. So you're saying..."

"We're saying we're all in," I add quickly. "All in on you and Lou. One hundred percent, little fox. Lou's one-of-a-kind, and we both care about him a lot. I don't think either of us can imagine life without him anymore."

Tom shakes his head. "Goodness, no. He hasn't even finished teaching me all the songs in *Frozen* yet. I've barely mastered the one about the snowman, and I think my harmony is off."

Gabe laughs out loud. Then he shakes his head.

"I still don't know what I did to deserve you two," he mumbles.

"I do," I tell him. "You bring light to the universe, little fox."

"Quite right." Tom nods and gently squeezes Gabe's other shoulder. Then Gabe takes a deep breath, and we start walking again, our pace slow as Gabe moves back and forth between grass and pavement on his crutches.

The whole winery property is really well-lit, because Bethany and Evelyn have got their shit together when it comes to details like that, and it's easy for the three of us to find our way to the back of the building, next to the large porch where I saw Gabe and Tom kiss for the first time. I wonder: if Gabe and Tom and I are together until old age, will I still remember that as the first moment when everything changed for us?

And there's Dave. The man I loathe.

Just to be clear, I've loathed plenty of people in my lifetime. I was a fucking race car driver, for hell's sake. I've hated announcers who trashed my driving choices, fellow drivers who crashed into me while making dumbass moves, and friends who took spots on teams I wanted to work with.

But I've never hated someone for very long. I've got a pretty short temper and memory when it comes to anger. I get pissed, I get over it. Pretty simple. Still, I'm pretty sure I'm going to hate this asshole until the end of my days. I see him standing there, next to the lake, between two benches covered in fake grapevines, and I immediately want to walk to him and pull him up by his shirt. I want to demand to know who the hell he thinks he is to try and make two amazing people like Gabe and Lou feel like lesser humans in any kind of way.

Fuck that. Fuck Dave.

"You're snarling," Tom whispers to me.

"So?"

"So while you snarling is one of the hottest things I've ever seen, bestie, you may want to tone it down just slightly. Gabe told us he wants to keep this civil."

I look over at Gabe, and I watch the way he straightens up on his crutches and stands tall as he nods at his former stepfather. "Hi, Dave," he says.

Dave clears his throat. "Hey, kid." His eyes narrow as he looks over to me and Tom. "You didn't mention they'd be coming."

Tom smiles. "Worried I might get some queer on you?" he asks lightly.

"So much for civil," I whisper to him as Dave's face turns red. He's shorter than I expected, maybe five-four, with a wide frame and a head that seems just a little too small for his body. He's got the same hair and eyes as Lou, the same pale skin, and he's wearing a polo and jeans with a hat bearing the logo of Montreal's hockey team. I wonder if he knows that team hosts an epic Pride night. I know, because Tom took me once.

Dave cocks an eyebrow at me. "Couldn't believe it when I read that article," he said. "You're like, a legend, man. Racing championships, all that shit. Is this really the way you want the world to remember you?"

I take a deep breath. *No throat punching allowed. Gabe said so,* I remind myself. "Do I want to be remembered as a man who had the privilege of loving two of the best people in the entire world? Sounds like one hell of a legacy to me," I tell him. Dave's eyes darken.

"I didn't come here to meet with you two f—fuckers," Dave says, and the word he chose not to say hangs in the air just as heavily as it would have if he'd said it. "I came here to talk to the kid."

I open my mouth even though I've got absolutely no idea what's about to come out of it, but Gabe answers Dave first. "I'm not 'the kid,'" he says steadily. "And they're my boyfriends." Dave bristles at the word, but he doesn't respond. "If you want to talk to me," Gabe goes on, and he's so fucking calm and relaxed I want to cheer out loud for him. He's not going to let Dave get to him; that's clear. "Then you talk to them, too. So tell me what you want, Dave. Why are we here?"

Dave shifts back and forth on his sneakers. "Listen," he finally says. He looks directly at Gabe, ignoring me and Tom. "I know Lou worships the ground you walk on, Gabe. And I'll be real with you: I'm really fucking struggling to be the dad he probably deserves these days. But I can't just hand him over to you either. I don't fucking understand any of this, okay? You're really telling me you're sure you're into guys now? And you're dating *two* of them? None of it makes sense to me, Gabe." He shakes his head. "Your mom was too soft on you. My boys always told me that," he mutters under his breath, as I contemplate how many ways I might be able to avoid doing time if I decide to kill *his boys.*

Gabe frowns and tilts his head. "Dave, you were my stepfather for years. You loved my mother; I know you did. You bought me my first baseball glove and cheered me on at my first play. And then you left me on the curbside, all alone, after my mother died, probably because those 'boys' of yours thought I might not turn out to be exactly like you. Or them."

Dave opens his mouth, like he might be about to argue. Then he stops and looks away. Seems like he's got no argument to give there, and my heart cracks open as I once again imagine a grieving, teenage Gabe, all alone with a social worker, watching the father figure he grew up with drive away with his little brother in the backseat.

Gabe clears his throat. "So tell me, Dave," he finally says softly. "Why did you have to understand me, why did I need to be exactly like you, for you to just *love* me?"

We all hear the break and the drop in his voice. I fight the urge to rush to him and hold him, and I can feel Tom holding himself back next to me. He's not alone this time. He has us, and he knows that. We just need to keep standing strong for him while he says all the things he's never said to Dave before.

The question stumps Dave, that much is easy to see. His eyes go wide, and his mouth drops slightly. He's silent for a long moment, and then he clears his throat.

"It's just not right," he finally says. He's not yelling. In fact, his voice is quiet, almost resigned. "This isn't how things are supposed to be, you know? Men are men, and they're supposed to be a certain way. Women are women, and they're supposed to be a certain way. And women are meant for men, and that's it."

I do my best not to snort-laugh as I imagine all the ways Claire would make this asshole pay if she heard him talking like this. She's got one hell of a right hook, as several drunk assholes in clubs and bars have learned the hard way.

But Gabe's still calm, still staring down Dave with something between fire and sadness in his eyes. "You know," he finally says, "I used to want to be just like you. When you and Mom got married. I thought you were the coolest guy in the world. You could cook and throw a fastball, and you made her so happy. You made us both so happy." He shakes his head. "Then she got sick. And I remember going to doctor's appointments by myself with her because you weren't there. I was just a kid, Dave. And I was the one going to the oncologist's office with my mother because suddenly you couldn't do anything but play video games all the time."

"Hey!" Dave points a finger and takes a step forward, and Tom has to put a hand on my chest to hold me back. "My wife, the woman I loved, was sick, okay?" He shakes his head. "I never fit in up here in Vermont, or anywhere I lived. I never had anybody who supported me like your mom did. Then she was gone, and I was on my own again. I needed some damn support somewhere, and it was my gamer buddies who gave me that support!"

Gabe nods, slowly. "Yeah, I get that. Everyone needs a place where they belong, Dave. I really, really get that. And Mom was never mad that you looked for some time and space with your friends after she got sick." He frowns. "The problem was that you started spending *all* your time with them. You were sad and upset and pissed off, and all you did after that was play those games with your boys. It was like the only thing that mattered to you was how *you* felt about her getting sick. Your feelings came first, everyone else came after that. Even Mom."

"How fucking dare you—" Dave starts to growl the words, but Gabe interrupts him. He shakes his head.

"I didn't realize, until a little while ago, that you're doing the same thing with Lou. It's all about you, Dave. When Lou wears a dress or picks out an Elsa toy at the store, you don't think first about the fact that he's your son and you love him for who he is. Nope. You think about how *you* don't understand it, and how that dress makes *you* feel or look." He shakes his head. "Just like you didn't understand me, back then in Connecticut, so you just left me behind. Because your feelings had to come first."

His voice breaks completely then, and I can't do it anymore. I can't stand off to the side where he lays his heart out for Dave like this. Tom and I both move to place ourselves at either of his sides, a moat around the castle he's made himself into in this moment, and he draws in a long, deep breath before he starts speaking again.

"I had to accept that you put yourself first and me last back then," Gabe finally says. "It hurt like hell, but I had no choice. I wasn't your kid. But for the longest time after that, Dave, I was so convinced there was something wrong with *me*. Something broken in how I was that made you stop loving me." He shakes his head. "And I don't care how long or how far I have to fight you. I am never, ever letting you do that same thing to Lou." He sniffs and blinks hard, but then he draws himself up on his crutches again and keeps going. "Lou is kind, and sweet, and loving, and he likes beautiful things in the world. There's nothing wrong with him, and you shouldn't have to understand or appreciate all the things he loves to know that you have the best son in the whole world. He's your *son*. That's the only reason you should need to love him. That's the kind of love he deserves. And I'm going to make sure that's the love he gets."

And that's when Gabe turns on his crutches and starts to walk away, back toward the inn and the music floating out across the lawn from the party taking place there. Dave stands there, looking furious and sad and shocked.

Tom clears his throat. "Well, then," he says. "I hope you heard the message you needed to hear just now, Dave."

I nod. "And if you didn't," I add quietly, "just remember something else if you do end up staying in Lou and Gabe's life. Tom and I care a lot about their happiness. And I've got at least two MMA fighters as close, personal connections. So I hope you'll decide to make some better choices about your family moving forward."

His eyes go slightly wide, and I revel in the victory.

Then Tom takes my hand, and we follow our badass, beautiful boyfriend over to the celebration of the inn and event space that the three of us helped save. Together.

Chapter 32

1 Day to the Devon Falls Leaf Festival

I know what I need to do next. —Tom Evers

We get all the way to the door of the winery event space before Gabe sags against his crutches, breathing hard.

"Holy shit," he whispers. "Holy shit, holy shit, holy shit. I can't believe I just said all of that."

Colin helps him ease onto the edge of a nearby Adirondack chair—I swear, those things propagate on this property—and I hand him a small bottle of water from my pocket, watching carefully as he sucks it down. I run my hands through his hair and he leans into my touch, hopefully away from the shock he's feeling right now.

Colin kneels down in front of him and props his crutches up against the back of the chair. "You were fucking phenomenal, little fox. That was a goddamn masterclass in taking apart an asshole."

I nod in agreement. "That was inspiring, Gabe." I rub at his cheek gently with my thumb. "You should be so proud of yourself."

Gabe takes in a long breath, then lets it out. "But what if saying all of that was the wrong choice?" he finally whispers. "What if Dave takes Lou away from me for good now?"

Colin makes a low, growling noise in his throat. "I'd like to see him try," he says, his eyes narrowed and his gaze dead ahead. Gabe's eyes widen, and he looks over at me.

We both burst out laughing.

"What?" Colin asks as he straightens up.

I snort. "Nothing, love. I just forgot, until quite recently, that your pre-racing face translates a little oddly into the real world."

Gabe grins. "You sort of looked like a cross between a mafia henchman and a cartoon character."

Colin rolls his eyes, but he's laughing. "I'm just saying we're not letting that fucker win," he finally says.

Gabe sighs and shakes his head, then looks back and forth between us. He turns his head slightly to look over at the long, tall building behind us. "Sometimes I still can't believe we fixed this. Together. The three of us," he says softly.

The three of us. Colin looks over at me, and the two of us lock eyes in a conversation with no words.

"We did," I answer, and my voice is possibly a little hoarse now. I clear my throat. "I need to talk to you two, actually. When Colin first kidnapped us into the mountains—"

"Yeah, because hot tubs and faux fur rugs just scream kidnapping," Colin says drily.

"They do when they're on the right movie set, love. Anyway, when you first stole us away from reality after Gabe's accident, we said we'd try this out just while we were there, while Gabe healed and we waited to see what came of everything with Dave and Lou. But the leaf festival's tomorrow, and we're about to step into a room with the entire town. Our relationship has also recently gone viral. So I have to ask: are we all ready for this? To be fully out, in person, in public? The three of us, together?"

I find I can barely finish the sentence. Because I'm *fairly* sure I know what their answers will be. After all, the three of us really did go viral across the entire internet together. But then again, all of us know too well exactly how people like to cast cruel and unnecessary opinions onto others. And it's a great deal easier to hide the comments section of an article than it is to hide from angry or suspicious faces in a public place. Devon Falls is one of the kindest and most accepting towns I've ever lived in, but there's still nothing inherently easy or guaranteed about how any group of people will perceive the three of us moving forward. Two celebrities and their much younger boyfriend being out and about in the world is always likely to attract some kind of attention, either positive or negative.

Gabe pushes himself up, off the chair, and Colin hands him one crutch while I hand him the other. "I can do hard things," he says, his voice low and light.

Colin smiles. "Of course you can, little fox."

Gabe shakes his head. "That's been one of my affirmations for a long time. Something I always said to myself. But the truth is that I didn't always really believe it." He tilts his head slightly to one side as he studies us. "But then we rebuilt an inn and an event space together, and I told off Dave, and we're going to keep Lou safe, no matter what, and I just feel like..."

Colin looks to me, and I nod.

"We can do hard things together," I say out loud.

Gabe smiles. "Yes. That's what I want. I want to keep doing hard things. But those hard things never seem quite as hard with you two around."

Colin and I both move to kiss him, and soon the three of us are connected in an extremely sweet and hot, albeit somewhat awkward, makeout session, with Colin and I both supporting Gabe on his crutches.

Colin pulls away first. "That's what I want, too," he whispers breathlessly into the chilly air.

I nearly blurt them out, then. The three words I *really* want to say. But it feels too soon, too early, especially against the backdrop of everything else that's already happened tonight. So I just nod as I lean over to kiss them each on the cheek. "Me too," I whisper.

Eventually, I'll say the rest of the words hidden in the back of my throat right now. I'm sure of that.

"Wow," Gabe whispers as we step into the event space. I'm in awe myself, actually. I knew we had done a strong job of fixing up the damaged areas of the large, old shed that was set to become the winery's event space, and we were nearly finished when Gabe fell off that ladder. So logically, I understood before we walked through this door that the space would be done, perfect, and beautiful. Evelyn and Bethany never would have opened it otherwise. But still, there's something about standing here in the middle of the cacophony of music and the lights that really brings everything home.

We did it, the three of us. We fixed the inn. We fixed this event space.

We saved Gabe's job.

And we made this shed into something that will be used for treasured Devon Falls moments for years and years to come. Birthday parties, baby showers, and weddings will be held here. Sam's wedding to Malachai will be celebrated here soon, and that's able to happen because of me and Colin and Gabe. I take hold again of Colin and Gabe's hands as I look at the space around me, at the beams covered in fairy lights (I manage not to glare at the offending string that tried to kill Gabe), at the large potted trees in each corner of the room that are covered in red, yellow, and orange lights shaped like maple leaves, and then over to the long tables covered in white table cloths and trays of food. In the corner, Bethany is pouring glasses of wine at a large freestanding bar, and people are milling about the space, talking loudly, excitedly with one another as they relish in the spot that we have created for them.

And then, Bethany looks up from the wine bottle she's holding and spots us. She lets out a long wolf whistle. "Look who's here!" she shouts. "The three heroes who made today possible!"

The entire room bursts into loud applause, and I feel Colin's hand squeeze so tightly against mine it almost hurts. I've never really imagined that Devon Falls wouldn't accept us exactly as we are, and yet now, as I stand in front of this crowd, I realize just how much this means to me: to stand in front of a place full of people I respect and care about and hear that they know all the truths there are to know about me and my boyfriends (and it still feels strange to feel that word move through me when I refer to them), and to know the three of us belong here, fully, in the midst of all those truths.

Sam, Jack, and Benson are standing off to the side of the bar, cheering and clapping as loudly as everyone else. Sam nods and sends me the slightest wink, and I shake my head as I nod back. Colin clears this throat.

"You know," he whispers. "My brother always said there's something about the air in Devon Falls."

The party is long, beautiful, and entirely perfect.

Amelia magics up a wheelchair that we help Gabe into so that he can "dance" with all the rest of us as Elijah and his band move through and across different decades of music, playing everything from Bowie to Gaga. I'm on my way back from the bar with a glass of wine for Colin and a sparkling cider for Gabe, who's still on painkillers, when I notice the long line of framed certificates sitting above lined pages with dollar amounts next to them. I have always adored a silent auction. "What's this for?" I ask Sam. He's been almost quietly clingy tonight, hardly leaving my side since I arrived. I'm not sure if that's because he's without Malachai, who is apparently very happy to be home in a quiet house with Lou at the moment, or because his natural big brother mode requires that he be there to protect me from anyone who might decide not to wish me, Gabe, and Colin well in our polyamorous pursuits. So far he's had absolutely nothing to worry about.

"Oh." Sam frowns. "Devon Falls has an old opera house. It's a few streets down from Lancer Family Medicine. It used to be one of the best performance spaces in the state, but it hasn't drawn a crowd in a long time. It's a historical monument, so the town wants to save it, but it'll take one hell of an infusion of cash. This is the third or fourth fundraiser we've done this year."

I wonder if he even realizes he's just used the pronoun *we*. Devon Falls has clearly stolen my brother from the rest of the world, and I'm not at all upset about that.

I'm studying a package for a winter sleigh ride, and then another one for a bespoke knitted hat collection (and am I dreaming, or is Sam's name attached to that prize?) when my phone dings with a text. Sam's been pulled into a conversation with Jack's mother, so I step off to the side to set down the drinks I'm holding and see who it is. I'm glad I'm not holding any glasses of wine when I glance down at the name across the screen.

Dellie Shepard.

Dellie and I spoke before either of us spoke to Max, and I texted them after the articles came out, but I haven't heard from them since then. I immediately unlock my phone.

Dellie

Wanted to let you know I just scored a massive part. Feels so good to find my voice in Hollywood again and to know I have voices like yours behind me. Hope you're looking ahead to more success too, Tom. Enjoyed reading that article about you and your boyfriends and hearing how happy you are right now in Vermont.

Just like that, it's as if my entire world comes into focus, and I know what I need to do next. I pick up the pen next to the silent auction table, and I smile.

Chapter 33

0 Days to the Devon Falls Leaf Festival

There's something about the air in Devon Falls. —Gabe Gomez

"Mario should have called by now."

I mutter the words as I thump my way down Main Street, in between my two giant boyfriends.

Boyfriends. I wonder if I'll ever get totally used to saying that, either out loud or in my head. Then again, I also wonder if I'll get used to this giant walking cast a doctor at the hospital in Fairlington installed on my leg this morning. It's supposed to make walking a lot easier, and I think it eventually will, but right now the weight is hard to manage. Every step feels like a trip through mud.

Which is sort of how my thoughts feel right now too, if I'm being honest. It's been almost forty-eight hours since I told off Dave at the winery, and the Devon Falls Leaf Festival is now in full swing. The parade in an hour will be the big celebration of the weekend, and the streets are already filled with people: community members I recognize, strangers visiting from out-of-town, local TV stations setting up interviews with bystanders. Three small children whiz by carrying giant cones of what looks like maple cotton candy, and a tired man chases after them. "No more sugar if you can't listen!" he yells down the street.

I blink back tears as I try to imagine what Lou's doing this morning. He loves this parade. I'm sure Jack and Benson will bring him to see it, but without the okay from Mario, I won't be able to even wave or say hello to him. And that fact feels a hundred pounds heavier than the boot that's wrapped up around my broken leg.

We reach the edge of the town square, where Sam and Malachai are waving to us. They've got a line of camping chairs set up at the edge of the sidewalk, right in front of the giant poop emoji statue that isn't actually a poop emoji. I salute it, the way I always do when I see that statue.

I've decided I like it when art can just be fully itself.

"We got prime spots," Malachai said. "Amelia saved them for us."

"The mayor?" Colin asks. "What did you two do to deserve spots right across the street from the parade announcers? I didn't know Amelia liked you that much."

Sam shrugs. "She said she wanted to make sure her neighbor got a front row seat to all the floats." He passes over a bottle of water as I ease myself down into a chair next to Malachai. "Don't worry, those things get easier," he says as he gestures toward my cast. "And I've got it on good authority that an excellent orthopedist will be at the wedding this week. He wants to look at your x-rays and make sure everything's healing as it should."

"Milo's coming?" Tom beams. "Little one, you'll love Milo! Sam and Jack's other best friend," he adds when he sees my confused frown.

"He's so hot," Malachai whispers in my ear from the seat next to me. "I swear, between Sam, Jack, and Milo, the hospital where they all did their residency had to have looked like something right out of one of those medical dramas they all claim to hate because they're not realistic enough."

I laugh and take a sip of the water. "And the wedding's all set to go?"

Sam sighs. "Well, we lost the battle on not inviting the entire town."

Malachai rolls his eyes. "They put the wedding on the last town meeting agenda. And then they begged." He shrugs. "So we decided to keep the ceremony small, but then everyone's invited to the winery afterward for the reception."

"Softie," says Colin.

Malachai grins as he looks around the crowds gathering nearby. He waves to someone across the street—one of the Ryker kids, I think—and shrugs again. "Well," he says. "What can I say? I like how much everyone in this town cares about being part of my life."

"Yeah," I whisper. I've spent so much time in Devon Falls hiding my real life, my real self, from these people. I spent so much time here being afraid. And even though I still don't know exactly what's going to happen to Lou, it feels great to be able to sit here in broad daylight, next to the two people who have changed everything for me, and know that I don't have secrets from anyone here anymore.

And everyone's still waving and smiling as they walk by.

I wonder if maybe it's time for a new affirmation. I keep thinking of that line Colin tells me his brother used to say all the time.

There's something about the air in Devon Falls.

"Friends of Devon Falls!" Amelia's voice, projected loudly from the giant hanging speakers attached to the stage across the street, echoes across the park. "It's time for the annual Devon Falls Leaf Festival Parade!"

Cheers and clapping flow up and down the street, and I can't help but stare back and forth across the crowds as I search for a glimpse of Lou.

"Don't worry, he isn't missing it," Malachai murmurs to me. "He's with Jack and Benson and Jack's parents. They're watching from the porch of Lancer Family Medicine."

I swallow and nod. That's a good view, at least. Lou will get to see all the old antique cars up close. Those are his favorite part.

"And he's... good?" I'm not supposed to ask, not really, but I don't think Malachai's going to tattle on me.

Malachai sends me a half-smile. "He's doing okay. He's strong. But he'll be better when he has you back in his life."

I blink back more tears as Colin snakes a hand into my lap to grip my knee.

"First of all," Amelia calls out across the town, "I'd like to announce that we've had a slight change in theme this year. Parade participants have changed their floats for a new theme, one sponsored by the LGBTQIA2S+ society here in Devon Falls. This year, the society and the town have declared the parade theme to be... royalty!"

"Huh?" I say. I'm used to the usual floats and costumes in this parade, where everything and everyone is covered in paper leaves of some kind. Royalty? What's she talking about? "Why would they change the theme?" I ask.

Then the high school band starts marching up the street, leading the parade, with the first float riding slowly behind them. And then I understand.

The band is playing the song "Let it Go" from *Frozen*. And on the float behind them, the town council's float, every single person is wearing a Disney princess costume.

"Holy crap." Tears are falling from my eyes now as the float goes by, with every member, male, female, or nonbinary, wearing a dress that looks exactly like one of Lou's favorites. The next float comes by filled with people wearing prince costumes, and then another one filled with princesses, and then I'm *really* crying as the marching band plays on and another float rumbles by us.

It's the LGBTQIA2S+ society's float, and I can't take my eyes off the banner on the side.

DEVON FALLS: WHERE EVERYONE ALWAYS BELONGS

"Was this..." I swallow down on the sentence I can't finish. "Did they... I don't understand..."

Sam looks like he might be blinking back tears too. "We read the article," he says. "Everyone in the society, I mean. And we thought it might be time for a big reminder to the world of what Devon Falls stands for."

I stand up awkwardly on my walking cast, and Tom wraps an arm around the side of my body as Colin steps behind me to envelope me against him.

"Where everyone always belongs," Colin whispers in my ear. "I like that. I like that a whole fucking lot."

I do too. But there's also a snake of danger eating its way through my stomach. Is Dave seeing this? Will this parade make him want to take even bigger steps to get Lou away from Devon Falls? From me? I close my eyes and let the band's music flow through me, and I wish with every fiber in me that Lou were here right now, watching this with me, cheering for these princesses and princes and waiting for his favorite cars, and—

"Gabe!"

My eyes shoot open as a tiny voice I'd know anywhere echoes across the cheering. I turn toward it, determined not to let hope get too big of a foothold in me.

But there he is. Lou. He's standing right in between Jack and Benson, holding each of their hands and beaming from across the green. He's wearing his favorite blue dress—Cinderella, I think—and all I can do is stand there, shocked, as Jack leans down to whisper something to him. Then he drops their hands and runs, and I try to run too but realize pretty quickly that running in a walking cast isn't really a *thing*. It doesn't matter though, because my little brother is fast, and I lean down awkwardly on my good leg so that I can wrap him up in the biggest, hardest hug ever when he finally catapults himself straight into my arms.

There are hands on my shoulders, hard hands I know all too well, and I lean against them as I cry even more and hold on tight to Lou. "I missed you so much," I say into his ear.

"Bet I missed you more," he says back.

Behind us, a swirl of applause and cheering rolls through the crowd. Maybe it's for a parade float, or the end of a song, but in my head all I hear is the applause that everyone should get to hear when they're totally and completely surrounded by the people they love most in the world.

It isn't until hours later, after the parade, that Mario the social worker fills in the rest of the story of how Lou and I have been brought back together. He's sitting with all of us on the town's green, at a picnic table covered in corn dogs and fried dough dripping in maple syrup. Lou's so high on sugar he might never sleep again, and he and George Ryker are racing around the playground next to the poop emoji statue.

"Dave signed custody over to you," Mario explains. "Dropped all of the accusations that we'd already figured out were bullshit anyway."

"Why?" I ask as Tom nudges a corn dog toward me. Judging by the pile of food he and Colin put in front of me, they're both worried I'm not eating enough.

Mario passes me a sealed envelope. "He said he had his reasons, and he wanted me to give you this."

Colin eyes the letter with more than a little apprehension, and Tom's staring at it like it might be a snake. Everyone at the table has their eyes on me as I start reading aloud.

Because this message isn't just for me. I'm not going to be raising Lou alone. And all the other father figures who will be in his life deserve to hear these words too.

"Dear Gabe." I frown at the handwriting, which reminds me of birthday cards and refrigerator notes I haven't thought about in years. Then I start reading. "I want you to know that I heard what you said at the winery the other day. Mostly, I heard what you said about your mom. I'm not sure she'd be too proud of the choices I've made since she first got diagnosed."

"Not sure, huh?" Colin mutters. Tom nudges him.

I just smile and keep reading. "You've always had the best of your mom in you, Gabe. You remind me so much of her. I don't know if I ever told you that. And Lou deserves to have a parent as amazing as your mom was." I clear my throat, determined to get through this without crying again, and Tom rubs a hand over my knee. "So do right by him, kid. I know you'll give him the life I didn't know how to give you. In the meantime, tell Lou I love him. I always will. I'll visit once in a while, and I'll remind him that I love him myself. I don't want to abandon him the way I did you. But you're the one in charge of him now, Gabe. I think that's what your mom would want."

I fold the letter over, closing it. It feels like I'm closing so many other things too, but I can't think about that now. Not without sobbing again. "Gabe!" Lou shouts from across the park. "Look how high I can swing now!"

"Great job!" I call back. I shake my head as I slide the letter into my pocket. "So this is all real?" I ask Mario. "I'm really his full guardian now?"

Mario smiles. "Yes. There will be some involvement on our part while the details are finalized, but yes. You have custody of your little brother." He glances back and forth between Tom and Colin. "And maybe we should talk, later on, about whether you ever want to look at adoption opportunities."

"Yes," Tom says, before I can answer, and I realize Colin's nodding aggressively from the other side of me. I wonder: are throuples allowed to triple-adopt a kid? But that's not a problem for today.

I clear my throat and look down the table, to where Jack and Benson are passing pieces of fried dough back and forth. "Thanks," I tell them. "For keeping him so safe. And so happy." I point at Benson. "And you're getting a hug the next time I get up from this table, whether you like it or not."

Benson shrugs and rolls his eyes, but he's smiling. "I suppose I'll allow it," he says.

The entire table bursts out laughing, Lou squeals across the park, and somewhere behind me a marching band starts playing something that sounds distinctly like a song from *Cinderella.*

Tom and Colin both lean into me hard from either side, and I take a moment to look around me: at this festival, these people, this community. This place we've all created, where right now, everyone belongs

Chapter 34

One Week After the Devon Falls Leaf Festival

Tom opens the door, and Colin shoves me inside. —Gabe Gomez

"Can I wear my Superman costume?"

Lou tips up on his toes as we look together through the outfits in his closet. His *new* closet, in his new room. The one at the end of the hall in the house Colin renovated, the one he insists I stop calling "Colin's house."

"It's your house too," he keeps saying. "Yours and Lou's. Our house, little one."

I smile as Lou pokes at the blue and red stretchy materials. "I'm not sure, kiddo. Let's ask Malachai, okay?" I type a quick message into my phone.

I wasn't sure whether or not Malachai would be answering texts on his wedding day, so I'm surprised when he answers in about five seconds.

Malachai

> Sure, of course. I've always wanted to be married in front of a superhero.

"It's a go," I tell Lou, and he squeals excitedly.

"Yes!" He pumps a fist in the air. "And then I want to wear my new Snow White dress for the party after the wedding!"

And of course he wants costume changes. Because that's my little brother: bringing the swagger to every event. And now in any damn outfit he feels like wearing.

He and I haven't talked much about Dave. I told him he was going to live with me from now on, and he was thrilled. But then I told him his Dad would only be able to visit with us from now on—Mario said that Dave's charges of child neglect make it unlikely that he'll ever get full custody of Lou back even if he does want to be in Lou's life again—and Lou frowned in that sad, thoughtful way he sometimes does.

"Well," he said. "Daddy's been sad. I hope the next time I see him that he's as happy as I am."

I hugged him hard and tried not to cry as I hoped for the exact same thing. And then I immediately signed both of us up for family therapy with someone that Mario recommended. I don't know yet if my insurance will cover it, but Colin said not to worry about that.

I wonder if I'll ever get used to having him and Tom standing behind me. I've been on my own for a long time now, I guess, just me and Lou, and standing up with other people doesn't come naturally. But maybe that's something to talk about with the therapist.

I help Lou into his outfit and spend another minute fighting with the bow tie Tom bought for me that still seems like some kind of bad practical joke. I finally give up and head down the stairs with Lou at my feet, convinced that this tie is some kind of ploy to lure me into a closet so Tom can have his way with me. Which I wouldn't mind, except that Lou's right behind me and we're going to be late for the wedding. "Can you help me?" I call out as I walk into the kitchen. "I think this tie is trying to strangle me, and I—"

"Hi, little fox," Tom says as I stop talking the moment I see who's standing next to him. "My mothers are here! They're so excited to meet you. And yes, I'll help you with the tie."

I can do hard things. I whisper the words to myself, and I do my best not to hyperventilate. Both of Tom's mothers have kind eyes, and I've heard nothing but good things about them from Malachai... and yet I'm frozen in place, all words sinking from my body. Nasty, cruel thoughts run through my head.

What if they don't like me? What if they tell Tom he's too good for me, or that he and Colin should be together without me? What if they don't like Lou? What if they—

"Oh, we're so excited to meet you!" One of them, a tall, large woman with pale skin who looks so much like Tom and Sam, rushes up to shake my hand. "I'm Francis, but the boys call me Mother. You can call me that too, if you like. Can I hug you?"

"Don't scare him, love." The other woman, who's equally tall with dark skin and long, cornrowed hair, joins her next to me. "I'm Evelyn, also known as Mom. And handshakes are perfectly fine if you're not a hugger."

"Or no touching at all," Francis—Mother?—adds.

"But I want a hug!" Lou darts between us, now carrying a video game controller in one hand and a giant stuffed bunny in the other. I have no idea where either came from. "Who are you?" he asks.

They both beam with delight as they lean down so he can wrap each one of them up in a hug. "We're Tom's mothers," Francis says. "And we'd love to be your—" she looks up at me, and it's clear she's asking my permission.

I nod, hard and fast. As quickly as I can.

"Your family," Evelyn finishes.

"Yay!" Lou leans against her neck. "Then come play videogames with me!" He disappears down the hallway, and I choke back a laugh.

"It's Colin's fault," I manage to choke out. "He made chocolate chip pancakes for breakfast today. Those always give Lou extra energy."

"Hey, now," says Colin. "The only thing we had in the fridge was milk, eggs, and maple syrup. What else was I supposed to make?"

Evelyn leans across the counter to kiss his cheek. "It's so good to see you, baby," she says. "So good to finally see you both again... together."

"Finally," Francis murmurs, and Evelyn pokes her in the side.

Colin nods and tilts his head up slightly. "Well, yeah. It took us a little while. We just needed a little help." He winks at me, and every cell in my body feels like it might be contracting in embarrassment.

"Who, me?" I ask. "I mean, I didn't—"

"Yes, you," Tom interrupts gently. "Mom and Mother, Colin and I can't wait for you to get to know Gabe. I'm afraid you already know Colin a little too well."

"Please don't tell the story about the time I tried to water your begonias by peeing all over them," Colin mutters.

"I think you just told it yourself, babe," Tom says. "Anyway, meet my other boyfriend. The talented and kind Gabriel Gomez. Oh, and that was Lou you just hugged."

Francis beams as she reaches out a hand to me again. "Welcome to the family, Gabe."

I swallow down the lump that won't quite leave my throat as I look back and forth between her and Evelyn. "Actually," I finally say. "If you're still giving them out, I'd really love a hug."

The wedding itself is small and quiet, just the way Malachai wanted it. He and Sam say their vows under a giant wooden arch covered in maple leaves next to the lake behind the winery—the one that separates the winery from *our* new house.

"I promise you'll always come first in my world," Sam tells Malachai.

"I promise to never let you forget that you deserve to be happy," Malachai responds.

Then Amelia, who's officiating, pronounces them husband and husband, and the small crowd claps excitedly as Sam takes Malachai's face in his hands and the two of them kiss long and hard.

"I don't know if I want to kiss when I get married," Lou says from where he's perched on Colin's hip, head leaning into Colin's shoulder.

"That's okay," Colin tells him. "You never have to kiss anyone you don't want to, Lou."

"And if you ever do want to kiss anyone," Tom says, "that's okay too, as long as you have their permission."

Lou nods, and I blink up against the mostly sunny sky glittering over the lake's waters. My mind wanders to visions of the kind of wedding Tom and Colin and I would have, if we ever got married. Would we get married at the winery too?

It definitely feels strange to even think about the three of us having a wedding. We've been together for like five minutes, after all. But then again, we've already moved in together, and I didn't even think twice when Colin asked me if I wanted to. Dave's house had never felt like home to me, even with Lou there. Colin's house felt like home from the first time I stepped inside of it.

Nope, not Colin's house, I remind myself. *Our* house.

The wedding moves over to the event space, where basically all of Devon Falls has assembled. "Hey," I say to Benson as we eat pigs in a blanket off of fancy paper plates together by the bar. "You never wore the leaf costume at the festival!"

"I shamelessly used your little brother as an excuse," Benson says as he hands me a napkin. "I told Amelia I was too busy with him to do it."

"Shameless," I agree. But... I've seen that costume. It's basically twelve pounds of cloth with slits for eyeholes. "Also understandable," I add.

"They'll try to get me into it next year." He shakes his head. "But maybe I'll have a different excuse." He looks over at Jack, who's dancing around the floor with Lou. My brother forgot about wanting to change for the reception, so he's still in the Superman costume. "Turns out we both really liked having a kid around the house," he adds softly.

My mind drifts back to that day Dave drove away from me, back to the cold worry that filled my body as I was taken to my first foster home. I wish I'd had a Benson and a Jack in my life back then. "Any kid would be so lucky to end up being in your house," I tell Benson. He almost blushes, I think.

"Gabe?" Bethany peeks her head up from under the bar. "I know you're not working today, hon, but we're out of cocktail napkins. There are more in the storage closet near the bathrooms. Could you grab some?"

"Sure. Keep an eye on Lou for me?" I ask Benson. He nods and heads over toward Lou and Jack, and I make my way across the room toward the back area, where two bathrooms sit next to the large storage closet. Colin and Tom and I rehung the door of that closet, I remember.

A hand finds its way up the back of my suit jacket just as I open the door of the closet. "Hiding from us?" Tom whispers in my ear.

I turn to see him on one side and Colin on the other. "Nope, just getting napkins. Where have you two been?" Last I saw they were dancing together with Jack's parents and Tom's parents.

Colin rolls his eyes. "Just reminding the world what a terrible dancer I am." He shrugs. "Then we saw you coming over here, and we missed you."

I'm not sure my heart will ever stop swelling in my chest when one of them says things like that. "Missed me, huh? I went to get food like ten minutes ago."

"Too long," Tom admonishes. "Especially when I'm thinking about how big that closet is, and how we always wanted to have our way with you on the giant craft table that's stored in there."

My face burns. "No way," I whisper. "How did you know?"

"Know, huh?" Colin leans down to kiss me on the neck. "What is there to know, little one? Do you have a thing for getting it on in public?"

I choke back a little bit of a gasp as his lips hit my skin. Have I ever fantasized about getting ripped apart and ravaged somewhere where I could get caught at any moment? Okay, maybe I have. But that's dumb, right? "I mean," I say. "Uh, we can't. This is Malachai and Sam's wedding reception, and—"

Just like that, Tom opens the closet door, and Colin shoves me inside.

"No making any noise," Tom whispers in my ear. He points to the giant wooden table that's taking up the majority of the storage space. "On the table, little fox." There's a soft clicking noise of a lock, and then a fluorescent light bulb above us clicks on, illuminating the small room in eerie yellow light. "We're in charge now," Tom whispers in my ear. "And you'd best hope no one walks in and catches us, or they're going to find out all about the things you let us do to you."

I manage to hold all the noises that want to escape me down to a whimper as Colin lifts me up, walking cast and all, and sets me down on the old dining table Bethany got from somewhere but has never found space for.

Now I'm glad as fuck it got left in here.

"That's it, baby," Tom whispers as I lift my hips and he helps me slide my pants and boxers down my legs. "You like this, don't you?" he whispers. "You love knowing that half the town's outside this room right now. It turns you on knowing they could hear us at any moment. Catch us doing unspeakable things to you."

All I can manage to get out is a whimper, because he's absolutely right. This is sexy as hell. Off to one side of the table, Colin's got his jeans open, and he's slowly jacking himself in his boxers.

"We love when you make those noises," Tom says. "But you have to stop making them now, or we might get caught. So Colin, dear bestie, you're going to need to put your cock down our little Gabe's throat."

My cock goes so hard when he says those words that I actually thrust up into the air, desperate for someone to touch it. But Tom shakes his head and makes a *tsk tsk* noise. "Such a little minx," he says as he starts unbuttoning his own pants. "Now be a good little one, Gabe, and suck Colin's dick until he comes down your throat."

I nod eagerly, as Colin helps me lay down across the table. He runs his fingers through my hair as he palms the back of my head and slowly pulls me toward his body. He threads his dick into my mouth, and I suck eagerly, watching Colin's eyes roll back in his head as I sigh against his skin. Holding Colin or Tom in my mouth always just feels so *right*. So comforting and safe and sexy as all fuck.

Tom's at the other side of the table, next to my legs. He starts caressing the nerves around my hole now, and he's still whispering pure dirt into the dim light of the closet. "Remember," he whispers. "There are so many people out there. They can all hear you. So you have to be very, very quiet when I do this." Then I hear him spit, and then two damp fingers are rubbing up against all the sensitive nerve endings there with his fingers just as he leans down and takes my cock all the way into his mouth.

I very nearly scream, but Colin pushes deeper into my mouth, and all I can think about is how easy it would be for someone to unlock that door and catch me here, with my pants literally down and Tom's mouth wrapped around me and my mouth wrapped around Colin—

Tom pulls up off of me with a pop and licks his lips. "He's so beautiful, isn't he, Colin? Always responding to every touch." Then he thrusts his tongue into me, and all the nerve endings there light on fire at once as Tom plays and teases. He pushes in just far enough with his tongue to bring me to the edge as he wraps one of his big hands around my cock. Colin holds on tightly to the back of my head, and it's like every inch of me is being cemented in their steady heat and comfort. I moan around Colin's cock.

"Shhh," he whispers above me. "Remember, no one can hear us, little fox." He rubs gently at the back of my neck. "Just feel. Feel how much we care about you."

Tom's lips disappear from my body, and it feels lonely and cold there until I look back down my body to see him slipping on a condom that seems to have appeared out of nowhere. Pre-lubed, I'm sure, because Tom thinks ahead like that. He slides it on and then, slowly, pushes my legs back, and then he begins to push into my body.

I'm holding onto every muscle I have as tightly as I can, determined not to scream as Tom slides in deeper at the same time that he takes my cock in his hand again. He closes his eyes as he pushes in just a little farther and I bear down, moving in between flashes of pleasure and pain. I stay hard the whole time, which isn't surprising given how incredibly turned on I am just thinking about what the three of us are doing right now.

My two boyfriends are making love to me together in a supply closet with most of the town right outside the door.

Tom bottoms out in me as he hits nerves that have me thrusting up and off the table into his hand. "Perfect," he whispers. "You're both so very perfect. I want to be this close to you both for the rest of my life. In supply closets. In every bedroom we ever walk into. In kitchens and bathrooms and dressing rooms. I want to be with you in every space we can find together, all across the world."

He lets out a gasp, and then he starts fucking into me, hard and fast. Just as Colin starts fucking my mouth at the exact same pace. "Colors, little fox," Colin says sharply. "Squeeze my hand if you need to change colors."

I nod around his cock, but there's no way I'm squeezing his hand right now. Every cell and nerve in my body is on fire. I'm hard as a rock and desperate to lose myself with both of them inside of me. The off-color light in the room is bouncing against them as they move in and out of me, giving me pure pleasure as they take it from me, and then Colin leans down and over my body, toward Tom.

"I want the same thing," he says steadily. "You've been the most important person in my life for years, Tom, and I'm not sure I've ever told you that. I think you've always deserved more from me. I can't wait to be the person you've deserved to have by your side all of these years. And I can't wait to be the person Gabe deserves, too."

Maybe it's how weirdly sexy it feels to have sex in a supply closet. Maybe it's the fact that two of my wet dreams of days past are both inside my body at the exact same time. Maybe it's the gravity of the words Tom just shared with us, or that Colin just promised the entirety of himself to me and Tom. Maybe it's knowing how much those words must mean to Tom.

All I know is that I come right then, and I come so hard in Tom's hand that it hurts, and I do half-scream around Colin's cock, but he thrusts into me and keeps me quiet as he loses himself down my throat, and at that exact same moment I feel Tom's body stutter in mine as he, too, falls down over this beautiful cliff we're all standing on.

The three of us stumble out of the supply closet minutes later, hair only a little disheveled but clothes tucked back in. We double-checked. Still, Bethany smirks as we arrive next to her at the bar.

"Forgot the napkins, didn't you?"

"Oh, shoot." I start to stumble back toward the supply closet, but she just laughs.

"Never mind, Gabe. We thought you might be... busy, so Evelyn grabbed some from the dining room."

I'm sure I'm blushing harder than I've ever blushed in my life. "Sorry, Bethany! When I'm back at work on Monday, I promise I'll be—"

She laughs again. "It's fine, Gabe! I know you're a model employee. Try not to worry so much. Be more like your little brother!" She gestures to the dance floor, where Lou is learning the Macarena with Tom's mothers.

"Look, Gabe!" he shouts excitedly as he gets the hand motions all wrong and flips them down while he should be flipping them up. "I'm doing it!"

"You are!" I call back.

"He's a natural," Tom tells me over the music. "We'll have him signed up for dance classes next week. Acting too, of course. Possibly singing. He'll be the next triple threat."

"Don't forget go karts," Colin adds. "The world needs more princesses and princes in go karts."

Bethany pours another glass of wine and pushes it into my hands. "I know you're on painkillers," she says, "but I'm sure you can have just one glass. That's the new cab sav, and it's fucking delicious. Drink it," she says, "drink it and enjoy your new life, Gabe." She lifts her own glass to me in a toast and then steers her chair down to the other end of the bar.

I take a sip and let the wine slide over my tongue. Colin wraps his arms around my waist from behind me, and I lean back into his touch as Tom circles his arm around both of us. "I knew this would be a good day," I tell them. "Lou had thirteen purple marshmallows this morning."

Colin kisses me on the cheek as Tom laughs and rests his head on mine. "Well," Tom says. "I've certainly never been one to argue with signs from the universe." He clears his throat. "I have something to tell you both. I bid an utterly absurd amount of money on a spa day I don't even want or need. But I did so to keep the opera house alive and intact. I'd like very much to revive the damn thing, and I've told my agent I won't be coming back to Hollywood anytime in the near future. I need a break from that town. A long one." He smiles. "Would the two of you like to stay here in Devon Falls with me while I bring this town's community theater dreams back to life?"

Colin hums against my neck. "Only if I can fix the place up with you. And maybe buy some old furniture for it and restore it, the way Gabe's mom used to. I think I'd like doing that."

"And maybe Lou can be in your plays," I add. "But only if he wants to, of course."

Tom lets out a long sigh. "That all sounds so very lovely. Don't you both think?"

"It sounds like home," Colin says softly.

It does. It really does. I hold up the glass of wine Bethany gave me. "To home," I say.

I snuggle into the two of them as I watch the scene in front of me. This scene, filled with people who accidentally became my home when I had none, where I'm wrapped up in the two people who gifted me with something I never, ever thought I'd have again.

A family. A family full of acceptance and caring and... well, a word Tom and Colin and I haven't said to each other just yet. But we will, soon. I'm sure of that.

The view of Devon Falls has never looked better.

Epilogue

Thirty-five Days After the Devon Falls Leaf Festival

My protectiveness where Gabe is concerned appears to have few boundaries. —Tom Evers

"You know, I'm actually perfectly capable of looking at a few x-rays."

My brother grouses from the corner of the exam room, but I just smirk at him and smile sweetly. "I'm sure you are, Sammy. But Milo's an orthopedist, remember? There's no need to be jealous of your best friend simply because he has skills you lack."

Milo bursts out laughing, which makes it a touch easier to take in the scene in front of me: him standing over Gabe as he carefully examines Gabe's leg, newly freed from the large walking cast (Sam keeps calling it a walking boot, but the thing was never even close enough to fashionable to be considered a boot in my opinion) that's been holding him hostage for weeks on end. Milo was kind enough to drive back up to Devon Falls from New York to do an examination and make sure the bone healed properly. Jack thought that was an excellent idea; Sam insists on pretending to be annoyed.

"You know these GP docs," Milo says, winking at me as he runs his hands up and down Gabe's ankle. And logically, there's no reason that should bother me. Milo's been a friend for a long time, and I trust him implicitly. But my protectiveness where Gabe is concerned appears to have few boundaries. "Always so territorial."

Sam rolls his eyes. "If you'd finally take me and Jack up on our offer to move up here and join the practice, then I'd be happy to have you barge in and take over my office, Milo."

Gabe looks up with surprise. "You might move to Vermont, Milo? I thought you loved New York."

Milo shrugs. "Shit changes, sometimes," he mutters.

Jack and Sam glance at each other sharply, and it's clear there's more of a story behind that phrase.

"Well," I say, "just a general reminder that the grand re-opening of the Devon Falls Opera House is in a mere two months. We're having a variety show. If you can get here before then, I'll make room for a tap dancing routine."

"You tap dance?" Gabe's eyes go wide. I'm not surprised. Milo's giant, muscled physique generally leads everyone to assume he's a natural athlete across the board—which he is. But people are sometimes surprised to learn that some of his strongest athletic pursuits were in tap and modern dance.

"I haven't put on the shoes in a bit, Tom." Milo grins. "But I'll come back up for the show. Sounds like you and Colin have been working overtime getting that place back up and running." He twists Gabe's ankle gently. "Any pain, man?"

"No." Gabe grins. "Wow, I can't wait to go up and down stairs normally again. Run. Damn, I may even try tap dancing."

"Let's maybe wait a few weeks for that," says Colin from where he's holding up the wall behind me. "We can start with stairs."

"Fine." Gabe holds out his hand. "Thanks for coming back so soon after the wedding, Milo. You really didn't have to do that."

Milo skips the handshake and wraps him up in a hug. "That's what friends do."

Gabe blushes. He still seems surprised by how easily the larger circle of people Colin and I have always had around us has accepted him and Lou. It never ceases to amaze me how much Gabe Gomez underestimates his own charm and kindness. People are easily drawn to him.

Gabe hops down from the exam table and tests out his leg. "It feels really good," he says. "Just in time for sledding season, too. Lou's going to be so happy."

Sam opens the door to the office and the five of us head out together, down the main hallway of Lancer Family Medicine and into the bright reception area where Jack's looking at a tablet screen. "Did I hear something about Lou and sledding?" he asks as he looks up at the crowd of people now taking over his waiting room.

"There's snow in the forecast this weekend," Colin tells him. "Lou wants us to take him up to that defunct ski area outside of town. He says it's the best place to sled. Ever. There was a whole lot of emphasis on the word *ever*."

"There's a hill at the bottom of the ski area where all the local kids have always gone," Gabe adds. "Lou loves it. Actually, I do too." He shrugs. "It's a cool little place, that ski area. I hope it doesn't stay closed forever. I wouldn't mind working there someday."

"Cheating on Northern Stars Winery, are you?" Sam asks, his voice teasing. Gabe laughs.

"No, not cheating on them. But now that I'm going back to school in the spring for hospitality management, I've been thinking about the kind of places I might want to work besides the winery someday. Bethany and Evelyn are great, but I think I want..."

He hesitates, because our little fox still struggles to have faith in himself and his dreams. Colin and I glance at each other. "He wants to be his own boss eventually. Run his own place," Colin finally finishes for Gabe.

Gabe blushes. "It's stupid, I know," he says quickly.

"Why would it be stupid?" Sam asks. "You're a very intelligent man, and you've got your whole life in front of you, Gabe. Anything's possible."

Gabe frowns for a moment. Then he looks back and forth between me and Colin, the way he does sometimes. Like he's still trying to convince himself we're a hundred percent real. "Yeah," he says slowly. "I guess I do." He shrugs again. "Anyway, we definitely have to take Lou sledding at the ski area now that I've got my leg back. It's one of the few things Dave and I used to do with Lou together that we all liked, actually."

Jack nods. "Heard anything from Dave?" he asks softly.

"He's written Lou a few letters. They've been… nice. I think he's trying to figure some things out."

Colin lets out the noise he often does when Dave comes up in conversation: a low, marginally dangerous growl. I nudge him in the side. "And he doesn't dare come near Devon Falls again until he's in a good headspace, because he knows Colin might kill him with a glance," I tease.

Colin shrugs, unrepentant.

"Do you think anyone here will ever buy that ski area?" Gabe asks. "I mean, I know it's been closed since… oh." He stops and claps a hand over his mouth. I'm sure he's just remembered how the closure of that ski area connected to a very, very dangerous experience for Benson, but Jack doesn't look bothered by Gabe's question.

"I'm not sure," he says. "It's such a big monetary and time investment. No one's been very interested after everything that happened there, and anyone who is interested hasn't had the finances to take it on. But it would be nice to see it open again," he adds. "Who knows. Maybe we'll get more interest now that a resident of Devon Falls will be an announcer for open wheel racing around the world."

Everyone turns to look at Colin, who rolls his eyes.

"It's not that big a deal," he says. "I'm just doing commentary for a few races this year. Like five of them. No one even fucking cares, honestly."

Gabe comes over to lean into Colin's side, pulling him close. "The internet cares. We care," he says.

"Are you traveling alone?" Milo asks. "Where are the races you're going to?"

Colin shakes his head. "Definitely not alone. These two are coming with me, and Lou. I only agreed to do races when he doesn't have school, and we're going to get some sightseeing in together. We're going to show Gabe and Lou London, and Rome, and Japan."

"I can't wait," Gabe says excitedly. Colin smiles, but it's a tight smile. I know he's looking forward to Gabe and Lou seeing all the amazing sights he and I have been able to take for granted over the years—I'm looking forward to that as well—but Gabe and I both know that returning to the racing circuit will be a very big deal for Colin. It won't be an easy transition back.

And that's why Gabe and I will both be by his side.

Gabe turns to Jack. "Do you and Benson want to come sledding with us at the ski area this weekend? Lou would love that," he adds. "He loves that place even more than I do."

And then an idea comes to me. One that's nearly as brilliant as my idea to save the opera house.

I look to Colin and tilt my head up in question. He knows immediately what I'm asking, and he nods slowly.

Yes, Tom. Excellent idea.

I don't even finish the sentence before Gabe tackles me. —Colin Templegate

A few nights later, Lou's tucked into bed, and the three of us are lying together across the large faux fur rug in front of the fireplace in our house. *Our* house. I still have to correct Gabe on that, sometimes, when he calls it *my* house. But he's getting there.

Once upon a time, I remember, I struggled to think of this house as my home too. Now, with Gabe and Tom and Lou here? I can't imagine it as anything other than our home.

Snow's starting to lightly fall outside of the window, bright as it drifts down through the darkness and into the glow of the outdoor lights I've installed up and down the front walkway. Some light jazz music is playing through the smart speaker on the mantle behind us, and the scent of the brownies we baked with Lou for dessert still hangs through the air. "Tonight reminds me of being at the cabin," I tell them both softly.

Tom smiles. "Ah, that place. It will always hold a special place in my heart. Should we think about installing a hot tub here?"

"Yes," I say at the same time Gabe says, "aren't those expensive?"

Tom smiles at Gabe. "They can be. But we're lucky. Our sugar daddy here is about to pull in serious bank after he goes back on the racing circuit."

I roll my eyes. "It's just broadcasting," I mutter. But there is something I've been wanting to ask them both... something I've been thinking about. "Actually, about that." I sit up on the rug, and Gabe sits up too, while Tom props himself up on one elbow. "My agent passed me a message from the network I'm working with. They'd like to do an interview with me to kick off my return. And they asked how much I'd be willing to discuss and what should be off-limits."

"Oh wow," says Gabe. "That's huge, Colin. Are you going to do the interview? What do you want to tell them?"

I look out the window, at the falling snow that might be enveloping me and these two men in all the safety and security available in the world. "Well, that's what I wanted to ask you," I finally tell them both. "I'd like to talk about a lot of things. About how I'm not ashamed to love two men, and I—"

Gabe makes a strangled noise, and I realize what I've just said. "Shoot," I add, shaking my head. "If that was too soon, then I'm sorry. I've just been thinking a lot lately about—"

I don't even finish the sentence before Gabe tackles me, knocking me back against the floor with a long kiss. Tom then lands on top of him, and Gabe's giggling and laughing when he finally pulls away. "I've been wanting to say it too!" he blurts out. "I love you two so much. Both of you." He looks back and forth between me and Tom. "Everything we have now... I want it forever and ever. And ever."

"Emphasis on ever," I tease him.

Tom grins. "Yes. Me too. I love you both with all my heart, Gabe Gomez and Colin Templegate." He leans over to kiss Gabe, and then me, softly and slowly. Sweetly. "And Colin, I hope you shout that sentiment to the world. Other people don't need to understand our love. Only we do."

My heart swells. I'm sure he's taken his share of heat in the public discourse for his decision to retreat to Vermont, away from Hollywood, and restore an old opera house with his two boyfriends rather than go back to movie sets. But my best friend is happier than I've ever seen him. And I'm determined to make sure that happiness grows, day by day by day.

"Thank you," I tell them both. "Then I'm going to fucking tell the world everything they want to know. And some shit they maybe don't want to know. The racing world's been filled with a lot of closed-minded people for a long time. So I'm going to get a little bit up in their business. Talk more about mental health and self-care. Queer rights that get ignored in a lot of countries we race in. Rights for transgender and nonbinary people that are getting ignored all around the damn world right now."

Gabe smiles and raises an eyebrow. "I can't wait," he says softly. "Lou's already talking about what he wants to wear to the first race you're calling in England. We'll have to take him shopping."

"Oh, maybe we can match!" Tom claps his hands excitedly. "I've been dying to get Lou and the three of us all matching ensembles!"

"Nothing that shows off my ankles," I tell him. "I have the worst ankles."

"You do," he agrees, and when I roll over to tackle him back into the rug, taking him with me, he folds eagerly against my body.

"I love you," I whisper to him. Then I look over at Gabe as I grasp his hand. "And I love you. And I've been wondering—well, there's something else I want to ask you."

"Did we put something in the wine tonight?" Tom murmurs to Gabe, who giggles.

I pull Gabe into another long kiss. "I was just thinking," I say as I let him go. "We've all been tested. We're all negative. We're all committed to this relationship. Living together. Raising a kid together." Tom nods. "So I was wondering," I go on. "Maybe it's time we stopped worrying about condoms." I drop a finger slowly down Gabe's cheek. "I'd like to be inside you, little fox. And you," I add to Tom. "With nothing between us. Just skin on skin on skin."

Gabe's eyes widen.

And then it begins. —Gabe Gomez

I've never had anyone inside me without a condom before.

I guess that goes without saying, since I never had anyone inside me at all before Tom and Colin, and we've always worn protection for anal sex. But I'll admit, part of what I love so much about all the other types of sex we have is that there is nothing between us for those moments: just their bodies against my body, and it always feels so perfect. So right.

"Yes," I blurt out. "Yes, yes, yes. Can we do it right now? Please?"

Tom bursts out laughing, then reaches for me to lower me gently back down onto the rug. "Someone's eager."

"It's been weeks since I had full mobility," I remind him. "My cast is off, and now Colin wants to lose the condoms? Um, yes. I'm a little eager!"

Colin laughs out loud, then leans over and picks me up off the floor, like I'm a ragdoll or something. Every time I start to forget how strong he is, he finds a way to remind me. "To the bedroom, then," he whispers in my ear. "Just in case Lou wakes up."

Tom claps excitedly behind us. "I'll get the whipped cream!"

"We don't need whipped cream," Colin tells him as I wrap my arms around his neck.

"We always need whipped cream!"

The bedroom is glowing in soft light when Colin sets me down on the bed and then falls onto it next to me to wrap his arms around me. "You sure you're ready for this?" he asks softly. "It's kind of a big deal, little one."

"For you, too, I'm guessing," I reply, then nibble gently at his neck. "I'm ready," I finally answer as I nuzzle against his skin. "You know," I go on, "after my mother died, I always sort of felt like I was living a half-life, just waiting to find the rest of my real family again. Besides Lou, I mean." I can feel Colin nod above me. "Now you're here," I whisper. I look up at him, surprised to see wetness at the corners of his eyes. "I love you, Colin Templegate. Thank you for being one-fourth of the most perfect family I could ever ask for. And yes, I'm absolutely ready to be even closer to you."

Colin maneuvers us so he can wrap me tightly in his arms, our cheeks pressed together.

"You did that for me, too," he murmurs in my ear. "Gave me the rest of my family. I hope you know that."

"Did you two start without me?" There's the sound of the door closing, and Colin loosens his hold as we both look up to see Tom setting a metal can down on the bedside table and then sinking down onto the bed next to us. "I should have guessed." He sighs and shakes his head. "It's my own fault for having two such attractive boyfriends. I can never possibly expect you to keep your hands off each other while I search for almost-expired dairy products. The whipped cream was behind the broccoli, by the way. Why on earth someone put it there is beyond me, but I—"

Colin leans over to press his lips against Tom, and I start to get hard just watching the two of them make out, all soft and sweet and so sure of each other's bodies. "We were just saying," Colin says when he finally pulls away, "how special it's been, finding the rest of our family." He traces a hand gently down Tom's cheek. "And to think," he adds. "Part of mine was standing in front of me this whole time. I love you, Tom Evers."

I fall across Colin to land gently against Tom's chest. "I love you too, Tom Evers," I add. "So much."

Now Tom's eyes go slightly wet, and he blinks rapidly. "Sweet talkers," he murmurs.

"Damn right. You deserve all the sweet talk in the world." Colin stands up from the bed and starts unbuttoning his shirt. "You both deserve everything I have to give you. All of me. Starting right now."

He drops his shirt onto the floor and crawls back across the bed, his broad, nude chest begging for touch. Tom and I waste no time giving it to him.

And then it begins.

We take our time undressing each other, letting clothing fall slowly and mouths drift across skin in the heat of the room. We pull up the covers on the giant bed and snuggle together beneath them, turning off the light and making every single touch a mysterious experiment in the dark. We suck and touch and tease and drift fingers everywhere, and the poor whipped cream gets wholly and completely forgotten as we turn each others' bodies into playgrounds. And then, just when I'm sure I'm going to lose myself before we ever even get to the main goal we set out to achieve tonight, Tom pulls me tightly against his body and tilts my legs open behind me. "Colin," he whispers in the silence of the room. "Show Gabe just how very, very much he matters to us."

And so Colin does.

He and Tom kiss above my head as Colin prepares me slowly, dripping lube across my body and pushing it into me with finger after finger. Then I can feel him stiffen above me, dropping his head down to murmur into my ear again as he holds himself ready.

"Ours," he whispers. "You belong to me and Tom now, Gabe Gomez. Ours. Forever."

"Ours," Tom adds in my other ear. And then Colin thrusts deeply inside of me.

Specks of bright light seems to swirl in my vision as Colin's bare skin moves in and out of my body while Tom holds our bare cocks together and plays, teasing and whispering in my ear, words about how special I am and how lucky he and Colin were to find me. "Bestie and I might have drifted forever," he says at one point, while Colin takes every nerve in my body apart from the inside with his slow and steady movements, "circling around each other, never knowing what was missing between us. When all along what was missing was…"

"You," Colin says in one long breath as he thrusts hard, and I come with a cry as I burst out across Tom's hand seconds before he does the same. Only a few moments later, Colin lets out a short, tiny shout (and in moments like these, I'm so glad the walls in this house are thick and Lou's bedroom is all the way down the hall). Then I feel Colin pulsing and shuddering inside me, feel his liquid filling me all the way up, and I close my eyes against the utter completeness of the moment.

So much perfection. So much rightness.

I fall asleep nuzzled between them, sandwiched as they kiss above my head again.

"Should we tell him tomorrow?" Tom whispers at one point. *Tell me what?* I wonder, but I don't have the energy to even open my mouth and ask.

"Tomorrow," Colin agrees. I listen as they kiss again, and the sound of them pressing together and then away lulls me more deeply into the peace I can't be dragged away from right now. "Tomorrow we'll tell him everything."

So. Tomorrow. Tomorrow they will tell me things. I drift further toward sleep, and I wonder. I wonder what news they could possibly have for me.

I wonder, but I don't worry. Because whatever news Tom Evers and Colin Templegate have to share with me, I know one thing for sure.

From now on, we'll do every hard thing together.

THE END

Thank you so much for reading *Fanboy in the Falls*. Want to know what Tom and Colin tell Gabe? Find out in the bonus epilogue for *Fanboy in the Falls*. This hefty bonus scene also includes hints about the next Devon Falls book, and you can read it here: **https://tinyurl.com/fanboybonus**

Curious about Milo? His book, *Found in the Falls*, is the next story in the Devon Falls series.

Want more of Devon Falls? Benson and Jack's book is *Fauxmance in the Falls*, book one in the Devon Falls series. Sam and Malachai's book is *Forbidden in the Falls*, book two in the Devon Falls series.

Turn the page for more titles from J.E. Birk!

More Books by J.E. Birk

Find all of J.E.'s books at www.jebirk.com.

Want more of Doug, Zeke, and Max? Check out *ILYBSM* and *TMI*.

Want more Vermont-y kisses and happy endings from J.E. Birk? Check out *Booklover* and *Counterpoint*. (Benson makes his first appearance in *Counterpoint*.)

If you're looking for a darker, angstier read, you may enjoy *The Worst Bad Thing*. Please heed the content warnings in the author's note.

Happy reading, everyone!

About the Author

J.E. Birk was raised in Vermont and is now adulting in Colorado with intermittent success. She is a long-time lover of stories, and she writes and reads in worlds where imperfect characters find their happily ever after. Snag free bonus content and stay up-to-date on J.E. Birk's news and releases by signing up for her newsletter at www.jebirk.com.